IRON SNAKE

PETER WYNN NORRIS

Copyright © 2019 Peter Wynn Norris

All rights reserved

All characters and events in this publication, other than those clearly in the public domain, are fictitious and any resemblance to real persons, living or dead, is purely coincidental.

ISBN: 9781090377258

DEDICATIONS

This novel is dedicated to the memory of Erinayo Oryema, the first Ugandan Inspector General of Police. He had a nice sense of humour and of occasion. In 1960 a local chief was murdered. I was sent to the area in case rioting broke out. A European and a Sikh from Headquarters CID came to investigate the murder and Senior Superintendent Oryema, who was in charge of policing the whole District, arrived. On the final day together 'Ernie' Oryema said, "It's our last night so why don't we have a curry. Since we should each do what we are good at I will shoot some guinea fowl, Manohar (the Sikh officer) knows more about the spices than any of us so he will be in charge of the cooking. But what should our two Europeans do?" He hesitated – rather theatrically – then with a smile he said, "You can buy the beer."

After Independence, dictator Idi Amin had Oryema moved from the Police to be Minister of Water Resources. Later, he and Archbishop Luwum were arrested on questionable charges and were both murdered, 'trying to escape'.

Cover picture by Ray Coles.

Railway across Africa. In the 1950s some still call it 'Nyoka ya Chuma' (the Iron Snake). It feels its way, inching up the hills, sunning itself in the plains, sliding by the swamps where it threatens to take to the water like the sinuous pythons of the forests. Riding astride this, testing its strength with her weight is the gari la moshi – the wagon of smoke – a marvel of Manchester-made machinery, towing an assortment of rolling stock in its train. Big as she is, but never gross, the engine carries her weight with an elegance that no photographer can resist.

By day, people using the track for a footway wave and laugh as the driver and fireman gesture. Then, in that fifteen-minute period of equatorial twilight she is at her best. Cruising serenely, smoke and steam merging, her silhouette against the colours of the sky – blood reds, oranges, the rich grey blues vividly changing. Yet by night she hauls herself through the mile-long hole bored through the darkness by her searchlight, no recognition of anything outside its beam. For all her show of mechanical muscle, it is then that she is incapable of protecting her charges. Masked by the night, the wagons stretching out half a mile behind her are vulnerable and open to plunder.

Illustration by Peter Wynn Norris

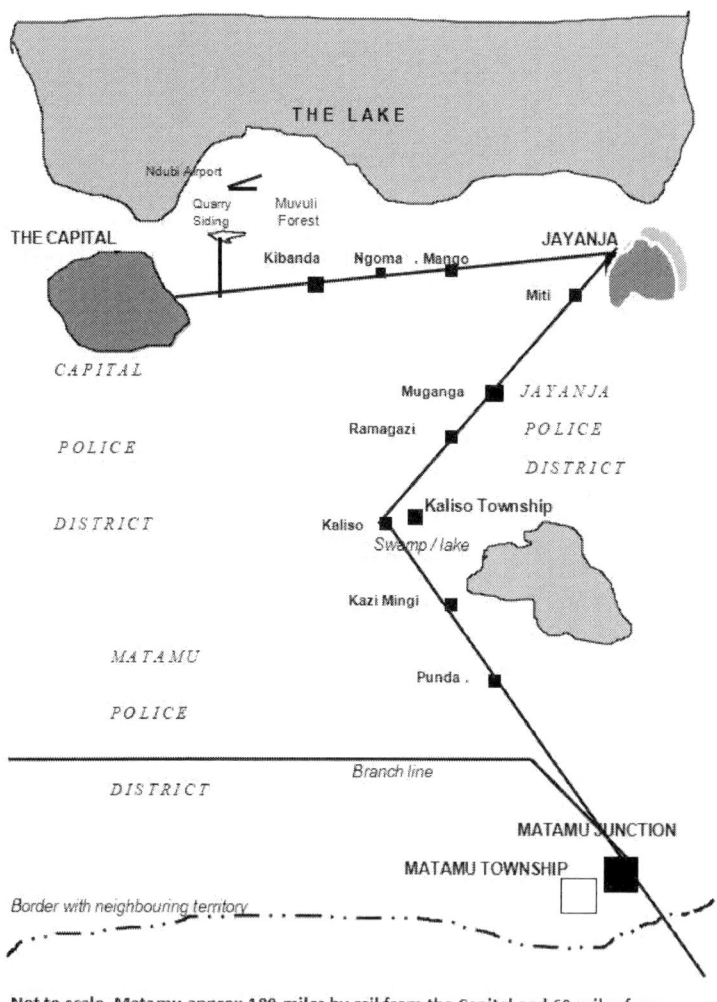

Not to scale. Matamu approx.180 miles by rail from the Capital and 60 miles from Kaliso

1942

Marika had pleaded with her husband to allow her to visit the place where she was born. She had been so young when he had found her as he travelled as a tobacco buyer and taken her back to his home as his wife. Now a minor chief at Kaliso, he had given in to her pleas, saying she had only delivered him one son and since she was past child bearing she might as well go.

She had given up hope of seeing her home land again. Her son was in the army, a long way away, so there was little to hold her to Kaliso until he came back. But now she was actually going. By train. Then by steamer across the lakes, a journey to that remote place where there would be such a welcome. They were people of the North, taller and darker of skin than the people of her husband's area and they were hardy folk used to drought and the hunger this brought. Her husband's people never knew such hardship. Stick a twig into the ground and it was a tree within weeks. She couldn't take food for them – they would reject what her husband's people ate, anyway – but she had some money wrapped in a piece of cloth. The local Indian trader would find enough for more than one feast.

The train travelled slowly and its rocking as it moved along the track was restful. "I know you," said the man sitting alongside her. He had used her own language. "You're Chief Wamala's woman. I work at the sugar crusher near Muganga, but I come from the same place as you. I'm taking leave to visit home." Travelling would be safe now with a fellow clansman with her.

She could see the steamer moored alongside the wooden jetty, the smoke drifting up from the tall funnel. The massive paddle wheel would soon be churning the water into weed-laden froth, pushing the vessel out into the main stream. The train stopped close to the jetty. Everything she had brought was in a bundle wrapped in cloth which would serve as bedding for later when she had found herself a comfortable corner on the long steel-hulled passenger lighter.

The cry went round that they were ready for boarding. She hoisted the bundle onto her head and walked easily along the swaying planks until she was able to drop down into the body of the vessel. "Over here," called her fellow traveller and she saw him setting up a nest near the bows where a canopy provided welcome shade. There was a long ululating blast from the steamer's whistle and the crew started casting off the mooring lines.

The steamer's master knew the lakes well. The only tricky bit was drawing away from the jetty, ensuring the lighters were riding correctly. Once satisfied with this he could hand over the wheel to his African mate. The level of the lake was low – the drought in the north was having its effect – and heaven knows it was shallow enough at the best of times. Still, the soundings he had called for showed there was no cause for alarm.

He looked down at the lighters. Properly secured, no hazards, but oh, the passenger lighter. Too many on it for his liking. The Lake Services Commander had simply said there had never been any difficulties and who was he to argue with the chief. He watched as the bubbles surfaced in the water ahead of them. The sun penetrating the shallow water heated the rotting debris that covered the lake's floor. Pockets of marsh gas were the result. He had been told by a Fisheries Officer that the ssematundu – huge catfish – probing around on the lake bed were the probable cause of the gas being released. Just nature in action.

Marika was comfortable. The cooling breeze swept in from the lake. The man from the train lit a small charcoal stove and cooked goat meat bought from a trader at the back of the lighter. They shared their food and congratulated each other on the fare. With the meal finished, the man used two pieces of wood to pick up the hot stove and tipped the last of the glowing embers into the lake. It was at that moment a string of huge bubbles burst alongside the lighter. The marsh gas erupted into sheets of flame which the breeze blew straight into the lighter. The cloth of the canopy flared and fell on passengers. Clothing was alight. Screams, splashes, passengers were jumping overboard.

The Master heard the screams and raced to the back railing. His lighter men had the flames under control, but he could see the string of bodies in the water being left behind in the wake of the vessel. He screamed for the Mate to stop engines. The steamer's lifeboat was launched and one after one its crew pulled living and dead from the lake. Three hours later it was dusk and he knew there was no chance of finding any more. Twenty-two passengers had been saved. Five dead bodies had been recovered. He radioed ahead to the port for the steamer to be met by the police. It was going to be a long night.

The generator at the port pounded away to give sufficient light for the bodies brought from the steamer to be laid out in the goods shed.

The police sergeant in charge stood making notes when a man tugged at his sleeve. "Do you want to know who she is?" he asked, pointing to one of the bodies.

The sergeant nodded and lifted his clip board.

"She is Marika, woman of Chief Wamala in Kaliso."

Chapter 1
1955

Stations
Matamu Junction - Punda - Kazi Mingi - Kaliso - Ramagazi - Muganga

The Beyer-Garratt locomotive stood in Kaliso station at the head of the goods train, panting, willing her driver to unleash her power. "We're going now," yelled the driver, in tune with her moods. The velvety darkness of the night shrouded all but the centre of the train where the oil lamps of the station reflected from the metal walls of goods wagons. A pneumatic hissing signalled the release of the brakes and the driver's movement of the regulator in the cab jerked the train forward with a start.

They had been late tonight. Samwiri always boarded the goods train at Kazi Mingi, the previous station, and now he would have to work very fast. He should have had all the seals removed by now, but he'd had difficulty in climbing on top of the wagon and had only just started his work. Still on his hands and knees, he stretched down for the heavy wire seal on the first door of the wagon but couldn't reach it with his hacksaw. He leant further over the edge and it was then that the jolt of the starting train caught him unawares. He tried to cling on but there were no hand holds. He fell back along the curved roof of the wagon where the surface was slippery with a light covering of dew and grease from the locomotive's smoke. With the second heave he was sent sprawling further backwards along the roof.

He was falling, desperately clawing, but his hands slid down the end plates of the wagon. His left foot hit the flange of the buffer. One more lurch of the train and the buffer of the following wagon closed up crunching the bones of his foot. He was sprawled on the coupling as the train started climbing the gradient outside the station, his screams drowned by a long wail from the locomotive's whistle. Another jerk of the locomotive sent Samwiri down past the coupling and he was now being dragged along the permanent way.

At last he fell free of the train. The pain brought a haze to his eyes. Though he wanted to screw them up in agony, he was mesmerised by the sight of the red tail light disappearing into the night. The jackals and hyenas would smell the blood and what would happen then?

The train was well clear of Kaliso station. He lay between the rails for what seemed an eternity. Where were the others? Now hands were picking him up. He was floating. He was being taken to the gods. Someone spoke. "Samwiri, you have cost us a night's work for nothing." He was carried to the level crossing a mile further up the gradient. Every time his bearers stumbled on the loose ballast the pains swept up his body. "You are too heavy, Samwiri, too much banana beer." Samwiri heard nothing. The pain had wrung his senses from him.

"Is he dead?"

"No. But he will be if someone doesn't do something soon. Keep going."

Luka Wamala stood by the lorry near the level crossing. The train had passed an hour ago. Even with a good haul someone should have appeared by now. There were eight of his men spread out along the line from just outside Kaliso station to short of the level crossing. He cocked his head as he picked up the sound of movement. Someone was coming. He could smell the rank smoke even though their last shared cigarette had been hours earlier. There should be the sound of bales and boxes being moved. There was something wrong. He sensed their presence before he saw them.

"What are you carrying?"
"Samwiri."
"Why?"
"He is hurt."
"How did it happen?"
"He fell from the wagon and his foot was crushed. It's bad. I said you would know what to do."

In the darkness Luka felt Samwiri's foot.

"There's nothing I can do for him. We will see the mganga in the village but I think he needs a daktari. We will probably have to wake up Yusufu at the dispensary."

The hammering on the door brought the dispensary attendant to his senses. He lit a lamp and opened the door and saw the men from Kaliso village.

"We need the help of a daktari, Yusufu. What do we do?"

"Why do you need a daktari?"

"Samwiri's foot has been crushed. There are bits of bone sticking out. Luka says he will die without a daktari. The mganga has used some of his potions but we don't think they will save him."

"Samwiri's in luck. There is a daktari staying in the Rest House. You can ask him in the morning."

"You ask him now. It will be too late in the morning."

"He is an important man. I can't just walk in and wake him up and say here is Samwiri wanting you… of course…."

The negotiations were brief.

James Cameron, a Government Surgeon, had arrived at Kaliso late that day to inspect local dispensaries. He had booked the Government Rest House in advance and the attendant had cooked his evening meal. Now it was 5.30am. The attendant padded into his bedroom and tugged gently on the mosquito net.

"Bwana Mkubwa, there is someone who says he needs your help. I told him to go away, but he persisted."

Thirty minutes later Yusufu once more opened the dispensary. Cameron did his best for Samwiri. It was well into the morning by the time he had finished.

Luka was informed.

"The Muzungu says Samwiri will be well again but there isn't much of his foot left. He isn't going to climb wagons for us."

Luka frowned. It took skill to do that part of their work and none of the others in his gang had this.

He thought again; there was someone. But was he the right person? He would have to find out. And very quickly, if honouring his mother's memory wasn't to fall apart.

Chapter 2

Railways and Harbours Authority

Office of the Regional Controller

P.O. Box 111

9th November 195

The Commissioner of Police
Police Headquarters

My dear Commissioner,
    I confirm our conversations about the seriousness of the thefts of goods in transit. While each incident may not seem major the cumulative effect of such persistent theft is affecting the smaller traders in the bazaars. They are demanding action and I therefore ask you to treat this as urgent.
    Reports to local police have brought no results. I strongly recommend that the police commander of Matamu area, where the Authority's line enters the territory, be given special responsibility for initiating action to put an end to these thefts.
    I am, Sir, your obedient servant,

C G Craigie

C. Gordon Craigie B.Sc.(Econ) OBE

The Police Commissioner picked up the phone. "Charles? Hello. Got your note... I'm not making excuses, but I have to say your railway is a world of its own and a mystery to my men... The man in charge of Matamu District retires soon and maybe that was part of the problem. I'll look into your idea of his relief being given responsibility for investigating these thefts... Yes, I'm sure we'll be able to crack the problem... Bridge?... I'll be at the club tonight. I'm looking forward to getting a bob or two back."

The Commissioner replaced the phone. He called for his Staff Officer. "Denys, I've just had Charles Craigie on the phone about thefts from the Railway. I didn't realise how bad they had become. Get on to Capital District for an up-to-date."

The Staff Officer reported back to the Commissioner. "Capital have seen the Chief Goods Agent. About once a week when offloading, their daily main goods train consignments have been missing from one wagon. They say they reported these losses to police at Matamu and here in the Capital. The Railway does all its communicating by telegraph in code which means a host of irrelevant telegrams burying those reporting goods missing. Every so often someone has telephoned Central Police Station then CPS sent a detective to the Goods Shed but they have got nowhere. Matamu have done nothing about it."

The Commissioner pushed his chair back and steepled his hands. "However slapdash the Railway are, we've got egg on our face. What's the value of the losses?"

"The least value for goods missing from one wagon has been two thousand eight hundred shillings and highest has been ten thousand or more. It's a tidy sum considering it has been going on about once a week for over a year."

"I can see why Charles is getting a bit shirty. If the seals are always correct and the tallying at Matamu is correct, he's probably right about making our man at Matamu responsible. Who did you have earmarked to take over from Maltravers at Matamu?"

"I've got Inspector Williams in the frame for it."

"He's a bit of an old soldier and his wife's a bitch. She'd ruffle too many feathers in a small up-country station."

"There's no-one else immediately available, sir."

"There's got to be. Get onto Capital District. I want their brightest inspector for posting a.s.a.p."

*

Nearly 10.00pm. Inspector Paul Carver parked his van behind the Capital's Central Police Station, a cluster of typical colonial design single storied buildings with green painted corrugated iron roofs and long verandas. It was Friday, and pay day, and Carver knew it would be a long night. During the day it was peaceful enough but from 7.00 pm or thereabouts the pace of the station's life changed, particularly at the end of the month. Pay day mayhem fuelled by liquor brought bodies, both dead and alive. Police trucks came and went with victims, witnesses, and prisoners. The cells filled, and the Occurrence Book and the Charge Register were in constant demand.

By 4.00am Carver completed the charging of all the night's prisoners, thanks to a Station Sergeant who knew his way around procedure and spoke enough languages to deal with the assorted tribesmen who made up that night's clientele. He stretched, stood up, poured himself a cup of tea from his flask, and looked out through the door of his room. He could see the Station Sergeant sitting on his tall stool, dozing, his head resting on a pile of books on the counter. He deserved his moments of peace.

He continued to think about one of the night's events. Was it going to rebound on him? Should he have done anything different? Well, he did what he thought right at the time and that was the end of it. *For now.*

What more could happen before eight o'clock when his shift ended? How different it was to the little English city. A bike or two without lights and some drunken labourers kicking up a rumpus in a pub was about the size of a night's law breaking. He well remembered the time that he decided the mind-numbing boredom of being a constable in a County Constabulary had run its course.

He could still feel the blast of rain-loaded wind that dashed against the door of the Police Station and blew it open with a crash, his long blue greatcoat blackened by the unremitting rain. Rivulets, not drops, flowing from its hem and down onto his already sodden boots. Constable 513 Paul Carver was off the streets for half an hour. There he was, removing his boots and wringing out his soaking socks, putting his bare feet up on a chair as he reached for the copy of the Police Review lying on the table. It fell open at the page with the job advertisements. *Inspectors of Police for East Africa.* Then back out on the stormy street, but the torn-out advertisement went with him. Yes, that really was two years ago.

Dawn was not far away. Carver stretched and walked out into the fresh morning air. His mouth tasted foul. He had drunk all his tea during the long night and the water from the tap was unfit for drinking without boiling and filtering. Six o'clock. The incident in the middle of the night still nagged. *Two more hours before Superintendent Glennon would appear. And what would happen then? Disciplined for insubordination or worse?*

The sparkling new Ford Zephyr pulled into the parking area. Carver watched as a dapper man with glossy black hair stepped from the car and started to move towards the offices. As he caught sight of Carver he shouted, "I want to see you. Now. In my office."

He was sitting behind his desk when Carver arrived. "What the hell do you mean by it?" Superintendent Glennon's face was red. Small blue veins stood out at the base of his nose.

"Mean by what, Sir?"

"Releasing those villains, that's what I mean. Detective Sergeant Ogwang told me you had six of them banged to rights and you let them go."

Carver hesitated. The Metropolitan Police jargon jangled in his ears. "With respect, Sir, I don't think you know the full story…"

"The story is Ogwang's informer told him a gang of thieves planned to break into a warehouse. I arranged for observation to be kept and when the thieves came they were caught in the act of breaking and entering. Ogwang was one of the witnesses. The informer was with them in case of a change of plan. And what do you do…? You charge the informer and let the other six get away." The Superintendent paused. Carver said nothing. Glennon continued, "That man has been responsible for the arrest of four gangs in the past month. Your action has been incompetent and insubordinate. You haven't got your knees brown yet and you think you know better than me."

"When you read the file, sir, you will find that Ogwang's informer collects half a dozen green country lads from the bus station as they arrive. With the promise of work and the sort of money they've never seen, he gets them to go with him to a break in. It's all in their statements. Six arrests. The informer gets paid from the

Information Fund and Ogwang gets a healthy cut." *And it makes your crime figures look good, too*, but thought better of saying it.

The Superintendent's nostrils flared. He opened his mouth to speak but Carver continued, "I went through the charge register last night. Ogwang and this informer have brought about the arrest of twenty-two men in the last month. Identical circumstances – they were all set up in the same way. These will have to be looked into but there's enough evidence against the informer this time. He has been charged and is ready for court."

Carver saluted, turned and left the office. He let out a long, deep breath. *What have you done? You've just told a Superintendent he is supporting a corrupt detective.* He pulled himself into his Peugeot van and drove slowly away. *Success mattered to Carver. It drove him; was he going to fall flat on his face with this one?*

*

The Senior Superintendent commanding the Capital's police leant back in his chair. Every morning at ten he met his Secretary for coffee and an update.

"By the way," she said as she was leaving for her own office, "there's some bad blood between Superintendent Glennon and Inspector Carver. I heard some of the African ranks saying that Carver read Mr. Glennon's fortune this morning. I'm told Inspector Carver takes a bit of stopping when he gets the bit between his teeth."

"Mmmm..." The SSP looked at the ceiling for a moment. "Thanks for telling me. I need to look into this straight away. I'll make a few enquiries then see Carver."

Paul Carver was in a fitful sleep when the phone rang. "The SSP wants to see you at midday," was all that the Secretary would say. As he drove to the Police Station, the altercation with Glennon loomed over him. He tucked his shirt into the waist band of his shorts and knocked on the door.

The SSP looked up. "What happened between you and Mr. Glennon?"

"We disagreed, sir."

"What was it about?"

Carver's mind whirled. Tell the whole story, accusing a Superintendent? Keep it to the bare minimum and low key and hope that would be enough? Sweat ran down his spine. His thoughts were jarred by the SSP.

"Well?"

"We disagreed about my action after the break in at MM Patel's godown. I thought I was right, sir. I still do."

He spotted the case files he had prepared during the night on the corner of the SSP's desk. The old man had done his homework.

"I think you've been in the Capital long enough. I've told Headquarters you will be available to take over Matamu District in two weeks. Before you go you'll have to learn about the railway. See the Commissioner's Staff Officer. That's all," and before Carver had left the office the SSP was working on the papers on his desk.

Chapter 3

Luka Wamala's presence was felt wherever he went. He was a big man; in many respects. He was physically powerful. Tall and muscular. His activities allowed him to spread money around the local people and although most guessed what these activities were none dared to look any further than that. Furthermore, he was the son of the chief.

He had been born in the area adjoining Kaliso station. His father had been the village chief, a person of some local standing then, but Nubian gin and syphilis had combined to eat away his vital organs and he had died painfully, a demented man. Only one of his wives – Mamayangu – had outlived the old man. She was now a shrivelled hag of indeterminate age who had long since rejected the customary role for wives past child bearing of digging and carrying water and firewood. She had two prongs to prick the conventions. She was a distiller of excellent Nubian gin and a practitioner of healing. And of blacker arts. With these talents she had acquired wealth and status which generated both deference and fear.

The Chief's only other offspring was Yowana. Luka was unusually tall for his people and this was attributed to his mother, Marika. She came from a distant people whose men folk were all six feet tall or more. When Luka was young she would say, "Look what I have given you. Height and strength. Standing among these little people here. Look at your brother Yowana – same father different mother – and you see what I mean. He is too skinny to come to much. Your father is a chief, but you will be much more than that. I know." And Luka never doubted his mother's words. He loved her for them. He said them to himself time and again. How he missed her wisdom.

The Austin A40 pick-up truck that left Nyangule village was loaded high with long bunches of cooking plantains. Oily smoke blew freely from the exhaust. Luka Wamala drove slowly until he reached the tarmac road leading into Jayanja, the main town of the Region.

He glanced at Yowana, slumped in the passenger seat. The heavy rains made the country roads treacherous with glutinous mud and Yowana was his safeguard against being stuck. "Your only value is as a donkey." He said the words loud enough for Yowana to hear but there was no reaction.

"Pretend to sleep. You've got nothing worthwhile to say, anyhow. No wit, no conversation to keep me happy while I drive." He started to sing in a deep bass voice, songs he had learned when he served in the Kings African Rifles.

Luka's destination was a village near the town's boundary. There, all the houses looked the same, single storied, mud reinforced with cow dung plastered over wicker frameworks and roofed with corrugated iron. The rutted way was barely wide enough for a vehicle and the wheels spun in the mud of the overnight rain sending the pick-up lurching into the long grass. Where the track ended was the house he rented. He switched off the ignition.

Yowana stretched and eased himself from the vehicle, stiff from the journey. Luka had money so why couldn't he get a bigger bright coloured Americani car with shiny metal like the Muhindis had, but he never dared voice this.

Luka gathered the skirt of his long white robe. "I will see you at Joyce's bar in the afternoon," and without waiting for an answer went to the house. It wasn't as grand as the one at Kaliso but it was distanced from his own village and it gave him the anonymity, privacy and storage for the items of his various trades, away from the eyes of any who knew him.

He pounded on the door. Where was Bulandina? He heard the sound of the bolts and she appeared, bleary-eyed with a coloured sheet wrapped round her, looking no more than the fourteen-year-old child that she was. He pointed to the pick-up truck and she knew what had to be done. The plantains would go to the market later but she would have to store all the other things in the house, hiding them in the pit below the floor boards.

The sun climbed and the market awoke. Everyone came for their vegetables. A butcher hacked chunks from a dead goat hanging head down from a mango tree and wrapped the pieces in banana leaves. People began to fill the market, feeling and weighing up the produce and haggling, always haggling.

Left in charge of the stack of plantains, Bulandina felt important. To be a seller of cooking bananas was such a rise above the trade she left her native village to ply that she was still unable to believe her luck. And even if Luka was bad tempered and beat her he always had money for her, and... he was a powerful lover. While she played her new role to its full, he made his way through the village, carrying two heavy cans of spirit with muscular ease. The gin was far better than the stuff brought in on bicycles, hot from the stills hidden in the swamps and it fetched a higher price here than in Kaliso. The fiery spirit was illegal, sometimes lethal, but in the village its trade was plied openly. It brought him a steady flow of money but its real value was in finding the right outlets for his more important business.

He sold the spirit and made his way back to the house and a few hours sleep. He awoke as Bulandina came in, babbling with pride at her success as a trader.

"I am a real market lady," she crooned, shuffling and moving her body in a dance as she accompanied herself in a high-pitched trill. "They all sold well," she sang repeatedly. She unknotted the large spotted handkerchief that served as her purse, taking three attempts at counting out the notes and small change before handing it over to Luka. Then she joined him in his bed.

Luka's business was done and now he was impatient to return to Kaliso. As he entered Joyce's Bar, heads turned to glance at him, then turning away quickly before he caught their gaze. He spotted Yowana in a corner, playing cards. He put the cards down and followed Luka out of the bar.

Luka had to remind himself of the main reason he had brought Yowana with him. He was not used to this. It was the first time he had actually needed Yowana. He would have to treat him differently – at least for a while. He waited until they were clear of the market area and then he said, "Little brother, you are about to do a man's job."

What was this? Luka's tone was honeyed, not the usual rasping sarcasm. Yowana waited. Luka liked to wave a flaming torch in front of you and see if it singed.

"Did you hear what I said?" Yowana grunted. Luka persisted. "Do you want to do a man's work?"

For once Yowana felt brave enough to confront his brother. "You must be in trouble or you wouldn't be asking me. What do you want?"

"I have watched you. You can climb like a colobus. Could you climb a railway wagon?"

"Of course."

"When it's moving?"

"Samwiri's work? I have watched him. I have ideas how to do it quicker."

Yowana's fantasy world was about to have substance. He would be someone, wear stylish clothes that would show who he was. Of course he could do it. Then Luka would have to treat him with respect. Everything he had, which wasn't much, came from him. The food he ate, the beer he drank, the bhangi he smoked. It wouldn't be like that again. And he wouldn't be Luka's donkey any more, pushing the pick-up out of the mud.

"I will have to tell the others. And keep yourself sober. No more crushed feet."

Bulandina was still savouring her success as a trader. Luka had said she had done well and that meant everything. Settling down, she brewed herself some tea, shook the ground herbs into it and noisily sucked it from a wide enamelled dish.

Chapter 4

With his van loaded with all he possessed, Carver arrived in Matamu in the late afternoon. The Britannia Hotel was built in the 1920s of whitewashed concrete blocks with long verandas and a galvanised iron roof. In the cramped reception area stood an elephant's foot, hollowed out as a stand for walking sticks and umbrellas.

The Hotel stood apart from the bazaar area of the Township. A thick hibiscus hedge separated it from the dirt road, which linked the Asian populated bazaar to the European houses. The road was flanked with jacaranda trees, tunnel-like under the canopy. When their bright blue flowers fell on the grass verges and on the rutted red earth of the road there was a semblance, for those who looked for it, of bluebell time in England.

Carver stood before the counter. He banged the bell with his palm. He felt grimy and the sooner he could get a bath the better. The red dust of the road penetrated everything. The navy blue of his uniform cap was coated, and it billowed out in a cloud as he shook it. From the shadows came a voice. "Watch what you're doing, man. The place will look like the road outside. You're our new policeman, I suppose." And with these welcoming words he signed the register.

There was little for the visitor to do in Matamu once the sun had set. Nearly all the Asian dukas, which lined the four streets of the bazaar, were closed for trading by seven in the evening. No cinema, the two bars were uninviting; a walk brought on a mass mosquito attack. Whether he liked it or not The Britannia was Carver's retreat until he was allocated one of the Government houses.

*

Over the following days he was busy getting to know his staff. They were the mixed bag he had expected. A few 'old soldier' constables, who had been stationed in most part of the Territory at some time, but most were younger with little experience. The sub-inspector was fresh from the Police College in the Capital. His education at a Mission school distanced him from most of the other men and he seemed unaware of this. And then there was the Station Sergeant. He stood no more than five feet six inches and he smelt of stale liquor. The Detective Sergeant had left for long leave before Carver arrived and had not been replaced yet. There were three Detective Constables, all non-English speaking, little use for such a complex enquiry as the Railway thefts.

The Sub Inspector knew nothing of the workings of the Railway. "They send us little pieces of paper. They are in a language we can't understand, so the Stores Corporal files them. We have many other things to deal with."

Carver went to see the Stores Corporal, Tomasi Ngirenga. He had a battered filing box. In it were several bundles of buff forms, many inches thick. He explained, "A Railway messenger brings some most days. The sub inspector tells me to file them. I said I should go to the station and ask them what they mean but he told if they were important the Station Master would tell us. I thought it was not right, but the sub inspector wouldn't listen to me."

Carver thumbed through the bundle; the earliest of the telegrams was over a year old. Only the Railway people could help now.

"Get your hat, Corporal We're going over to the station now."

The Station Master, Mohamed Akram, rose from his desk. "It is a pleasure to welcome you to Matamu station."

Carver looked at the tall, thin Asian man, hair greying and dressed in an immaculate white drill uniform.

"We are sad that we hardly ever had the opportunity to welcome Inspector Maltravers. He must have been a very busy man." There was a twinkle in the Station Master's eye.

"I'm told that the Railway is a world of its own that's hard to enter, Mohamed."

"Oh, it is, Mr. Carver. Do you know that many of the Africans who work here say they are 'Mu-lerway'? Their way of saying they are of the *Railway tribe*."

"Then if I'm going to win, I'd better join that tribe too. We're not going to leave the station until we understand all the ins and outs of how goods are dealt with."

"I have sent for some tea for us and then we can get down to the business."

Three hours later, Carver and his Corporal left the Railway station. They now knew that most of the goods reported missing by the Capital – about three hundred and fifty items in all – had been transhipped at Matamu from wagons coming through the other territory. After being held for a short time in the Matamu Goods Shed, they were loaded into wagons for onward shipment. All the missing consignments were for the Capital. Most were high value goods and these were always sent in steel covered goods wagons.

They had visited the Goods Shed to look at one of these trucks. "You say it's the most secure but I can't see any locks for the doors."

The Goods Clerk shook his head. "We have hundreds of these wagons. Locks would be too costly. You see the long tower bolt. It has a hole in it at the top and when the loading is complete very thick wire is screwed up tight in the hole so that the bolt can't be pulled down. Then to show where it was last loaded, lead seals are put on the doors. These are crimped with the loading station's code. Matamu is 'MTU'; the Capital is 'CPL' and so on."

"But in the Capital, I was told all the wagons from which goods were missing were correctly sealed. I watched porters remove the heavy wire seals. They needed ladders and big bolt croppers to do this. And that was while a truck was stationary at a loading bay."

"I know. And that is the big mystery. The seals being intact says they could not have been opened anywhere between here and the Capital."

When they returned to the Police Station Carver and Ngirenga went over what they had found.

"There's just a chance the lead seals might tell us something. I want you to go to the Capital Goods Shed and find the lead seals from as many as possible of the wagons from which goods were missing. The offloading clerks there wrap the lead seals around the wagon labels and throw them into tea chests which they keep in the store."

*

Now there was a new arrival to meet. At last, a replacement for the Detective Sergeant. When he considered his staff – the greenness of the sub inspector, the drink-jaded station sergeant and the detectives who were no more than thief takers – he realised how much rested upon the quality of the newcomer. He didn't know the man's name yet since his papers had not arrived – the post from the Capital took ages. Whoever he was he would be more than welcome.

Carver stood by the station tea stall. The third class mail train was due in shortly from the Capital and the detective should be arriving on this. There was always banter between the tea stall proprietor and his customers, the sparky, raucous humour that made Africa such an enthralling place. The throng showed its delight when Carver joined in and with courteous corrections they polished his Swahili for him.

The train glided into the station and soon he was watching hands rising from unseen bodies pushing wooden suitcases and bundles through the carriage windows to other hands waiting outside. Soon those bound for Matamu were clear of the station. Carver's attention was drawn to the last person climbing down from the leading carriage. Detective Sergeant bloody Ogwang. He couldn't be the replacement he was expecting. *What the hell is he doing here? A bent informer. The row with Glennon. I thought I'd seen the last of the bastard when I left the Capital.* He stood back and waited until Ogwang had nearly reached him. The man was looking down as he trudged dragging his kitbag towards the exit. He stepped out in front of the detective. "What are you doing here, Ogwang?"

The detective looked up, startled, his drinker's bloodshot eyes squinting against the light. Then recognition. "I am posted to Matamu."

So this is who they have sent me. Ogwang. Ogwang. Ogwang. What will he be up to when I send him out on line?

Is this Glennon's revenge?

Chapter 5

9th December 1956

The hotel was wearing thin. Most days Carver returned there around dusk, took a bath and early meal and made a quiet night of it. Now, for one evening, he was determined to forget crime and the Railway. He went to the bar. Jonathan Morley, a tobacco company representative who was also staying in the Britannia was leaning against the bar.

As he sipped his beer, Morley said, "I travel light. Bare essentials only. A suitcase of clothes and these." He pointed to a wind-up gramophone and two record cases. "Do you like Fats Waller? You do? Good man. He tapped the record cases. In here is every record by Fats ever released in the UK." He sipped his beer again. "These new fangled thirty-three-and-a-thirds don't give you the same authentic sound as the good old seventy-eights. I doubt they will ever catch on. You're a policeman, here's one for you, 'Your Feet's Too Big'," and he already had the handle of the Columbia gramophone cranking.

Dinner was served on the verandah. It overlooked the junction where the road from the bazaar met that from the railway station. The long shadows were quickly absorbed by the night and the cicadas had started their fiddling. With no street lighting it was now pitch black beyond the light from the veranda's lamps. The two men talked and listened to the mellow voice on the gramophone record that poked fun at the world. They had finished the onion soup. The waiter had just placed the main course before them when Carver was conscious of a light wobbling its way up the long incline from the station. As it came nearer he saw a cyclist with a hurricane lantern dangling from the machine's handlebars. The white drill uniform of the Railway became clearer. Ashabhai Patel, the Goods Clerk, was bent over the cycle like a human question mark. He spotted the policeman in the verandah light and waved frantically.

"Mr. Carver, sir. I must most urgently talk with you."

"Mr. Ashabhai, you'll do yourself a mischief straining away like that on a bicycle."

"Sir. There is trouble at the station," Ashabhai blurted out, struggling to regain the breath cycling had wrenched from him. "The up mail is held up. There is a drunken man stopping it."

"One man stopping the train?"

"Ah, but he is having a gun also." Ashabhai stood leaning against the cycle, mopping his forehead with a large red handkerchief. "You are so right, Mr. Carver sir. There is mischief at the station. The Station Master has sent me to get you. You must come and sort it out."

"You say there is a man with a gun holding the train up. Is he trying to rob it?"

"Oh no. He is a policeman, with a rifle, and he is very drunk, sir. He is not letting the driver and guard do their business."

"A policeman? Who's there now?"

"The sergeant, sir, but he is not making much success."

"Give me a moment," he said over his shoulder as he went back into the hotel.

He took his uniform jacket and cap from the coat stand, and as a passing thought picked up his silver knobbed swagger cane from where he had left it in the elephant's foot. Carver took the drive to the station slowly. *Never rush to a dust-up, the old hands in Hertfordshire had always said. Let them tire themselves out.* Down the hill, no buildings, scrub right up to the edge of the road and hyenas' eyes reflecting in the headlights. He arrived all too soon. He passed his police station, fifty yards back from the railway buildings, and parked his van. He took a cigarette from a packet in his tunic pocket, lit it, drew strongly on it for a moment and then flicked it through the open window. He pulled the peak of his uniform cap down, picked up his swagger cane, and climbed from the van. He stood looking at the station entrance for a few moments, taking deep breaths. And then he willed his reluctant feet down the steps past the ticket office, firmly closed now, even though the mail train stood alongside the platform.

The train, the flagship of the line, filled the length of the station and more. The locomotive idled gently almost out of sight beyond the end of the platform, pluming out steam, ready to go. The Travelling Ticket Inspector had secured as many doors as he could reach and inside the third-class heads bobbed up and down from the safety of the locked carriages, relaying their accounts to those who couldn't get a clear view.

Station Master Mohammed Ashraf, stood just inside the office door midway along the platform. What would normally be a noisy thronging concourse was unnaturally still.

Fifty yards from Carver was the police constable, tall, muscular, dressed in khaki drill uniform, creased and dishevelled, the tall tarbush askew on his head, enlarged pierced ear lobes looped and swinging. The constable lunged at the walls of the nearest carriage with the butt of a service rifle, bellowing out at the same time.

"What will we do if Mr Carver is not arresting him?" asked the Assistant Station Master.

"We will wait and see."

"But what if he fails?"

"Then I will put on my hat and go out and take charge. After all, I am Station Master. Look. Carver is very calm and confident. The mail train will be on its way in no time."

Carver had spotted the Station Sergeant crouching behind a pile of crates and mail sacks. He wore no uniform but shorts, a loose shirt, and sandals made from old car tyre.

"Sergeant, here quick. Who's the constable?"

"He's PC Kipchai. He is from Special Force in the Capital. He was on money escort and he should be going back on this train, but he got drunk somewhere."

"He looks familiar…"

"Everyone knows him. He's national boxing champion."

The atmosphere had now changed, and Carver felt it. When he had arrived all eyes were on Kipchai. Now they were on him. *What the hell do I do? In his state he won't see reason. If it comes to an arrest I'll lose, get slaughtered. The sergeant's useless. I don't need this.* He clenched his fist to stop its shaking being obvious.

A quick mental rehearsal, then he tucked the swagger cane under his left arm and mustered as much military bearing as he could. He stepped forward into the light and stamped his right foot down. He marched towards PC Kipchai, the swing of the arm exaggerated.

"Constable Kipchai," he yelled, a parody of his drill instructor during National Service.

He halted six feet away from the constable. Kipchai stopped beating on the carriage and slowly looked round, the rifle hanging loosely from his right hand.

"Constable Kipchai, *atten – SHUN!*"

The constable pulled himself up to his full height and although still holding the rifle, adopted a boxer's stance, peering though half closed eyes. Carver felt the movement in his stomach. He re-tasted the onion soup. And then

Kipchai's right boot stamped into place, the rifle held stiffly in the attention position.

"For inspection, pooo…rrrt arms!" Carver yelled as though commanding an entire Aldershot parade ground.

Kipchai flung the weapon up across his chest.

"Ease bolts!"

The constable fumbled but then worked the bolt backwards and forwards until the rifle rounds had all been ejected, brass shining as they dropped onto the platform. Carver felt his breath forcing itself out. He hadn't realised he had been holding it so long. He shouted the drill sergeant's commands to march PC Kipchai along the platform, up the steps, and across the road to the police station. The cell door was open and Kipchai marched in. Carver took the rifle as the constable entered and the door clanged shut.

He went to the charge office, removed his cap and wiped away the sweat with the back of his hand. From the station came the long drawn out whistle of the Beyer Garratt. As though the cork was taken from a bottle of sound the noise of the passengers, the hawkers, the tea stall servers, and those who just came to look, swelled and the tramping beat of the locomotive was almost drowned as it pulled away on its journey to the Capital.

He went out to where he had parked his van, sat in it and it was only then that the full impact of dealing with a drunk with a loaded rifle hit him. *You're a sham. What on earth are you doing in the police in Africa if you feel so gutless in a situation like this? How will you be the next time, and there will be a next time, and the time after that?*

He had no answer. He started the van and drove back up the incline to the hotel, savouring the cool evening air through the van's open windows. It seemed impossible that only twenty minutes had elapsed since he was called out.

"I told them to put it in the oven," said Morley as he got up from reading a paper. "How do you fancy this one?" and Fats Waller's voice boomed out.

"The joint is jumping, it's really jumping… check your weapons at the door… don't give your right name, no, no, no!"

With the meal over, he excused himself. Even though the encounter had lasted a few minutes, he sensed there was something about Kipchai and he wanted to know more. After forty minutes trying he managed to get a phone call to the constable's O.C. in the Capital.

"Kipchai? Four years service, comes from a small tribe. Two commendations and no disciplinary record. Good lad. Not just because he's an outstanding sportsman. What did you say he's been up to?"

Carver related the evening's events.

"Right out of character. I thought he didn't drink. Trains every day and the National Championships are in a few weeks. His father makes a living as a professional hunter. Said drink didn't help his aim. I thought his son was the same. You can take him to court – there's enough evidence – or take action under Police Regulations. It's up to you."

The disciplinary hearing at eight the following morning was short. Kipchai had been up at 6am and persuaded the duty corporal to bring him a charcoal flatiron. He pressed his uniform, polished his boots and belt and brushed his tarbush. He stood rigidly at attention, towering over Carver's desk. He pleaded guilty. He spoke in Swahili.

"I took strong drink, Effendi. I came last night on the train to guard money for the Gavamenti office. I gave the money and it was then I met two fellow clansmen. They insisted I drink with them. I took one drink with them. It was good to meet fellow clansmen. There are not many of us and they found more drink and then more. That is it, Sir."

First disciplinary offence. The hearing was over quickly. "You are fined one month's pay, to be paid over three months. Fall out."

And that's that, Carver said to himself – *just as well Glennon wasn't around. He would have thrown the book at Kipchai and then at me too.*

Chapter 6

Carver had hoped for Ngirenga's swift return from the Capital, but he was beginning to realise not much happened quickly in Africa. He had put all his hope into what the seals might tell him. It was the only ray of light he had.

And then the corporal arrived. Ngirenga was carrying a canvas bag which he clutched to him.

"I found out that goods were missing from fifty-nine wagons." His broad grin said he had good news. "I found fifty-one labels with seals," and he tipped them all out over Carver's desk from the bag he was carrying. And then his mood seemed to change. "Finding all these was hard but what are we going to do with them now?"

"The Station Master said they use one seal press in the Goods Shed and one in the station office, and they have two spares in the Station Master's safe. Go and get two samples from each of the seal presses. We'll see if they tell us anything."

An hour later, Ngirenga was back with the sample impressions, mounted on cards and neatly labelled and certified. Together they compared these samples with some of the seals brought back from the Capital. At first sight they were identical. Carver took a magnifying glass from his drawer and it was then that very slight differences were apparent. Was this the first ray of hope?

Carver made a phone call and then called Ngirenga back in. "It's a journey back to the Capital for you but this time to Police HQ Scenes of Crime Department."

Ngirenga was back in three days. The message from the Scenes of Crime specialist was that the impressions on the seals were fakes. Every one of them. Carver's delight was obvious.

"Now we know someone is using a fake seal press, sir, but where is it being used? It could be anywhere between here and the Capital."

The corporal had brought Carver down to earth with a bump. How were they going to find out where the fake seal press was used?

Chapter 7

The Bayer Garratt locomotive ran at the steep gradient as it left Kaliso station and then settled to its muscular tramping beat as it hauled the half mile of trucks into the African night on its journey to Ramagazi, twenty-one miles and an hour away. Almost everything sold in the city and in the dukas of the up-country townships found its way into the country on the railway.

Ramesh Patel sat in the Station Master's Office. He had seen the train off. It had come and gone, leaving nothing and taking nothing away other than greedily drinking its fill from the water column. He felt very alone. The next train, another goods in the opposite direction, wasn't due until 6.30am. Nearly midnight and it was still 75 degrees. Stickily humid. When wasn't it? The swamps around Kaliso made sure of that. The Tilley pressure lamp hissed, spluttered and the light dimmed. Ramesh pumped it so the hissing grew though the light remained a modest glimmer on his desk.

The irritation of being posted to such a place gnawed at him. His comfortable job as the Assistant Goods Agent in the Capital had ended abruptly with his posting to Kaliso. In the city he had standing, a good social life, and the opportunity for extra earnings through manipulating a service that could swell a trader's profits. Now here he was without anything that made life more than drudgery. The nearest township was three miles off, a dirt road lined with Asian shops – the universal 'dukas' of this part of Africa. And what was there when you got there? A drink of cold Pepsi with a duka wallah chewing betel nut, edging him towards his daughters, and hoping all the time to keep the dowry as low as possible. No entertainment other than the card and gossip schools and a daily game of volley ball for which half the male population crammed the red earth court an hour before dusk. Ramesh did not fit the life of such a rural community.

It was gone midnight.

He had taken over Kaliso station when old Maganlal retired. The administration and the paperwork was a mess which assaulted Ramesh's need for order and tidiness. Everyone talked fondly of Maganlal but *they* didn't have to clear up the unsorted documentation for the District Traffic Inspector's visit. He shifted the pile of waybills and invoices, payment vouchers and receipts, requisitions and delivery notes from one pile into another. He yawned. He would have to go to bed.

He was not alone. He squinted into the darkness.

"Nani huko, *who is there?*"

The up-country Swahili had the abrupt intonation that marked the Asian way of speaking the language. There was slight movement in the shadows.

He called again, more petulantly this time. "Wewe. Nani huko?"

He peered and as his eyes became accustomed to the gloom, he made out the figure of an African moving forward.

"Wewe nani? Taka nini?"

"I speak English, Muhindi."

The brazenness of the tone turned Ramesh's unease to fear. "Who are you? What is it you are wanting?"

"I came to say you must not to come to the station at night time."

"I am Station Master. I come to the station at any time I wish." He did not feel as brave as his words.

The man moved closer. Ramesh recognised him – a short thin man, the marked cast in his right eye – as one who had spoken to him at the station platform a few days before. He had not made sense then and Ramesh had pushed the incident from his mind.

"This office is closed until morning eight o'clock. You will now please be leaving it."

The African continued to move towards the table. Ramesh felt the sweat on his forehead and his palms were wet. He inched his hand across the desk towards the heavy round ebony ruler a foot in front of him. He hardly saw the panga coming down on his wrist. For a moment he stared at his severed hand, his mouth open.

Ramesh fell forward as his life blood was pumped away. He died some minutes after the African had slipped out through the fly screen door.

The body was discovered by the Assistant Station Master when he came on duty at 5.30am. It was pouring with rain when he came to open the station for the first train, the down goods. With the collar of his white cotton drill uniform tunic turned up against the weather and his head down as he shook out his umbrella, it did not register that the station office door was unlocked. It should have been secured as soon as staff went off duty on the departure of 119up. As he realised this he went cautiously through to the back office, past the 'line clear' tablet machine and through the fly screen door.

The dawn was slow to break through the leaden rain clouds and he could see nothing clearly. He reached around the table for the Tilley kerosene pressure lamp he knew should be there and it was then that he touched the cold softness of Ramesh's hand.

He found the lamp and as he tried to light it he could see the shape of Ramesh. The lamp was empty. Another match confirmed what he thought he had seen. The station master was lying across the table, congealed blood on the floor. Like most Africans, the ASM was accustomed to violent death, but that someone had dared to attack a railway official in his office was unheard of. Beer party fights in the railwaymen's quarters, but not this. No, not this. He ran from the office, oblivious to the rain, calling for the night watchman who patrolled the goods shed area the other side of the track and well away from the station building. "Hamisi, Hamisi, where are you?"

The watchman rose from the nest he fashioned nightly in between the cotton bales awaiting shipment. As the Assistant Station Master came closer, Hamisi straightened his red tarbush and saluted.

"Hamisi! Come quickly! You must go to the police post in Kaliso. Tell them the Station Master is dead. He has been killed."

The watchman stood, inactive, bemused. The Station Master dead? Could that be?

"Don't you understand? Get the bicycle. Go man, go, go on. Go fast."

It took thirty minutes for the sub-inspector to arrive in a police truck with two constables, the watchman and the railway bike in the back. He looked inside the office and was out in seconds.

"No one is allowed to go in."

"But I've got to give line clear for the down goods."

The sub-inspector wagged his finger at the ASM and posted a constable at the door and went back to the police post where he radioed the District Police HQ. An Asian killed. This was well outside his scope. A day of frustration and confusion was about to start for railwaymen, passengers and traders all along the line.

Chapter 8

Saturday 6.18 a.m

In the early light of morning, Inspector Gurbachan Singh, officer in charge of Crime Branch for the police district of Jayanja, washed himself under the running water of the tap on the outside of his house. He was looking forward to the end of his stint as duty officer and as he sluiced the water over his head, face, hair and beard, and then over his upper body, he anticipated the pleasure of the hockey that afternoon. The Sikh Union against the Goan Sports Club for the league leadership. And then came the message about Ramesh's death. He stood and considered this. On this Saturday above all days. There had been a note from the Commissioner's Office a couple of month ago – Inspector, what was his name, Carver was it? – had been posted to Matamu and thefts from the Railway all the way from the border to the Capital were his responsibility. Let him take it on. A phone call would land it in his lap and Gurbachan would be free to play.

No; this was a bit more than a theft. It smelt of trouble and there was no way he could avoid starting the investigation. He set out for Kaliso, forty-five miles of wet, slippery red laterite roads to negotiate, and maybe some flooding from the swamp. His Chevrolet Sedan, heavy with a high clearance, was as good a vehicle as any for these conditions. An African detective sergeant sat beside him and two constables were already dozing on the back seats.

"An Asian murdered," he said to himself as he drove. "And a railway official, too."

As soon as he arrived, he set up his Olivetti typewriter in the station's front office. He didn't see the need for all the other paraphernalia of 'modern investigation'. His methods hardly ever varied – very personal enquiry, leading to rigorous interrogation, which in turn would bring a confession. But this one was different. The file would be scrutinised at Headquarters by senior officers who put more importance on well-ordered paper work than he did. It was just as well he had thought to request a Scenes of Crime man from HQ before he left Jayanja. His viewing of the scene gave him only the basic information necessary in court if the killer were caught. And now he could do no more than wait for his detectives to question the railwaymen whose quarters were at the station. Perhaps he would strike lucky. Maybe a detective would come across someone of his own tribe among the railwaymen, a lever to press for information.

Gurbachan had investigated a hundred or more homicides. Most had been Africans killing Africans. He had only ever handled two murders of Asians and there had been no mysteries in those cases. And now here was this Hindu babu lying in a remote railway station with his hand chopped off. It wasn't a robbery – the safe was closed and locked – and enquiries showed no other reason. He took as many photographs as his supply of flash bulbs allowed and then arranged for the body to be taken to the mortuary at Jayanja. The sooner the better, flies were already swarming.

If he had to wait for the Scenes of Crime man he might as well go to the township of Kaliso and wait in comfort. As he arrived he looked for the sign saying *'C.K. Mistry Fitter & Engineer Living Frontside Working Backside.'* Mistry owned and ran the only garage within forty miles. The high corrugated-iron-clad workshop stood in a compound full of old cars and lorries, which yielded spare parts. Though the outside looked dilapidated, inside there was a well-equipped machine shop – a re-boring machine for engines, a lathe, a grinder and drilling machine which Mistry, trained in India by the RAF, used with an expertise rare in this country. His large diesel generator powered the tools, gave his house electric light and was the envy of all Kaliso.

Gurbachan used Mistry as his eyes and ears in this part of the District, but the garage owner was a businessman and there was always a quid pro quo for quality information. They retired to the back room of the living quarters. Mistry made a sign to his wife. She reappeared a few minutes later with a bottle of brandy and two glasses and a pile of samosas on a tin tray. The two drank and ate as they talked. After an hour Gurbachan knew a little about petty crimes in the area and more about the frailties of members of the local Asian population but knew no more about the station master's death. Mistry was shocked by the news.

"It is a bad thing, I am telling you, when they go around killing people like us."

"Who are 'they', Mistry?"

"I don't know. They... Africans... none of us would do a thing like that." He added, "We didn't know him. He was different."

That was true. Ramesh, with his manicured hands and bow tie, could not have been less like the Asians of Kaliso, with their flapping shirts and dhotis and betel nut stained fingers. He ate the lunch prepared by Mistry's wife and after a little more conversation drove back to the railway station. The garage man was on edge but so were all the other Asians in Kaliso.

By mid-afternoon the Scenes of Crime officer from Police HQ had completed his examination. He had lifted fingerprints found on the safe handle and brass doorknobs.

He looked for footprints and found none. He had taken scrapings of the dried blood from the table and floor and prepared scale drawings of the scene. He worked quickly to get clear of the muddy dirt roads and onto tarmac before dark.

"I could have done a better job if the body had been left, Singh."

"You should have come quicker. You headquarters people think there's no crime outside the Capital."

"You will have a report in forty-eight hours."

"Eight, eight hours, no more. The Assistant Commissioner will not want any hanky panky with this."

With the Scenes of Crime Officer gone Gurbachan started to collate the reports of his detectives. It was midnight before he returned to Jayanja, leaving the detectives to continue enquiries. He climbed into bed a tired and puzzled man.

Mistry didn't sleep well. If they didn't arrest the murderer soon the police would keep on coming around and this could be difficult for some of his business.

What to do?

Chapter 9

21ˢᵗ December

Noon. Another week over. Paul Carver closed the last case file he was going to look at for a week. It was hot in the office. Christmastime was always hot, so the old stagers said. He poured water from the tall enamel jug on the table by the window into the bowl. As he bent to swill the lukewarm water over his head and face, he heard a raised voice coming from the Charge Office. A female voice. A European female voice. Just one of the wives making a fuss about her houseboy. It happened. While he was still wiping the water from his face he saw the Station Sergeant standing by the door.

"There is a lady here wanting to complain. I tell her, but she will not go away."

A woman in the uniform of a Nursing Sister pushed her way past the sergeant. "No, I will not go away. Not until I have some answers."

Carver hastily buttoned his tunic. "Won't you sit down and tell me what's wrong."

Her anger bubbled. "I'd rather stand, thank you."

The policeman sat down behind his desk and looked at her. White starched head-dress, spotless white tunic dress, blue elasticated belt accentuating her narrow waist, fob watch pinned above the breast. The new Sister for the hospital. Baird, that was the name.

"Miss Baird. I'd feel more comfortable if you would sit down… Please."

He indicated the chair in front of the desk. She sat stiffly on its edge.

"My name is Carver. Paul Carver. I…"

"I know who you are. You have arrested my Senior Orderly, Justin Matovu…"

"I've just finished looking at the file."

"They say he has been pretending to be a doctor in one of the villages. I don't believe it. I know he wouldn't do that. He's been in Government service too long." She looked for a reaction in Carver's face and found none. "Besides, I need him at the hospital."

"If you'll be patient…"

"Patient. I'm past being patient!" Her voice was rising. "I can't get any sense out of anyone. He is essential for the hospital. You've got to understand that!"

He took a file from his desk drawer and leant forward. "Look," he said, with exaggerated patience. "In this file there are twelve witness statements all saying the same thing. He regularly sets up as a doctor in Malaba village, giving injections. When he was arrested he had a Government marked box containing four syringes and three phials of penicillin. All contaminated. And, by the way, he had over three hundred shillings on him when he was arrested. That's a lot of money."

"There will be a good explanation."

"Can you think of one?"

"Well…"

"No, there isn't one."

"Doctor Walsh is away until next week. There's no-one else. I'm in charge until he comes back."

"You'll just have to trust…"

"Trust. Trust… trust a policeman?" She glared at Carver. "At least let him out on bail or whatever it is you do."

"Matovu's not a local man and I can't risk him absconding. The charge is a serious one. So far no one has died. If he carries on doing this, who knows?"

"You've arrested him and now you're talking as though he is already convicted…"

"On Monday he will go before the Resident Magistrate and he'll decide if there's a case to answer. If there isn't, he'll be released. If there is, his trial by the RM will go ahead. It's not me who tries him. I'm sorry…"

"You're sorry. Well, that's all right then!"

She sprang from the chair, slammed it back against the desk and was through the door before he could say anything.

Carver caught himself sighing. *I'm doing a lot of that lately.* He took his tunic off and hung it over his chair again. He pulled the file towards him. Half an hour later he had gone through it – twice. Matovu was still going to court.

*

31st December 1956

Rap, rap, rap went the spoon on the hard wooden table.

"Quiet please. Please. Thank you."

The throng around Rod Stern, District Commissioner of Matamu, eased back.

"According to my watch it is two minutes to midnight." He scanned the room. "I am glad you all were able to come to say goodbye to 1956. It hasn't been too bad, so let's drink to its painless demise and welcome the new born 1957." He lifted his glass. "To 1957."

Dougal McLean, Matamu's bank manager, inflated his bagpipes and 'Auld Lang Syne' droned around the room. Those who could move burst into the rituals to accompany the song.

Carver stood in the arched doorway between the verandah and the lounge. watching the gaiety. He could see that all the government officials of Matamu District and their wives had been invited, plus the Bank Managers, the leader of the Asian community, and four of the senior African chiefs and their wives. With the singing over conversations picked up again.

"My houseboy Kasmiri's a treasure. Does a better soufflé than I do…"

"You know what they're like with the spirits. Well I always used to mark a bottle when I put it away. But then he was watering it up to the mark. So now I turn the bottle upside down before I mark it."

"… you wouldn't believe he could have gone four no trumps with that …."

"… no they're not too dangerous but watch out for the black mamba. Now they're like greased lightning…"

Rod Stern watched as Carver stood back, weighing up the room. He had met the policeman shortly after he arrived from the Capital and he had hardly seen him since then. He realised he knew little of the man, and as DC he felt he should know more. Hell, he was the District's police commander after all. Word of the encounter with Constable Kipchai had gone round the bazaar and by the time the story had reached the European population of Matamu it had grown to resemble a shoot out in a Hollywood western.

Carver saw Stern motioning to him with his glass. "Thanks. I was wondering if I could elbow my way in somewhere. I'm only on nodding terms with most here."

Donna Stern, the District Officer's wife, appeared at their side with a striking dark-haired woman.

"Margaret arrived late and is on her own, so I thought I'd steer her over to you. Mr. Carver has been in Matamu only a little longer than you."

Carver looked at the newcomer. There was something familiar, but he couldn't place her. Until she spoke. "We've already met, haven't we Mr. Carver." The edge was still there in her voice.

"Well, nurses and policemen always seem to get together, don't they?" With that, Donna left to play hostess elsewhere.

Margaret; was this the same woman who had stormed his office and didn't trust policemen? She looked so different now that the anger no longer distorted her face. Now he could see the dark shiny curls which were hidden under her starched head-dress that day in his office. Then she had worn her uniform as if it were a suit of armour.

"It's Maggie, by the way, 'Margaret's a bit too formal for my liking," she explained to those around her. The throng of people swayed like the tide and now she was pushed closer to Carver and with the closeness he was aware of her perfume, light and fresh.

As the night lengthened, and the crowd thinned, conversation with her became easier, though it was still only at surface level; why they had come to Africa, Matamu and its people, what she did at the hospital, and what it was like in the Capital before they were posted up-country. Her soft Ulster accent and way of speaking fascinated him. He found himself rehearsing what he wanted to say. But then when he was ready it was too late.

Suddenly she exclaimed, "Heavens alive, it's nearly two-thirty. I must go. I've got a heavy day ahead. Two bush dispensaries to visit. So I'll love you and leave you."

A few minutes later he heard the sound of her Morris Minor pulling away. Through the fly gauze of the verandah he watched its headlights cut through the night.

He was still staring when he felt a hand on his shoulder. "When she's off duty she's quite stunning, isn't she?"

Donna Stern, obviously much younger than her DC husband, stood alongside him nursing an empty glass. "If you've got over absent friends, you might help out present company. Another Pimms would do nicely. Not too heavy on the gin, though."

Chapter 10

Justin Matovu was convicted and sentenced, and Carver was relieved that the case was now completed. Matovu's offences had taken far too much of his time. It had nothing whatever to do with the Railway, where he knew he was losing ground. If it hadn't been for that damned Nursing Sister, he would have left it to the sub-inspector. He resented her intrusion. Damned Nursing Sister! He grinned as he recalled the words that had run through his head. That was the starchy madam who stormed his office. It wasn't the New Year's Eve person by a long chalk. I wonder what she is really like, he thought as he drove to the hospital to tie the loose ends of the case up with the District Medical Officer.

Doctor Walsh was waiting for him, but Carver hadn't expected Sister Baird to be there too.

"I thought Maggie should hear what you have to say," said the doctor.

After Carver had finished giving them the findings of the Resident Magistrate, Walsh pushed back his chair and said, "I'm not surprised. That sort of thing is always on the cards. People in the villages know he works in the hospital. And he wears a white coat. They're torn between their own traditional medicine and what we have to offer at the hospital."

As he went to his van, Sister Baird caught up with him. "I owe you an apology," were her opening words. "I liked

Justin, but being new to Matamu I depended on him too much. I suppose that's why I led off. It wasn't you personally."

"It felt pretty personal to me."

"Maybe we can talk about it another time. Look, I've got to get on with my rounds. I'm already late."

With that, she looked at the fob watch, smoothed her uniform dress and strode off to the wards. She found herself thinking of this tall policeman with the corn coloured hair. She would make sure there would be 'another time.' Before she went home at the end of the day, she called in to the Medical Officer to give him a summary of the position in the wards.

"Well what do you think of our young policeman now, Maggie? Still angry with him?"

"No. I think I've got over it now. I apologised to him before he went."

"Good… Nothing more than that?"

"I think I know what you mean. A bit, maybe. He might be good company, though some of the old stagers here say he is too stand-offish for their liking. What do you think?"

"I'm not a Nursing Sister in her twenties. Most medical people think that psychology isn't a real science. Some think it is hokum. I'm not one of those. There's a feature of our personality which can tell us a lot about the way people act. At one end of the scale is extraversion and at the other end is introversion. The introvert goes inside himself to recharge his batteries and the extravert goes into the world outside himself to do this. In short, the introvert – which, by the way is what Paul is – is more comfortable dealing with a small number of people he knows. To people he doesn't know, he may well seem distant and hard to read. This might give you a few clues."

She recognised Doctor Walsh was putting her straight in the nicest – and most professional – way.

As time went by, it surprised her that she found herself thinking of Carver at the most unlikely of times, and – yes – what the doctor had said was beginning to help. She found herself thinking about what he had said. And then her past took over. In such a small place, where could she take cover if it didn't work out? She still had all those memories.

Their next meeting came sooner than she expected. Two days later she went to the railway station to collect a package for the hospital and Carver was there talking to the Station Master.

He smiled. "Good timing. I was going to find an excuse to come to the hospital."

After that, they saw each other most days but memories of their abrasive first meeting at the Police Station were still fresh for them both. In whatever they did together it was as though they were both feeling their way – a few minutes mid-morning at the hospital; a walk together along the Railway platform to watch the mail train come and go; early evening at the small club where they played tennis on the dusty court, with an impromptu dance later, Jonathan Morley playing the ancient upright piano and, as ever, cranking up his gramophone.

Some Sundays they climbed the Rock, a five hundred feet volcanic plug dominating Matamu, Carver bounding ahead and then turning to offer his hand to pull her up. It was cooler to sit and talk at its summit than stay in the township.

They met; they talked; he was beginning to realise he had never known a girl like her. But where was it going? He didn't want it to stay just as it was, but Maggie seemed reluctant to become more involved. In the quiet of the night as he lay in bed he told himself to be grateful for what he had got. When had he been happier?

After work they met at each others' houses and then in the dark of the evening they listened to records, dance music giving way to the husky tones of Eartha Kitt. *'I want to go on a loving spree... you just gotta keep me company...'* echoed from the high-ceilinged veranda.

One scorching Sunday they drove the forty miles to the cool foothills of the mountain, where a tumbling stream splashed over rocks. They found a spot near the water's edge where the grass was short. No village houses in sight, no cultivation. No people. They had eaten all the food they had brought with them and had opened the beer that had chilled in the stream.

"It's been a wonderful day. Even better if I cool my feet in the water before we go home."

She kicked off her sandals, jumped to her feet and gathered up her skirt. She splashed and danced in the foam. Carver propped himself on one elbow and watched her. This wasn't the serious nurse whose conversation so often centred matter-of-factly on injuries, diseases and death. Bending down to splash her face she lost balance and with a shriek slipped into the rushing water. For a moment she lay laughing as the stream rushed around her, over her face and hair. Carver jumped up to help her but there was no need. As she rose, her soaking blouse and skirt clung to her body. With both hands she smoothed her hair away from her face, sweeping it back behind her ears. She knelt in the shallows of the stream and looked at Carver. The invitation was in her face, her eyes, her body. He went over to the stream. She opened her arms and pulled him gently towards her.

Afterwards they lay peacefully, side by side at the water's edge, hands touching, while the sun and the breeze dried them. For once he didn't care that he could find nothing to say. There was no need for words. It was then they noticed the head of an African boy, eight or nine years old, peeping over the long grass twenty yards away, a knowing grin lighting his face.

Chapter 11

The following weeks passed quickly for both of them. Too quickly. That Sunday had changed everything between them. What they both now desperately needed was time. Time to be with each other. Uncluttered time. Time without hard edges; time to love. But their wheel of fortune was spinning out of control. The hospital was overflowing; an epidemic of measles in the District took all of the hours Maggie had, and more.

Carver became engulfed in a spate of serious crime. The murder of a minor chief and two savage gang robberies on remote Asian shops barely left him enough time to sleep. Though his thoughts were not on the Railway, the missing goods telegrams continued to arrive. Ogwang was the only detective available. A large number of high value goods was missing but the detective made no more than token enquiries and relished the thought that the Railway authorities would blame his Inspector if serious losses continued.

Carver was worn out, but he couldn't sleep. As he lay sweating in the humid darkness all his apprehensions about Ogwang plagued him. Apart from arresting pickpockets the man had achieved nothing. All the crime novels had smart detectives finding clues and making brilliant deductions from them. The real world was nothing like that. Once the first and basic steps had been taken, success came from information, usually from the fringes of the criminal world, and it irked him that he couldn't go out and get it himself. That was Ogwang's job. Only an African could do this. He needed success and it wasn't coming quickly enough. And it hurt.

*

Midnight. Punda station, the next up the line from Matamu; isolated, with a goods shed serving the few dukas in the surrounding villages and local coffee growers and cotton co-operatives. The 119up goods was late arriving and since a crossing with a down train had been missed, it was now going to be even later when it left.

The four men slid through the darkness from the scrub that marked the station's boundary and across the unlit yard to the train. A spluttering pressure lamp hanging from a standard barely lit the goods shed. One of the men crawled to the back of the platform, out of the reach of the feeble light, searched under a tarpaulin and eased a ladder out. Armed with a hacksaw, and now the ladder, the men moved to the side of the train furthest from the station buildings. The hacksaw was greased with mutton fat to make its work silent, and it cut steadily through the heavy wire seals of the Covered Goods wagon next to the fuel tankers. The man up the ladder tapped the wire from the bolts and they eased the top doors open. No sound. Then they grasped the bottom door and started to lower it. It slipped. The noise it made was not loud but in the clear night air it could be heard above the hissing and puffing of the locomotive.

The sound reached night watchman Okecho. He was used to the noise of steam and the clunk, clunk of the couplings but this was not one of those sounds. He stirred from the station bench where he had dozed until the 119up was ready to go, gripped his club, and stood in the shadows, listening. He walked lightly, quietly, as he had been taught as a child out hunting. He stood again and looked. He could see nothing on the station side of the train to worry him. He went around the back of the guard's van. No guard; he was at the station office. The caboose. No sound, no movement. The spare driver was asleep. He stood and peered along the side of the train nearest the bush. All he could see was the glow of the engine in the distance.

It was probably nothing. He would go back to the bench. Yes, but he had better walk along the train to the locomotive, checking the seals as he went. After all, that's what he should have done when the train came into Punda.

He only sensed the movement of the thief as the iron bar crashed down on his head, the felt tarbush giving scant protection. As he lay unmoving his attackers bounced three bales out of the truck onto the gravel by the track and rolled them to where the bush met the edge of the goods yard.

"What have we got? Is it any good?" asked one.

"We'll have to open them to see."

"We will do one. No time for the rest."

The locomotive puffed its steam in the distance.

"What about him?"

"He'll have a head like he has drunk too much waragi, when he wakes up – if he wakes up."

He slit the hessian baling cloth to reveal the blue material of imported woollen blankets. They pulled the cloth out, gasping at their luck. One wrapped the blanket round his shoulders and together they rolled the three heavy bales into the bush away from the railway goods yard.

When Okecho recovered his senses, the train was still there. He crawled through the dust at the side of the track and managed to stagger into the station office, rich, thick blood from the gaping scalp wound dripping onto the concrete floor. It didn't take the Assistant Station Master and the guard long to find the open wagon.

For police officers phone calls in the middle of the night are never good news. 4.30am. Carver padded through to the lounge feeling for the phone in the darkness. It was Matamu Station.

"I have just heard from Punda. During the night a CGB was broken into there; general goods on 119up, marshalled next to the tankers."

"Where's the truck now?"

"It was detached and still at Punda. 119 has gone on. You know how the drivers are about delays."

This was it. This was the break he had been waiting for. This time he knew soon after the event, not days later when a wagon had been checked at the Capital. Carver was eager to get to the scene as quickly as he could. He set off for Punda in his van with Corporal Ngirenga, leaving the Ford tender to follow on when enough men had been mustered. He bounced along the twenty-eight miles of rutted murram road at a speed that made Ngirenga grit his teeth.

Though not yet dawn, they could just make out the labourers' houses on the sugar plantation as they covered the last mile to Punda station. The approach to the station was through trees that formed a tunnel for the road. It was dark and felt hostile and set Carver's blood racing. In the glimmer of the station's oil lamp they could just make out the wagon standing by the goods shed.

The Station Master's story was short. Around midnight – 119 was running late – they found one of the wagon doors open. A check said three bales of textiles were missing. No, he didn't know what kind of textiles. Could be anything, khaki drill, dress material, carpets even. No, he couldn't have let Matamu know earlier. He had to get porters out and off load the wagon to know if anything was missing. "Would you have come out if nothing was stolen?"

The tender arrived. Carver spread his men out and searched. The marks on the ground showed the location of the wagon when it was broken into.

"Inspector!" It was Ngirenga who called out. "Look at this!"

Carver could see the tiny piece of blue wool glistening in his torchlight and then on the ground the track of the rolled bales. The track was easy to follow on the rough earth and it took them fifty yards to the edge of a wider path which was obviously well used from the human and animal tracks that stood out in the light of their torches.

By now dawn had broken and the light was improving rapidly. "This needs a hunter," said Ngirenga and he beckoned Constable Byakika.

A mile later along the road, the trail took them to the edge of the sugar plantation. They could see the workers' houses in straight lines ahead of them. Strands of the hessian baling cloth caught on low scrub were unmistakeable. At the third house they came to a thread of blue wool snagged on a crack in the door frame. A woman sat on the ground outside the house pounding maize in a hollowed wood dish. Ngirenga stood with his hand on the door frame. "Where's your man?" The woman looked up, shrugged and carried on pounding. He pushed the door open and in the darkness of the room could make out a figure under a blue blanket on a low bed. As he whipped away the blanket, a man tried to spring at him. His feet caught in the bedding and as he went sprawling, a panga clattered from his hand. They found three more men in the adjoining house. The search soon discovered an iron bar and a hacksaw that had been pushed up into the rush thatching of the ceiling. The search widened, and the three bales were found in the bush under a covering of banana fronds directly behind the houses.

The blanket in the house obviously came from one of the bales.

Now the tidying up, the collection of the evidence. A long day was coming to end, and Carver sat at his desk, frowning. Ngirenga knocked and entered.

"You look unhappy, Sir. We should be glad. At last we have caught Railway thieves. Four of them. And recovered what was stolen."

"I suppose we should. But our problem is still with us."

"I don't see…"

"These aren't the thieves who have caused so much trouble for the Railway… and us."

"They might be…"

"No. I found out they have only been working at the sugar plantation for three months. And before that they were two hundred miles away in their own area until they were recruited by the plantation's Labour Officer."

Ngirenga grinned. "But our luck is changing, I know it."

"Keep on saying it, long and loud, Corporal."

Chapter 12

A glance a month ahead in her diary made Maggie gasp and pick up the phone.

"Paul, it's just hit me, in four weeks time I'm due to go home on long leave." She was met with silence. "Are you still there?"

"Yes, I'm here. Just when we... this is all we need... can't you delay it?"

"I've asked the Department if I can put it off, but they say it will muck up their planning."

"To hell with their planning!"

"That's not helping. Let's talk about it this evening."

And talking about it changed nothing. The reality of going was emphasised when her belongings had been packed and taken away for storage. It was to be a special evening, one for him to remember all the time she was away.

Tomorrow she'll be on the train for the first leg of her journey to the UK but forget that. There's her coming back to look forward to. He busied himself. A final check in the kitchen, and then the table to be set. He knew it was her car from the sound and he hurried to light the candles on the table. He flung the tea cloth he had used as an apron onto the kitchen table and met her at the door.

"Hungry? Let's eat straight away. I've got something special to finish with. Gorgonzola cheese Khosla has freshly imported. He says he only lets his privileged customers have some. That's my standing in world gone up."

With the meal finished, he brought coffee to the table. Maggie stayed where she was sitting.

"Let's have it here, not on the verandah."

"Why? It's more comfortable out there."

"If that's what you want."

He looked more closely at her. She seemed tense and on edge. Was it just that it was her last night in Matamu? What else could it be? They had never been happier together and yet, here she was, toying with her coffee cup, no conversation.

"There's something wrong and you're not saying what it is. I don't think it's just that you're leaving tomorrow."

She sat looking into the distance. "Paul, sit down. I want to tell you something."

"This sounds serious, what is it?"

He could win her over when her temper showed. He was genuinely interested when hospital matters dominated her conversation, but this was so different. *My God, She's going to say she doesn't want me around when she comes back.* He leant forward to see her but her face was in the darkness. A light breeze sent the candle flames fluttering.

She stiffened. *If they were to be together he would have to know some time.*

"I've never told anyone of this so please try to understand…"

"I'm great at understanding."

The words fell from her mouth, in a hurry to escape. "I had an affair while I was in training. He was a houseman at the hospital. It was forbidden, of course, on pain of being thrown out. At that age the risk was part of the excitement, I guess…"

"Is that all? I'd hate to list the girls I've been out with…"

She hesitated again, "It's not just that…" Her voice was so low he could barely hear her. "Then I found I was pregnant."

She looked up, as if to gauge his reaction and he could see the redness around her eyes.

"And…"

"It was right at the end of my training and I managed to keep it from Declan – that was his name – and everyone else until I qualified."

"That must have been difficult."

"I knew my way around. It wasn't so hard to keep it a secret."

"What about the baby, was it all right?"

There was a silence that weighed heavily on the night air. She whispered, "It was terminated."

"You had the baby killed." His voice had risen, louder than he realised. He nearly choked on his words. He was accusing her of a crime and now he could never haul the words back.

She glared at him. "Yes, it was an abortion. Go on, say it. I broke the law. You think I didn't know that!" Her voice rose. "Much worse than that, it was morally wrong, and all my religion said it was wrong and… but I went ahead with it. Being in the medical world it wasn't difficult to…"

He couldn't hear her finish the sentence, "…to kill the child." He could find no words and she continued. "What made it even worse was I never told my parents. I couldn't. I wasn't thinking of myself, I was afraid what it would do to them." She looked up, silently pleading with him to understand. "I told them I'd been ill."

"There's still more, isn't there?" He was fearful of what might come.

"Yes. I still can't accept what happened."

"What? The abortion?"

"No, more than that. Declan was a Catholic. Some of the Billy Boys got to know…"

"Billy Boys?"

"Protestant strong-arm lads in Ballymena. They found out and Declan got a terrible beating. You see, I come from a Protestant family in an Orange area."

"What happened then?"

"I was told he was going to be all right, but they lied. He died. The police never arrested anyone. It was a small community in Ulster; they must have known who it was."

"What a mess. That's why you don't trust policemen?"

"I knew you wouldn't understand. You don't know Ireland and how things are."

"No and I don't think I ever will. How can I? The way you tell it, it sounds as tribal as Africa."

"Is that all you can say? 'Mister Logic' himself. Can't you appreciate what it took to tell you?"

The Maggie he first met at the police station was back, anger flaring, and this time he couldn't handle it. What could he say? He couldn't get it out of his mind – an abortion. She could have had the baby. *It was wrong.*

He hadn't realised she was standing. Her voice was barely audible as she said, "I knew there would never be the right time, but I had to tell you before I went away… That's it then."

She looked at him expectantly. There was no response.

"If you've nothing to say…"

He listened to the over-revving of her car engine as she drove off. The taste of the food rose in his throat. It was bitter.

*

8.45pm Saturday.

The mail train pulled in to Matamu on time. The platform hosted the usual assortment of people – trinket sellers, thieves waiting to snatch unattended luggage, bread and tea sellers, and the inevitable beggars parading their disfigurements to shock money from the travellers in the first and second class.

This evening was a special occasion. A European was departing and Matamu residents were on the station to wish her goodbye. Rod Stern held up a large Thermos of chilled gin and French and glasses were produced. Maggie's health was toasted. Carver stood at the fringe of the crowd, looking for a sign from her, conscious of the covert glances at him. He wanted to pull her away from the crowd, hold her and say he did care. He cared so much, but he just wasn't good at saying this. That he was clumsy, that he… oh what the hell. Now, with everyone milling around, the chance was slipping away. Here on this very platform he had sorted out Kipchai but there were no commands in the drill book that would help him now. He tried to push his way forward again.

The Beyer Garratt's whistle lowed, a gentle caution that the long haul to the Capital was about to begin. A group of African nurses broke out into a song of farewell. The hiss of steam and the sound of the brakes releasing was further warning, but by the time he reached the front of the platform the train had gathered speed and she was gone. All he could see was her head and shoulders through a departing window. The red tail light disappeared into the night.

Chapter 13

Manassi Kidu was a long way from home, but at the moment it didn't matter. Nothing mattered. He swayed as he moved from the cluster of huts that sheltered the bar which had provided the stewed goat with plantains and banana beer. There was good company and the drumming on the upturned kerosene tins and the singing had kept a boisterous crowd until late.

The moon was up and if the senses were not too dulled it would light the way home. But Manassi's senses were dulled. He navigated in that instinctive way that only a drunk can manage. He didn't see the path but moved along it. On he went, rolling on the balls of his feet. He turned right onto the well-worn path that followed the shiny steel rails, tripping occasionally on the rough ballast of the permanent way. He was heading for Kaliso where he shared the quarters of a fellow tribesman who worked as a watchman.

Oblivious to everything, Manassi tottered on, yard after yard. He didn't see the train crawling towards him, its searchlight blazing. The Long Train was slugging its way up the gradient from Kaliso station. The richness of the evening's fare overtook him and he dropped to his knees as he vomited. And that was when the packing case flying through the air from the train hit his head. It cracked the base of his skull and the metal binding securing the case ripped through his scalp as it travelled on to the ditch by the edge of the permanent way. As other bales and packing cases landed at further intervals, three men came from the ditch near where Manassi lay. One looked down at the inert body, clearly visible in the moonlight.

"He's already dead."

"What shall we do about him?"

"Nothing. Leave him. There are too many things to move without having to shift him."

They set about lifting and rolling the bales and packing cases further along the track to the level crossing. The lorry stood in the tall elephant grass a few yards from the road. Mistry started its engine and backed it to the level crossing. With the plundered goods and men aboard it started slowly towards Kaliso Township.

Manassi's body was officially found at eight o'clock the following morning by the Permanent Way Inspector and his gang as they were checking for loose sleeper ties, though it had been seen earlier by dozens more local people using the railway line as a thoroughfare. The PWI despatched one of his gang to Kaliso police post and when a sergeant arrived statements were taken and notes were made of the scene.

"I don't know why you are going through all this rigmarole. He must have been as pissed as a coot. Look where he's thrown up. Get someone to inspect the loco and all the wagons of 119up and I'll bet you'll find blood and skin," was the PWI's assessment.

The sergeant shrugged his shoulders and carried on with his enquiries, understanding little of what the European had said. Eventually the body was carried to the police post on a makeshift litter of branches.

Chapter 14

Gurbachan Singh's day had been frustrating. From early morning he had been in the CID office at Police HQ in the Capital to review the enquiry into the death of the Station Master. The Assistant Commissioner and Superintendent Glennon were already in the office when Gurbachan arrived. The ACP laid out Gurbachan's photographs showing the items on the station office table. Screw top pots for red and black ink, two pens, a stack of railway documents, some stained with blood, an eighteen inch round ebony ruler, and a bunch of keys. And the macabre reminder of the purpose of the enquiry – a severed hand.

"There's nothing in this lot that gives us any clues, is there?"

The ACP didn't wait for an answer. He hadn't expected one. Eventually he showed his impatience with the lack of progress. "Offer me a motive for this killing, someone. Mr. Glennon?"

"Word among some Asians has it that he was killed as a result of his dalliance with a married woman in the Capital before he was posted to Kaliso. Unlikely. It doesn't have the hallmark of one Asian killing another and it is said that they wouldn't go outside their community for a killer. Especially not an African. Pity, because it would be easy to get a result in a murder with this motive."

"I think it's unlikely too. What else?"

Glennon again. "Robbery has still got to be a runner. Nothing was stolen I know but perhaps he tried to stop the thief before he could get anything, and the man panicked and ran off when he found he had killed him."

"Mm… possible, I suppose," though the ACP was obviously unconvinced. "What do you think, Inspector Singh? It's your case."

Gurbachan had been through all of this in his head a hundred times. *Yes, it is my case while it's still unsolved.*

"I can see only two other possibilities. It's an African killing, so there may be some local grudge. Not likely. Such a killer would have struck the head or used some other weapon. More likely it was some passing drunk – smoking cannabis too."

"That sounds the best bet. So, it's still with you, Singh. Keep on making enquiries around Kaliso."

Gurbachan knew it was no good protesting that this line of enquiry was exhausted. His detectives had spent a huge amount of time in the area. His sigh and expression must have given his thoughts away.

"Keep at it, Singh. We have got to get a result on this one."

Gurbachan pulled himself to attention and saluted. It was all very well for the ACP sitting in the Capital. When did he last travel off the tarmac? Nor was it like the big city of London England, where the ACP was proud to tell you he had learnt his policing. There he wouldn't have depended upon a rabble of detectives with whom he could only converse in a language foreign to him and to them as well.

He set out to return to Jayanja. These thoughts occupied his mind as he parked his Chevrolet in the Police Station compound and went to his office. He now had to switch his thoughts to the pile of crime files that had accumulated on his desk, but first he reached for the new radio messages from the outlying police posts. Three homicides and several robberies. Let's hope there are no more station masters among any of these, he sighed. He paused over the report of a body found alongside the railway between Kaliso and Ramagazi. Kaliso again. That damned place. Still, it wasn't an Asian this time and Kaliso Police Post had it in hand. It was four thirty. Office hours were officially over, and he'd had enough of the day. Play some volleyball before it got dark, work up a sweat, drink a brandy or two. Play some cards, another large brandy and bed… and then, if he wasn't too tired… his beard hid the smile of anticipation.

*

The bales and packing cases had all been split and the contents distributed or hidden. Brightly coloured head scarves, clutch plates for cars, bone china crockery, lawn mower parts, an assortment of bicycle spares, khaki drill cloth and a bale of cardamom pods made up the plunder. Within the two weeks that followed, 119up was raided five more times and a similar amount of goods stolen each time. In Railway Headquarters in the Capital the Assistant Traffic Superintendent was becoming very concerned about the level of claims. This was the worst quarter ever. Time to chase up the police. It seemed Carver wasn't as good as everyone said.

*

Hamisi, the railway watchman at Kaliso, grieved. He had loved Manassi. He was always good for a laugh and for a sub when he was short of money for beer. And now he was dead. He was his mother's sister's son and they were about the same age. Hamisi sat cross-legged on the earth outside his quarters. He rocked backwards and forwards, low moans coming from deep within him. Even in his grieving, he asked himself how it could have happened. If the train had hit Manassi, the injuries would have been worse. Were *they* after 119up again that night? And if they were, why should they kill Manassi? He would have to find out. But how would he ever manage this?

Chapter 15

3rd June

The patchwork of bright green fields came up to meet the plane as it landed. The Emerald Isle at last and fresh chilly air after the stuffy aircraft. Luggage, Customs, Immigration and then she spotted them. Dad. Best Sunday clothes, looking sombre. Aunt Moira and Uncle Bobby with the Austin Princess which he used for car hire. And Mum. Mum, dabbing her eyes with a handkerchief. Greetings; hugs and kisses from everyone and then they set off on that familiar road to Ballymena, her mother's arm still entwined with hers as they sat on the back seat with Aunt Moira on the other side. Dad, more at home on a tractor, perched awkwardly on a narrow pull down seat. Her mother eyed her up and down and then pronounced, "You've lost some weight, dear." *Did she know? She wasn't likely to say so here.* Then she couldn't resist adding, "And isn't that the dress you went away in?"

She found the routines of farming life in County Antrim constraining and parochial after the freedom of Matamu. She was now at the end of her third week of leave and her seven-day wonder status with relatives was fading. She had taken to coming down from her room in the early hours so that she could sit and talk with her parents before her father started his work. Her mother fussed around, as she always had, getting breakfast and gossiping about the people in the area. Her father seldom had much to say but on this particular morning he was even quieter.

"Is anything wrong, Dad? You seem out of sorts."

He gazed at her for a moment, turned to his breakfast again and without looking up said, "You'd best be talking with your mother." He pulled his cap firmly down on his head, rose and strode out through the door to the yard.

"What was all that about, Mum? I know Dad's a man of few words but... what's wrong?"

"He and I were talking last night."

"That sounds ominous."

She had hoped to keep it light.

"We know you still have several weeks remaining of your leave, and they pay you for that, but we haven't seen you make any approaches to get a post yet. The time will soon go you know."

So that's what's wrong. They must have realised, surely. She had taken it for granted they knew.

"You were doing so well in the Royal Vic and it isn't all that far to come home from Belfast."

"Mum, I thought you realised I am going to go back to Africa."

"Oh." Her mother paused, looking down. "We, your father and I, thought, well... with us getting older and that, you would want to stay here."

"I don't want to seem unfeeling, but I really want to go back. I enjoy the work far more than I did in Belfast."

"You could do your midwifery training and all, like your Aunt Moira."

"Mum..."

"It's no good, I suppose, I can see your mind's made up. You'll have to tell your father. But wait until after supper. It won't help by upsetting him while he's working."

Supper over; her mother rose quickly to clear the table.

"Dad, I asked Mum what was wrong. She says you want me to stay and not go back at the end of my leave."

He coughed that irritating little back-of-the-throat cough and there was the steely look she remembered when she was a child.

"So, you've made your mind up. What made you go in the first place, we'd like to know? You were doing well."

Relief warmed her. So, this meant they didn't know about her and Declan. Without waiting for an answer, he continued.

"We had expected you to grow up in Ulster, marry a good Protestant boy and be part of the family. But what do you do? You go off to some heathen parts."

"Dad…"

"I suppose it doesn't matter to you that young Willie McArthur has been longing for your coming back, so he has, but you've hardly had a word to say to him. You've just left everyone guessing."

"Dad…"

"It just isn't good enough…"

Slowly and deliberately she stood up.

"Dad, I'm not a little girl any more. I don't want to live all my life here in the way you want. I've loved being back with you on leave but there's a wider world and I'm finding it."

She had run out of words. She ran up the stairs to her room.

After the confrontation with her father, she looked for things to take her away from the farm for as much of each day as possible. There are only so many times you can visit old hospital colleagues and relatives seemed to know about the row. She borrowed a car and took to visiting the coast at Carnlough, walking by the sea for hours on end. It was during these times she realised how much she had taken Paul's company for granted. Brooding, often funny in his dry sort of way, stubborn – very stubborn. Understanding? Well, he could be when he wasn't absorbed in his work. She wanted to think the best of him, but then she tensed as she remembered that last night in Matamu. It had taken so much out of her to tell him and he hadn't even tried to reach her at the station. Could they ever pick up the pieces and start again? And if that was the way he reacted, did she really want to? As she walked, hands deep in the pockets of her thick woollen jacket, she kicked the pieces of stone on the beach.

"I want to go on a loving spree. You've just got to keep me company."

Her singing out aloud startled her. The Eartha Kitt song they used to listen to. She looked around in embarrassment. *Is that what I really want? With Paul? She thought back to the mountain stream; what would a loving spree be like?*

Later that week, she stopped the Hillman Minx outside the cottage. The curtain flickered, and Aunt Moira appeared, pulling her coat on. A moment later she was settling in to the passenger seat.

"I haven't been on the Antrim Coast Road since George died."

After a twenty-minute drive, Maggie parked the car and the two women made their way to where the sea and land met, rocky, rugged, hardly a beach. They walked for ten minutes before either said anything.

"Why did you go to Africa?"

Maggie stopped, jacket collar turned up against the easterly wind, her dark hair blown round her face.

"Lots of things. Mostly because I wanted more responsibility."

They were moving forward again, oblivious to the blobs of rain carried across by the wind.

"Is that it? Now tell me what really took you away."

"Oh… I suppose… constantly being pushed towards marrying someone like Willie MacArthur. Oh, I know he is nice enough. Hard working. He will have his own farm one day; Dad's if I married him. But like all of them it will be on with the regalia and the bowler hat and pick up the rolled umbrella and march with the Orangemen whenever they say so."

"Yes, I know." They walked on further. "The real reason wasn't Declan Byrne was it?"

Maggie stopped. She couldn't brazen it out with her aunt.

"How long have you known?"

"There's not much an old-time Matron misses. You should know that."

They turned and faced each other. This is what she had dreaded.

"So, Mum and Dad know about it."

"That was a hard decision. I heard about it just as you told us you were going abroad. I kept it to myself. It would have been an unholy row. At a time like that it wouldn't have helped anyone."

They still stood together as the wind and the rain splashes threatened a storm. The once little girl threw herself on her aunt and sobbed. The rain fell, like driving nails into the beach. Thunder grumbled out at sea. Eventually she was able to wipe her eyes, but it was some time before the younger nurse could draw herself away from the comfort of the old matron's body.

"It's cold, we're soaked. I know a nice little tea shop where scones, soda bread, jam and cream will make life a lot better. Ten years ago I'd have said 'race you there'."

With the second cup of tea in her hand and the third scone inside her, Maggie did feel better. More than better, it was marvellous.

"Now, I'm sure you've got a man out there, so tell me about him. What's he like and how serious are you?"

Chapter 16

He stared at the pile of railway telegrams on his desk. It was now a month since Maggie had left on the up mail train. *Dear God, on the up Mail I'm even thinking about her in railway terms.* He had written to her but so far there was no reply. Even air mail took ages. He shuddered with embarrassment – no, not embarrassment, guilt – every time he thought of that last evening. Why couldn't he have found a way to clear the air before she went?

Other work was quiet – a ceremonial parade for the Queens Birthday to be rehearsed, a handful of thefts, and the inevitable fatal road accidents – and so he was able to give his attention to the railway.

Sixty-five items had been reported missing in the past ten days. Heaven knows what value would be put on them. At least you knew where a shop or warehouse breaking had taken place. Where do you start when you don't know the location of a crime? Somewhere over a nine hundred mile stretch of railway line, someone had spirited away eighty-five bales, crates, boxes, bundles.

Corporal Ngirenga's arrival with another batch of railway telegrams interrupted his thoughts. Among these were two from the Goods Agent in the Capital, reporting more missing goods. At least he knew that the seal impressions were likely to be forgeries, but this did not lead them any closer to where the truck breakings were taking place. He was finding the lack of activity unbearably frustrating.

"Do you think, Corporal, you might find out anything if you spent some time out on the line?"

"It is possible, sir. I do not know all the stations, so it will not be time wasted."

"How soon can you start?"

"Tomorrow morning. I will go looking like a cattle man."

Before dawn Ngirenga rode off to Punda station on his bicycle. He wore a tattered pair of khaki shorts, a brightly coloured length of cloth wrapped round his upper body, leaving one shoulder bare, and a pair of sandals made from an old car tyre. He carried a bundle wrapped in goat hide, a short spear, nine-inch blade at one end and a spike at the other, and a wooden club. His appearance was topped with a huge pair of white-rimmed sunglasses. He had stopped at each of the five stations between Matamu and Jayanja and now he sat in the shade of a mango tree at Miti. What had he got? Nothing. He spread his things out under the tree. Time to think. If it was not happening at a station then it must happen when the train was travelling slowly. He considered all that he had seen and kept coming back to the long gradient outside Kaliso. But there was still Jayanja and that was for tomorrow.

At Jayanja, he rode into the market on the outskirts of the town, close to the railway station. He had never been there before, but it was so typical of its kind that he felt at home. It was early and less than half of the stalls were ready for trading, although those selling tea were busy. These were the places for the gossip. He bought a hunk of bread made from yellowy maize flour and a mug of hot spicy tea, stuck the spike of his spear into the ground and settled down at one of the tables outside the hut. He was not alone for long. Two labourers on their way to work in a saw mill joined him and in between noisily drinking the tea from tin mugs they started to talk. As always the conversation centred on the availability of work and the pay.

"I suppose you are looking for work as a cattle herd," said one, and without pausing continued through a mouthful of tea and bread. "Your tribe always are. Don't you know anything else? There's not much of that around here. The locals are all growers with their little patches of land. They grow enough bananas to make good beer, though."

And they continued to praise the local alcohol and bhang. *Soon they'll be onto the quality of the women*, thought Tomasi, but he just nodded and lit up a herdsman's pipe.

"What do you people smoke, your cow's dung?" said one, waving the smoke away and pulling a face.

"And not yet dry," said the other. "If you're going to smoke that stuff, go and find someone of your own sort who will like it. There's a woman sells matooke near the entrance. She's the only one of your lot I know."

Tomasi smiled and, pulling his spear from the ground, picked up his bundle and wheeled his cycle away.

"You want to be careful what you say," said one of the men. "They may look skinny, but they know how to use those things," pointing to the spear.

Ngirenga strolled round the market place, appraising some paw paw here and some oranges there while making his way to the entrance. There on one of the stalls was a girl with coppery coloured skin, high cheek bones and thin nose. Tomasi greeted her in his own language. She looked up over her shoulder from where she was arranging the huge bunches of cooking bananas in stacks on the ground, her face lighting up in a massive smile. She replied to the greeting and then, "You are a long way from home, cattle man."

"So are you, market lady."

They talked about trade and the market and about the local people.

"Most are not much compared with us," said the woman with a wrinkle of her nose and a mischievous chuckle. "But there's more money here. I live in the house of a good man and he made me a market lady. I could not have done this at home."

She had obviously left their area for the reason that nearly always brought young girls to the towns. It was fortunate that she didn't come from anywhere near his village but as a precaution, he used the name of a herdsman, Tadeo, who had left the tribal area.

And then she said, "I'm sorry, I've got to get everything ready. Come back later when I've sold all these. It's nice to talk in your own tongue once in a while. I am called Bulandina."

One of his own tribe and working in the market too. She could know a lot. It was nearly mid-day by the time the woman had finished her trading. Tomasi called to her, "Bulandina, are you finished now? How about a little food for a fellow countryman?"

She wrapped her takings in a large red and white spotted handkerchief and swept her market patch with a bunch of thin twigs bound together.

"Of course, we will go to the house and I will find you food."

He followed her along a narrow track for two hundred yards or so to a large hut standing back from the track. She unfastened the padlock and pushed the door open.

"Welcome to my home. It is yours while you stay." Tomasi smiled at the traditional greeting.

He sat on a wooden chair in the middle of the room and looked around while Bulandina busied herself with the cooking pots. The pieces of furniture, the trinkets and the clothes hanging from the roof beams all said this was the house of a man of substance. Bulandina produced an enamel plate of stewed chicken and posho. It smelt good and tasted even better. It was the best food since… since… Flora had died. Curled up on the wide bed, Bulandina watched him.

"What is the matter, cattleman? Suddenly you look sad. I'm not only a market lady," she crooned, looking up from under her eyelashes, "but a maker of my men happy."

Ngirenga wiped up the last drops of gravy with a hunk of bread. He licked his lips in appreciation. He sighed. This young girl with the worldly ways made him feel good despite the memories of his loss.

"Your man is lucky. Where is he? If he comes he will be jealous and I don't feel like fighting today. Besides he might be bigger and fiercer than me."

"He's away. He said he would come tomorrow. He lives somewhere else, but I don't know where. It is true he is bigger. He is a big man in every way," and there was the coquettish look again. "He will bring me a present. He always brings me presents."

"I bet the only presents are bunches of bananas to sell."

"No, silly. I'll show you," and she jumped down from the bed, reached under it and pulled out a wooden case.

"Look."

She held up a small blue and white lacquered coffee cup and saucer to the window light. He could see the translucent bottom of the cup with the silhouette of a woman's head.

"Isn't that pretty?"

"Bit small for a decent drink. That would only satisfy a Muzungu," he teased.

"There's more. Look."

She rummaged in the case and pulled out an ornate leather belt of the kind European women wore.

"See. Only bananas indeed!"

His policeman's nose twitched, as it did when he was a herd boy long before the leopard came creeping near. The furniture, the clothes, the presents, not the kind he would expect of a local produce grower. He was probably a receiver of stolen property from burgled European houses; but that was for another time.

"Who is this giant of a man of yours?"

"Japani. He is known only as Japani."

Chapter 17

The Assistant Traffic Superintendent had brought his inspection of Matamu forward so that he could meet the policeman. After a day in the goods shed and the offices he called In at the Police Station.

"What are you doing this evening? Fancy a beer at the pub?"

Carver had received a letter from Maggie that morning and he would rather have spent the evening on his own. Ah, well. "Good idea. 7.30 ok?"

The ATS had bathed and smelled of Imperial Leather soap when Carver met him at the hotel, in the gloomy room nominated as a lounge. They talked of sport and anything but work until the railwayman suddenly changed gear.

"You don't seem to be getting anywhere, Paul."

"Hardly nowhere. I'm just not getting as far as I'd hoped. Let's see what we do know. That all the big thefts are from 119up and they are all from the first wagon after the tankers. That a rogue seal press is being used somewhere between here and the Capital. It took our going through all the old seals to find that out. Your people had said the trucks were properly sealed on arrival. Now we know that wasn't so."

"Mmm... I hope you're not trying to make too much of that. They handle hundreds of wagons in the Capital's sheds and anyone could miss the odd rogue seal."

Carver ignored the remark. "That's all we are sure of so far. I thought we had a lead with the truck breaking at Punda and although we got a conviction." No harm in reminding him of a success. "It wasn't done by those we really want, though it has probably stopped a new set of thieves starting up. Now, my corporal is out making enquiries at every station between here and Jayanja."

"Is sending a corporal out the best you can do? I'd hoped for something better than that."

"Look, I run a police district. I can assure you your Railway's important, but I do have a lot of other things on my plate. Like four homicides and half a dozen gang robberies, mainly on Asian dukas in outlying villages."

"All right, Paul, keep your shirt on. But I've got to say it's difficult keeping the old man from having words with your Commissioner. He thinks there ought to be some results by now. I'll tell him you're on the brink, shall I?"

By now Carver had had enough. "Tell him what you bloody well like! We shall get a break soon!"

He rose from his chair, left his half-drunk bottle of lager and said goodnight.

Here I go again, a repeat of my performance with Glennon. Without good informers... Ogwang... God, I'm off on the same old record. Please, Ngirenga, bring something back. Soon.

Chapter18

Stations
Matamu - Punda - Kazi Mingi - Kaliso - Ramagazi - Muganga - Miti - Jayanja

The third class down mail train pulled into Kaliso station as the evening slipped into night. The unofficial pedlars and beggars worked their trades in the yellowy light of the station's few oil lamps. Passengers came down from the crowded carriages to stretch their legs, looking for bargains in the temporary market set up in minutes before the train arrived.

Yowana Wamala passed among those waiting to board. Another traveller among many, his only baggage an old army haversack slung round his shoulders. The Beyer Garratt's whistle sounded its long blast and the station area started to clear. The down mail took thirty minutes to reach the next station, Kazi Mingi, a quieter place than Kaliso, with few waiting to board. If it were not for its water, which was free of the corrosive chemicals that plagued the locomotive power staff at the majority of the stations, and its position as a crossing point, there would have been no need for a station there. 119up stood waiting for the arrival of the mail train from the opposite direction. It spread its considerable length along the whole of the crossing loop waiting for clearance to enter the next section of line on its journey to Kaliso and eventually to Jayanja and the Capital beyond. Yowana stepped down from the mail train on the side away from the station lamps. The light from its carriages gave a dim glow which couldn't penetrate the darkness beyond the side of the train. The down mail started to pull slowly out of the station.

Yowana slipped through the gap between a petrol tanker and the first of the goods wagons climbing over the couplings and buffers. He felt his way along the side of the wagon until he touched the holder for the label, which gave its contents and the last station at which it was sealed. By the flicker of his small torch he could see it contained general goods, a term guaranteeing a worthwhile night's work. The label showed it was last sealed at Matamu and was now destined for the Capital. He climbed the petrol tanker's fixed ladder and crawled along the top of the rounded vehicle. No moon to pick out his movements, but who was there to see him? There was no watchman at Kazi Mingi, the train crew were all occupied, and the station staff had already checked the seals on the train's arrival. Yowana stood up at the end of the tanker and leapt the few feet to the flatter roof of the long Covered Goods Bogie. He could do this with his eyes shut. He knelt above the first of the two side doors and used a hacksaw from the haversack to remove the heavy wire seal from the top of the tower bolt. Done in seconds. "You ought to employ me, I could teach your porters to do this more quickly!" he shouted into the night, preening himself in satisfaction. He moved along to work on the seals of the second door.

The train's whistle blew and the hissing sound from the brake couplings told him that it was time to use other methods. From his haversack he took a short length of rope with a loop at each end and draped it over the top of the tower bolt. Using the loops as stirrups he hung on the side of the wagon to cut away first the thin wire seal and then the thicker securing wire from the hasp. Now the door was ready to be opened. Then the tricky bit. He pulled himself onto the roof and crawled along until he was above the second door. He repeated his work on this, swaying with the train's movement. Long before the locomotive wailed its warning as it approached Kaliso the first part of his work was done. The wagon was ready. Yowana sat enjoying the ride in the cool of the night. He crowed to himself about the way he now did the climber's job. Samwiri had been thick. A stupid mpumbavu. Samwiri had climbed on while the train was moving. Too risky. Moreover, Yowana's way gave him much more time to unseal the doors. And that meant two doors every time without fail. The Long Train flowed into Kaliso station. No passengers, no wayside market. No-one except the Assistant Station Master who reached up to the fireman in the loco cab to take the line clear hoop and then made his way into the station building. Hamisi, the watchman, had emerged from his nest among the bales of cotton on the goods shed platform. He stretched and walked slowly towards the front of the train to gather the down-the-line news from the fireman. The whistle sounded, short defiant whoops to say the locomotive was ready for whatever the night had in store for her.

Four figures moved from the shadows to the wagon on which Yowana was now lying flat, hugging its roof against being jerked loose and suffering the fate of Samwiri. Two of the men swung the third up the front door of the wagon and held him there while he pulled the tower bolt down. The door was opened. No noise. Forty-five seconds. They repeated the routine on the second door and as the train started to pull out of the station, ready for its climb up the long gradient, two of them swung up and clung on to the bales which stopped them fully entering the wagon. The third and fourth clambered into the front door and squeezed inside.

The train was clear of the station. The driver worked the regulator and gears and the locomotive snorted its way up the incline dragging its mixture of wagons into the night. Bales and crates were tumbling alongside the track. They hit the ballast bedding of the permanent way, spraying stone chippings into the air, and then rolled on into the drainage ditch. All fell within a short distance of the level crossing where the track crossed the road.

Three of the men jumped down as the train crawled to the top of the gradient and started to gather speed. The fourth remained in the goods wagon where there was now enough room for him to be comfortable. All the while Yowana sat on top of the wagon. His was the specialist work that required skill and nerve and agility. He was not just a porter like the others.

The train's whistle sounded again and once more, a deep-throated moan. Yowana could hear the brakes and felt the slowing down as they passed the station signal. They ran into Ramagazi. From his perch high above the train he watched the fireman hand the line clear hoop to one of the station staff. No one saw him jump from the goods wagon back on to the petrol tanker. He was far enough away from the station lights that he could slip unseen down the tanker's ladder. The other member of the gang who had boarded the open wagon at Kaliso was on the ground. Between them they closed both the doors, sliding the long tower bolts up into the flange on the top of the wagon.

Yowana flicked his rope up over the tower bolt. Hoisted up by his fellow gang member he re-sealed the wagon, adding the finishing touch by crimping the lead with a pair of pliers on to the jaws of which had been welded tiny mild steel plates engraved with the letters MTU, the code for Matamu station, the handiwork of CK Mistry, master mechanic. Mistry had also provided the special tool for screwing up the heavy wire seals. Yowana and his companion slipped away from the station to walk back to the Kaliso level crossing.

The Magirus Deutz truck was concealed by the tall elephant grass near the level crossing. All that could be seen from the road was its high wooden superstructure for its normal work of carrying cotton bales. The 119up passed by.

"Mistry, get your lorry nearer the railway."

The Asian had not heard the man approach and it startled him. He was about to protest that this would put him in danger of being seen, but he thought better of it and started the engine. The cold diesel engine rattled noisily in the still of the night and Mistry looked around anxiously as though a hundred hidden eyes were staring at him. He engaged gear and drove the lorry the fifty yards to the crossing. The tailgate had been lowered and the goods from the train were already being loaded – six hessian wrapped bales and four heavy wooden crates with green numbers hand painted on them showing they were rail goods traffic. Mistry drove the four miles to the Township as slowly as he could. Dogs barked but nothing more disturbed the night. He steered the truck to the back of his workshop, stumbling from the cab as quickly as he could to unlock the big corrugated iron sliding doors. Well greased, they slid easily, noiselessly. The truck's load soon covered the floor of his workshop.

"Burn the wood and the hessian now. I will see you tomorrow," said the African and with his three fellow thieves slipped away into the night.

A wiry man, Mistry was not muscular and he found the task of turning the bales to cut the stitching arduous; by the time he had finished he was sweating heavily. The wooden crates were easier. Tin snips to cut the banding, a crowbar into the joints and the boxes burst open. He stuffed the wrappings and wood into a forty-four-gallon oil drum that he used as a brazier for burning his rubbish, poured old sump oil on top of them and left them to soak. He would burn them in the morning when a fire would be less suspicious, and he turned his attention to hiding the goods. He removed the oil-impregnated planks that covered the vehicle inspection pit and put sheets of waxed paper salvaged from earlier raids along the bottom. Then he stowed the goods away carefully into the pit. As he replaced the pit's planks he looked towards the heavens and prayed. *Don't let that Sikh inspector come nosing around just yet.*

What was this work worth? In the past he had taken part of the spoils as payment, but now he wanted no more of it. He would tell Luka that he wanted to finish. And then what would Luka do? Pour scorn on him, no doubt. He was a man of violence too. Then he would ask him for a proper sum of money if getting out was going to be too dangerous. Three hundred shillings? Luka would recognise he was serious. And with that thought he closed the workshop and went and sat on the verandah and watched the dawn. The spicy tea appeared on the arm of his wooden chair by his wife's hand just as he started to slip into sleep.

*

Gurbachan Singh knew that he had done all he could. As the Assistant Commissioner had said, probably the killer was a drunk, mindlessly intoxicated. If this was so, then he had little chance of success. His only hope was that his detectives would pick up a boastful remark, but hours spent at beer parties had found nothing. And all the time Headquarters CID were looking over his shoulder. He had to do something, but what? All he could think of was to re-visit Mistry. He lived on the spot. He must know something. Where was he vulnerable?

It was ten o'clock when he drove into Kaliso. He stopped outside Mistry's garage, ran his fingers through his beard, gave his moustache a tweak and made his way to the building. There was the garage owner burning rubbish in an old oil drum at the back of the compound.

"Mistry, my old friend," he called as he came through the sliding door, "you want to be careful burning rubbish near so many oily things. You will set fire to your lorry."

Mistry stiffened, looked round open mouthed, and dropped the stick he was using as a poker into the oil drum. He started wiping his hands on a wad of cotton waste.

"You're rubbing so hard you'll skin yourself."

"I am so pleased to see you, Inspector Sahib," though the language of his body denied this. "You will be hungry and thirsty. Come through to the house straight away and have refreshment," and he steered Gurbachan away from the compound, up the steps and into the house. It was cool in the room shaded by the verandah. "Pepsi? Tea? Hennessy? What do you fancy, Inspector?"

"A glass of brandy and some of your wife's excellent samosas would be welcome."

The uniform encouraged fawning and Gurbachan found this pleasing. But wasn't this garage man a little too eager today? Mistry's wife appeared with the refreshments and placed them on the low table in front of them. After eating two of the samosas Gurbachan cleaned some crumbs from his beard, took a long sip of the brandy and looked hard at Mistry who was sitting hunched on the edge of his chair.

"I am back again," he said slowly.

"Yes, I can see that, Inspector Sahib," and then after a long pause, "Why are you back?"

"Why do you think, Mistry?"

"It is puzzling. There have been no crimes since you were here last. You must have more important things than to visit such an insignificant place as Kaliso."

He sipped again, eyeing Mistry over the rim of his glass. "I will come to the point, my friend. We are hearing nothing to help us capture the murderer of the Station Master. You traders here in Kaliso must want this as much as I do, but I need information and I am not getting it. You are so close to the scene of the crime you must be knowing something. So why are you not telling me?"

"We are as puzzled as you, Inspector. None of our community knows anything. It must have been an African who was smoking bhangi and drinking their strong drinks. Why else should anyone cut off a hand?"

They carried on talking while they ate and drank with Gurbachan probing all the time. After half an hour he gave up.

"Your hospitality is as fine as ever, but I must go. What will you be up to?"

"I have to prepare one of my lorries for your police Vehicle Inspector. It is annual inspection time."

"Ah," trilled Gurbachan, sensing a lever, even though it was a small one. "It is important for you to get your lorry through the inspection without being off the road and costing you much in repairs, isn't it? Some useful information from you might help with this, you understand my friend?"

In his heart Gurbachan knew that he had little sway with the Inspector of Vehicles, a prim Scotsman who took everything by the book.

"You know where to find me."

Mistry returned to his workshop. He crouched down on his haunches and lit a cigarette, smoking it cupped in his hands. Gradually his heart rate slowed.

"What did the police inspector want, Papa?"

Mistry's son, Chandra, was standing at the oil drum stirring up the remains of the smouldering hessian from the bales. He felt the sweat on his hands and the pain either side of his temple.

"Leave that fire, boy."

Chandra continued to poke the fire. "Why, Papa?"

"Leave it alone I tell you."

"Why are you shouting, Papa? It is only old stuff and not burning now."

"Do not argue with your father. Leave it."

Before he could say any more, a car horn sounded outside, its loose wiring allowing only a quivering noise. There was a familiar blue Austin pick up at the petrol pump. Luka looked from the driver's window and held up four fingers. Mistry. worked the handle of the pump until the four gallons had been pumped.

"Eight shillings."

"You are a thief, Mistry. You would not charge a European or an Asian as much."

"I am telling you that is one price for everyone." He leant forward until his head was inside the cab. "What about the things in my workshop? I don't want them found there. That Sikh was here this morning."

"I know. What did you tell him?"

"It was only chit chat, he was not here about the goods. He wants to know who killed the Station Master, that is all and I know nothing about that and that's what I told him."

"Come to the usual place. As it gets dark," and he drove off, the Austin squatting low on its rear springs under the load of plantains.

The day dragged for Mistry. Late in the afternoon he sent Chandra on an errand to the cotton ginnery four miles outside the township and then backed his lorry to the door of the workshop. He removed the planking from the top of the inspection pit and started to load the goods, feeling aggrieved at having to do this manual work. He was a 'fundi', an expert mechanic, and labouring work should be done by one of his African 'boys', though he knew he could not risk that. As he sweated away, piling the contents of the bales in neat stacks he was consoled by the thought that this was a good haul. Three hundred shillings would not be too much, and maybe some of the sari cloth for his cousin's shop in Jayanja. There was still a little daylight as he drove the lorry along the dusty road to the forest. The trees closed in rapidly. After a mile he turned onto the track to Mozin Khan's sawmill four miles deeper into the forest and then onto an even smaller track leading to an open glade.

From the bushes Luka and his half-brother appeared. Luka lifted the tarpaulin and used a torch to inspect the goods – suiting, delicate material for saris, Stockport khaki drill, brightly coloured printed cotton cloth, green knee length socks, and a large bolt of striped cloth, aluminium cooking pots and ladles, and chewing gum, masses and masses of chewing gum. Luka turned the piles over for a better view. Yowana reached for the striped cloth and draped it around himself, mincing as if in a fashion show.

Mistry was alarmed. "Be careful of that cloth. These are special colours for making the coats the Europeans in the Capital wear when they play cricket and drink. No-one else can use it. It will be seen sometime if you sell it and it will be traced to you."

Three more of the gang appeared in the glade.

"I want nothing left here after tomorrow."

Luka pointed to two of them. "You will take the khaki cloth and the pots round the village markets. I will take the rest." He turned to Mistry. "You can have the Muhindi women's cloth," he said pointing to the sari material, the last item left on the floor of the lorry. "It is for your work. You will know what to do with it." Then he added as he turned to leave, "You could wear it yourself."

Mistry was stung by the insult, especially since he could still hear the laughter from the five Africans as they were leaving the glade. He could take no more of this man's jibes. Though he could barely see Luka now, he shouted, "I want to be out of this thing, I am telling you. I cannot keep on like this. It is shameful to be living on a secret all the time. I have made up my mind. I will not use my lorry any more for you."

"You cannot refuse. I will not let you."

"If you make trouble I will see that the Sikh Inspector knows about you."

No sooner had the words left his mouth than the foolishness of his bravado hit him. Luka waved a panga at Mistry and bellowed in his own language. Mistry jumped up into his lorry and roared out of the glade, back wheels spinning on the loose leaf mould. He parked the vehicle in his compound and sprang up the steps to the house. As he slumped into the old steamer chair on the verandah, he hoped that none of the neighbouring traders would see him and come over. He had to grasp the tea that his wife brought in both hands to stop his shaking spilling it. Then he dismissed her with a wave of his hand. He was desperate to be alone with his thoughts.

What have you done, Mistry? He had long been assuring himself that when the time was ripe he would tell Luka he would not help him any more, but the time was never ripe. Now in panic he had blurted out the words. *Why am I sitting here, afraid for my life? That man is a thief, a rogue, a murderer even, and I am an engineer, an honourable profession, trained by the British air force, no-one in the country can re-bore a motor engine better than me.*

He and his family could not stay here in Kaliso, that was certain. He must get away as fast as possible, somewhere Luka would not find him. His uncle was down on the coast. He could go to him. That settled it then. He pushed himself up from the low chair and hurried down the steps to his workshop. He had no difficulty in finding the lock in the dark. He groped around until his fingertips touched the generator and then he started it and flooded the workshop with light. Regret gripped him when he saw his machine tools, his lathe and boring machine, his vertical drill and grinders. No, he wouldn't leave them. He took the block and tackle from the peg on the wall and he fixed it to the hook high in the workshop's roof. He laboured as he had never laboured before. He dismantled as much of the machinery as possible to lighten it and then backed his lorry in. Using lifting gear and wooden rollers he manoeuvred the heavy equipment, piece by piece, onto the back of the lorry, stopping at the slightest sound from outside, the sweat on his head and the palms of his hands coming not just from the heavy work. Then the drums of fuel. All that remained was his beloved generator, that piece of machinery which gave him such standing in the Township. Princely, it stood in the corner, dispensing its light. He lit a lantern and shut the machine down. The only electric light in Kaliso was out for ever.

He woke his wife and while she bundled up all their moveable possessions he went back into the workshop for his final act there. He took a long screwdriver and prodded around in the earth floor until he struck the hard metal box. This had been a welding test piece when he had passed his training in the RAF. He sighed as he unlocked it. Inside were his life savings, grubby notes bundled together with elastic bands. He bolted the box to the floor of his lorry, heaved until he had pulled a tarpaulin to cover the bodywork and went back into the house. At half past one Mistry, his wife and three children, all clustered in the cab of the lorry, left Kaliso.

An hour later the fire started. At first its flames licked up the sides of the wooden house. It started round the two doors and then engulfed the whole building until the corrugated iron sheeting of the roof, glowing red, buckled with the heat. The wind carried the flames onto the workshop and its flammable contents roared, bottles burst, oil and brake fluid cans exploded.

Although sounds of the conflagration could be heard in Nyangule village Luka waited impatiently for the men's report. "Is it done?"

"Yes. Everything is burnt. The house, the garage, everything."

"And the Muhindi? Is he dead?"

"He must be. We stayed and watched and no-one came out."

*

When his Superintendent told Gurbachan about the fire, the Sikh said, "I am not surprised. I told him he was careless lighting fires near his lorry, but he didn't take any notice."

"You'd better get out there and check. From what they say, Mistry and his family all perished in the fire and even if it was an accident it's four sudden deaths."

This cursed place again, he said as he entered Kaliso, eyeing the crowd standing in the dusty road near the still smouldering ruins. He parked his car and walked slowly round the compound. The house was now a pile of charred timber and blackened, buckled corrugated iron. He sighed. There was no way of telling whether the Mistry family had perished until the remnants of the building had been cleared and that was going to be a long and tedious job. He turned to the area that had been the workshop and its adjoining vehicle graveyard in the uncovered compound. All the old vehicles were smoke blackened, tyres had burned and glass had shattered, but where was the Magirus Deutz? It usually stood there. He called to the local policemen and Asian traders who had now gathered to watch the Sikh at work.

"Shift that metal. I want to look underneath."

An hour and a half later, the floor of the workshop was exposed. The concrete bases on which had stood the generator and the machine tools were clear, anchoring bolts pointing to the sky. However the fire started, there were no deaths. Mistry and his family were long gone.

"That's good. It means much less paperwork, too."

Chapter 19

Carver's meeting with the Assistant Traffic Superintendent had affected him more than he realised. Another signal of failure. He was worried that there was no word from Ngirenga. On top of this his day had been a mess. First, he had forgotten that one of the constables was retiring and he had done nothing about this. There were reproaching eyes throughout the police station. Then he found this man's replacement was none other than Kipchai. He tasted that onion soup again. What was strange, however, was that Kipchai had told the sub inspector he had applied for the posting to Matamu. It puzzled Carver that the man wanted to see the place again after his disgrace at the station. Still, he had seen something in the man. Now he could find out what that really was.

It was too late to worry about this now. Half past six, dusk, and he was hot and sticky. He went home, showered and drove to the hotel. A quiet drink and then he would treat himself to dinner. He could just about afford it, it was nearly pay day. Damn, Jonathan Morley was astride one of the two bar stools.

"You look like a man who needs a cold beer and a dose of Fats."

The wind-up gramophone was conjured into motion and the strains of 'Blue Turning Grey Over You' rang out across the bar. Carver wanted solitude and refreshment; Morley needed company and conversation. The extrovert prevailed. Carver's mind was miles away but as the talk slid past him he lubricated the interaction with sufficient nods and grunts to keep it going. So it was that Carver nearly missed it. He came to in time.

"What were you saying then, Jonathan?"

"You just don't listen do you? I was saying that I saw Joseph and his coat of many colours today." He changed the record. "Are you really interested?"

"Yes, but weren't you saying something about it looking like the colours of the Capital Sports Club blazers?"

"Yes, it was like their colours. It was weird, really. You don't expect to see a man dressed like a walking deck chair. It stood out from the universal khaki."

Carver was fully awake now. "Where did you say this was?"

"Let's see, I was coming back from the Lake, I'd been through Gombola – had a Pepsi there. Must have been Kaliso. Yes Kaliso, he was walking along the road near there."

Carver was beaming.

"Cat got the cream? What is it about a walking deck chair that's got you going?"

"You've given me my first break. A bale of Sports Club blazer cloth was stolen from a train last month. Why don't you put 'Jump for Joy' on the turntable?"

From then on Carver enjoyed the music and the talk and when he left they had both consumed a few beers too many. Fats Waller had confirmed that 'His Dreamboat was Coming Home'.

Chapter 20

The day was starting to fade and the 119up stood in Matamu station. Swathed in vapour gently curling up from the piston housings, it passed its steamy wind gently. Farnie de Hoek's stint as driver began here. He and his fireman, Ben Kagwa, moved round the locomotive with practised ease. The fireman slipped his long-nosed oil can in between the connecting rods and the driver listened for any noises that might mean trouble out on the track. Satisfied, Farnie swung lightly up onto the footplate. Copper piping glistened with the constant polishing lavished on it by the crew. Three years had Farnie and Ben worked locomotive 5901. For three years they had bought their own metal polish for her. "Like lipstick and rouge for the old girl," Farnie would say.

Carver looked up into the cab. "Are you ready for me, Mr. De Hoek?"

"We'll get on better if you call me Farnie."

He was as tall as Carver. Biceps swelled under the sleeves of the check lumberjack shirt and an oilskin covered driver's cap sat on blonde curls.

"You need a driver to show you what's what. These Traffic types, man, don't know what the hell goes on outside their little stations." He stretched and heaved Carver up the last of the rungs. "We've got to wait for line clear, when the bloody Station Master gets on to it." He watched Carver looking around the cab. "Make you a driver before the night's out. Then you'll be a real railwayman."

Carver heard the fireman's chuckle.

"This is Ben. Never shovelled coal in your life, have you Ben? Apart from that, best bloody fireman on the track and'll be the first African Garratt driver, too."

They were interrupted by the call from the Assistant Station Master as he held up the hoop with the line clear key. "You can go now."

"Course I can bloody go. See what I mean about these Traffic types? Think they run the bloody railway!" and the driver set his gears and touched the regulator gently.

Ben used the whistle to announce the Long Train had been in Matamu time enough. Farnie leant over to speak into Carver's ear. "What exactly do you want apart from a ride on the best part of a train? The Foreman said something about thefts …"

"You must have heard about all the goods that are missing. I've little idea where it is happening, so I thought another run down the line, this time on the footplate, might help. Also, I've had a bit of news and I want to check a few things out."

"Right, tell me later. Got to get her going now."

As the train moved along the track at twenty-five miles an hour, Farnie pointed through the forward window. "Look, man, the track's like a couple of little ribbons way down there. Don't look as though they could carry two hundred and fifty tons of loco, do they? Metre gauge, that's what we run on."

He wiped his hands on a ball of cotton waste and looked out of the side window. In a small plot near the railway line, an African woman bent to pick the ripe cotton bolls from the plants in that right-angled posture no European woman can contrive. A high-pitched whistle, the locomotive and driver in harmony. Farnie hung as far as he could out of the window, his left forearm raised in that universal gesture. Without stopping her picking, the woman looked up and the white teeth shone. Then a return gesture, just as lewd. The whistle sounded out again, gently, mellifluously.

The driver worked his gears and moved the regulator a touch. "Theft's not my line, man. But if you want a Railwayman's best guess, penny to a pinch of shit, man, it's the long gradient out of Kaliso. Why? You'll see when we get there." Another rub of the hands with the cotton waste so as not to smear the shining metal. "Out of Kaliso there is a mile of gradient. Trains can only crawl up it. Level crossing at the top. Right Ben?"

He shouted the last remark across the cab. Carver was sure that the fireman could not have heard above the noise of the wind and the engine but there was a flashing smile and nod of the head. Farnie busied himself with the locomotive's controls and the pounding noise was greater than ever as they started to climb a gradient. Carver shouted above the sounds, "How much longer to Kaliso?"

"It's eight thirty now. Get into Kaliso around eleven. Bit of shunting to leave two flat wagons. Out at eleven forty-five."

Carver nodded. "How did you get into driving, Farnie?" Carver was intrigued at the enthusiasm and the synergy between the two crew members.

"Born into it. Dad was Station Master at Victoria Falls in Rhodesia. He used to say, 'Farnie my boy, if you must be a railwayman be a proper one. Don't get into pen pushing.' So I got me a job as a fireman and then driver. Served in the war up this way and I joined to drive the big ones here when I came out, rather than go back South."

Carver watched ahead as the locomotive's searchlight cut through the dark. Kazi Mingi came and went and now the tramping beat of the locomotive settled into a flawless rhythm. The Kaliso home signal. Oil lamps glimmered in the distance. Run in slowly, coast to a halt by the water column.

A figure approached the fireman's side of the locomotive.

"Jambo, Ben. Habari gani (*what's the news*)?"

The man reached up and Ben handed him down the line clear hoop.

"Vizuri, Hamisi. Habari gani yako (*Good, what's your news*)?"

With a few more words the man disappeared into the night towards the station buildings. Carver couldn't see outside the cab.

"Who took the hoop, Ben?"

"It was Hamisi, the watchman. The ASM is getting lazy."

"There you are, Paul, see what I mean about Kaliso. For starters, the watchman's not watching. He can't be bothered, or he's too scared. He should be checking the wagon seals."

Ben had already released the water column and had climbed up on top of the front tender of the locomotive. There was the pleasing sound of water splashing.

"Once she's had a drink, I've got some shunting. No more than thirty minutes before we're off. We've got another crossing further up."

"I'm going to have a look around."

Carver climbed down, his feet slipping where the spilled water had made a muddy pool. He walked slowly along the train. Deep, deep darkness. *Anyone could be around here and I wouldn't be aware of them.* The first trucks after the locomotive were six petrol tankers, bulbous outlines against the night sky. Then the big steel Covered Goods Bogies, slab-sided, reaching up into the night. The flats followed, the first two empty and waiting to be shunted off here, the remainder loaded with new imported vehicles, still covered with their greasy coatings to protect them from the salty air on their journey from Europe. Then came a string of Americans, with their large sliding doors, loaded with bulk goods – of sugar in hundredweight hessian bags, paper sacks of cement, metal in all shapes and sizes, heavy vehicle parts. Tonight's train followed exactly the same pattern as all the other 119up's whose details Carver and Ngirenga had studied.

What was it about Kaliso? Something felt wrong but he couldn't define it. Was the murder of the Station Master colouring his view of the place? As he entered the station buildings, he came face to face with an African, the new Station Master. This was the man who had found the body of Ramesh Patel.

"Station Master. What are you doing here at this time of night? I thought your assistant would be on duty."

The Station Master didn't seem surprised to see Carver. The telegraph would have been buzzing along the line once he had left Matamu. "My assistant has gone to a funeral. There is no-one else at Kaliso who has authority to give the line clear."

"It was you who found Mr. Patel's body, I believe. What has it been like at Kaliso since the murder?"

"We are all frightened. The man who killed him hasn't been found. There was no reason for it. But I have told all this to Inspector Singh."

"Yes, I know. I'm more interested in the theft of goods. I'm narrowing down the area where they are taking place."

In the dull light of the office oil lamp, Carver watched the station master's face. Fear, but was it fear because of the murder or was there something else?

"Why is the watchman collecting the hoop and not checking the seals on arrival? And shouldn't he be patrolling the train now rather than helping with the shunting?"

The Station Master looked shamefaced. "This only happened tonight because I am suffering from malaria. There's no-one else on duty but Hamisi. There is no harm in that for one night."

The sweat was dripping from his forehead. Maybe it *was* malaria, but everything said that the conversation was over. The buffers clanged as the shunting continued and then the heavy metallic noise stopped. The whistle of the Beyer Garratt shattered the quiet with three long blasts. 5901 was becoming impatient.

"If you want to continue, you must go now. 119up must leave on time."

The Station Master was keen to be rid of the policeman. He finished clearing the line to Ramagazi. As they walked the two hundred yards to the locomotive, Carver could feel the tension radiating from the man.

"Come on Paul, I thought you'd got lost."

A long arm came out of the cab doorway and pulled him up on to the footplate. The oil lamp showed green behind the signal glass and Farnie de Hoek coaxed the Beyer Garratt into smooth movement, ready to run at the long up gradient. Carver settled down to watch as much of the track as he could. The searchlight picked out the edges of the permanent way and a little beyond. Despite its enormous power, the giant machine could only move the snaking wagons up the gradient at ten miles an hour, even slower as the train neared the level crossing at the top. Carver had to agree with Farnie. It was a perfect location. He leant out and tried to look back along the train. Pitch blackness, his vision was all the worse for having peered along the headlight beam. Neither driver nor fireman would see anything happening, even if only a few wagons back from the locomotive.

The Station Master did not see the man until he was about to lock the door. Dressed only in black shorts he was nearly invisible in the dark.

"I'm glad you didn't tell the Muzungu anything."

"You heard us talking then?"

"I heard all that you said. The Muzungu says he knows where the goods are being stolen. He was testing you to see what you would tell him. You shouldn't be on the station at night. Do you want to end up like the Muhindi?"

"I had to be here. There was no-one else to give line clear."

"You want to be careful. Very careful." The man was gone.

"I don't go much on the Station Master!" shouted Farnie over the noise of the locomotive. "The bastard's probably taking a back hander to keep a blind eye, and now he thinks you're on to him. Do you reckon the thefts are taking place at Kaliso?"

"I haven't seen a better spot. The conditions are perfect. What do you know about the watchman?"

Farnie shouted across the cab, "Hey Ben what do you know about Hamisi?"

"He's a good man," Ben yelled back. He left his window and came closer to Carver. "He's honest. He wouldn't be involved in any thefts himself, but there are none of his people around here and it wouldn't be difficult to make him close his eyes. Who would help him if he gets into trouble?"

"You're a bloody marvel, Ben. You're capable of doing half Mr. Carver's work for him. I wish you were as good at being a fireman."

The rest of the Kaliso to Ramagazi section offered nothing, though it was notable that no one was checking the wagons of the incoming train. The wait was short, line clear was given and they continued their journey. By now Carver was nearly asleep on his feet.

"Here, man, sit on this for a bit before you fall on the firebox," and Farnie gave up his small round padded seat to the policeman. Carver was vaguely aware of the cattle pens at Muganga and then the glimmer of dawn light exposed the vast sugar fields that surrounded Miti station. Carver was in and out of sleep until the home signal of Jayanja.

"Christ man, you don't half bloody snore!" was the driver's morning greeting as he handed the policeman a chipped enamel mug of strong tea, sweetened with condensed milk.

Carver climbed down at Jayanja. He had seen enough. He was certain about Kaliso. But how did they do it? He still remembered seeing the porters in the goods shed at the Capital – ladders and big bolt croppers and all of this while the wagon was stationary at a level platform. And not having to reseal with the heavy wire and the small lead seal.

There was a lot more he needed to know before he could plan the next step.

Chapter 21

Yowana sat smoking bhangi, his thoughts spiralling, spiralling away from him with the smoke. The land on which the station now stood was theirs. It had always been so. His father, the old chief, had told everyone round the fire late one night. The old man had been dead for many years. So who was the guardian of the village's interests now? Someone had to do this; through the haze in his mind he convinced himself that his father's cloak had landed on his shoulders.

He knew there was something he had to do and at last his wits settled. The Mzungu policeman had been nosing around the station. Perhaps he knew something, though he might have just been fishing. Matamu was far away, why should he be interested in them? This Muzungu could be dangerous and he needed a lesson; that was sure.

His thoughts drifted off again, but they kept coming back to the same thing. Should it be like the Muhindi Station Master? No, that was too careless, clumsy, he hadn't thought, but there wasn't any harm done, was there. Well, only to the Muhindi and that was of no importance. Then it came to him. This was what he would do. No need to tell anyone else. It was his secret to boast about when the time was right.

*

Carver sat on his police station veranda, drinking an early morning cup of tea. The compensation for not sleeping well was in the beauty of the sunrise. When it rose clear, uncluttered and bold he felt invigorated, but even when it was misty from the overnight rain there was a peaceful, soothing quality. The information from Jonathan and the trip on the footplate had helped him to regain the confidence that had sagged so badly. Why hadn't he thought of talking to a driver like Farnie before? Early rising had also given him the bonus of a quiet period at his police station from six thirty until the place filled up at eight o'clock.

The third class down mail train pulled into Matamu just before Carver drove his van to the car port at the back of the police station. He strode round to the steps of the building, stopping to root out some weeds from the canna lilies in the flower bed, before climbing up to the verandah. As he stopped to take mail from Livingston, the office messenger, the man – one of the many leaving the train – nodded in satisfaction. The first part of his task was done. Never having been to Matamu before, he had worried that he might have difficulty in finding the Muzungu and here he was in front of him. He swung his old army kit bag, tightly laced with a leather thong, up over his shoulder, and wandered off, one unremarkable traveller among all the many others.

Carver was pleased with himself. He had read twenty-three case files, added his notes, and they were now ready for further action. Eight o'clock and the police station was bustling. No more peace for a while.

Next item, ceremonial parade rehearsal, at least an hour leached out of his day. The last thing he wanted to be was a drill sergeant. But it had to be done. He took his Sam Browne belt with his sword in its scabbard from the cupboard and started off for the red murram parade ground behind the police station. He was back in seconds to look quickly at the drill manual. *How stupid can you look when you've forgotten the commands?*

The sun was now high, the parade over, and he set out to return to his office. He stumbled, cursing the archaic piece of weaponry that had nearly tripped him, smiling at the letters VR in relief on the hand guard. *Victoria Regina* – that says it all. At least Livingston was cleaning his van. The thick red dust had been washed off, the windscreen had been polished and he could see he was starting on the inside.

Carver was about to enter the building when he heard the scream. He looked back to where the messenger stood by the open van door clutching his forearm shrieking "Nyoka inuma mimi!" – *the snake has bitten me*. Carver raced back to the van to see the green of a snake, forked tongue darting, wound round the steering column. He whipped the sword from its scabbard, leant over Livingston, and thrust the blade into the reptile, swinging it out of the vehicle and onto the ground. A boot stamped on its head and he turned to see the Station Sergeant picking the snake up.

It was a green mamba, one of the most dangerous of Africa's snakes. If the messenger didn't receive the anti-venom serum soon he could die.

"Get Livingston over to the hospital! Fast!" he shouted, and he watched as he was whisked away in the Police tender. As he sat in his office he thought of his luck. How had the creature got inside his van? It was often said that if you ran over a snake on the road it might cling under the vehicle, then entering it once the vehicle was stationary. The Station Sergeant appeared in the doorway with the dead reptile slung over a broom handle. Carver judged it to be about four feet long – at its killing prime.

"You must have made a bad enemy, sir."

"Why do you think that, Sergeant?"

"Look at this piece of wool. It has been tied round near the head and there's another piece near the tail. It was tied to keep the snake in a circle. Whoever did it knew it would break the wool in a short time, but he would be safe as he put it in your van."

The consequences were obvious. Carver shuddered. He had never thought of himself being targeted. Now he had to be more careful.

"Take it away, please, Sergeant, and find out how Livingston is."

VR had her uses after all.

Chapter 22

It had been against Carver's better judgement when he sent Ogwang to Kaliso. Corporal Ngirenga was out on line and he had no idea when he would return. Jonathan Morley's surprise information about the striped cloth being seen at Kaliso had to followed up and quickly. He had no-one else to send and so he briefed the Detective Sergeant as well as he could and dispatched him.

The Up Mail pulled into Kaliso station at mid-day. Detective Sergeant Ogwang, waking slowly, realised this was his destination. Carver knew too much. Someone had told the Inspector about Mzungu cloth being seen near Kaliso and that he should not come back until he had found out about it. So how should he handle this? Might be tricky. He'd think about it later. He stretched, shook himself and still felt the ague that had set in overnight, the first sign of a bout of malaria. He swore to himself and slipped two of the tablets from Matamu hospital into his mouth. He had less faith in European 'dawa' than in traditional remedies and as a precaution he eased the tablets down with a swig from his bottle of Nubian gin.

He made his way to the door of the carriage, barely touching the floor as he stepped in between the people, chickens, the bundles and cooking pots, and animal and human excrement. He followed the track that led to Kaliso. On the outskirts of the township he could hear the sound of hammer on metal long before he could see the man he sought. He found him bending over his anvil – the cylinder block of a worn-out lorry. The sweat shone on the blacksmith's heavily-veined biceps as he beat the glowing metal into a spear head. He gave a few more taps, looked approvingly at the metal, straightened up, thrust the spear head into water, and wiped his hands down the cow hide apron.

The blacksmith produced two chairs and a gourd of banana beer. "This is all these local people are good for," he said as he handed Ogwang a mug fashioned from a baked bean can. They drank and talked of their home land and times past.

At last the detective broached the subject. "I want to know about some striped cloth. Someone was seen wearing it here."

"Yes, I've seen it. Not to my taste, mind, but fine enough if you like that kind of thing. I last saw him three days ago."

"Do you know who it was?"

"Of course. He's well known around here. It was…" and the blacksmith leant over and whispered in Ogwang's ear.

They carried on talking for a while, catching up on gossip. It was now getting dark and Ogwang's malaria submerged beneath the liquor. He bade his farewell and made his way along the track to Nyangule village. The sounds of the early stages of a beer party would have directed Ogwang even had he not known where to go. He entered the large compound, lined with a dozen or so mud houses. Mango and banana trees filled in the background and the fires gave the shiny leaves an orange glow.

Groups of men sat on locally-made chairs. One of these had collapsed and its dumped occupant was lying on the ground, kicking his feet in the air and roaring with laughter as his drinking companions made ribald jokes about his position.

Ogwang stood back in the shadows. In the corner of the compound was a group of men. In its centre was the one he sought. Luka, long khanzu with a dark jacket over the top, dressed in the manner of a minor chief. There was loud talk and laughter, but all the time sideways glances towards the main figure. Ogwang edged his way round the compound towards Luka. Theatrically he entered the lighted part of the compound.

"21068041 Rifleman Ogwang reporting for duty, Sir," and his arm swung up in an exaggerated salute.

Luka stood, a mock stern expression on his face, swinging his fly whisk up under his arm. He flicked with exaggeration at Ogwang's greatcoat, a parody of a military inspection.

He barked in English, "Buttons not polished!" He flicked up around Ogwang's chin. "Dirty flesh and unshaven, you biralifulu. *A bloody fool; what the Wazungu sergeants always said.* What are you?"

"A biralifulu, Sir."

The act developed. The pair marched around the compound side by side, singing the marching song of the King's African Rifles. "*Funga safari, funga safari, amri ya Kayar…*" We're off on a journey, we're off on a journey, orders of the King's African Rifles.

The Swahili words rang out across the compound. Three circuits and they stopped, convulsed with laughter. Luka embraced his former platoon mate. "A seat for an old askari," he called to no-one in particular but in the knowledge that someone would comply. A young girl scuttled from the houses with a chair. Ogwang settled in, anticipating a long and enjoyable night.

Musicians filed into the compound. A bamboo xylophone, hand held African harps – wooden boxes with springy metal prongs plucked with the thumbs – drums of hollowed tree trunks covered with stretched cow hide. Cow and gazelle horns reamed out for blowing.

Ogwang drank well. The blacksmith was right. The banana beer was good. Then the gin. Mamayangu's juice was fit only for the connoisseur. At last the musicians tired and dispersed. The flames from the fires dwindled and the light came from a few oil lamps spitting away round the compound. Now the vigour of chanting, the drumming on empty five-gallon kerosene tins, and the shaking of gravel-loaded gourds moved some to dance. Solo acts of shuffling feet, bared torsos, rib cages, and stomachs palpitating to the rhythm of the cruder, more urgent substitute music.

Ogwang leant closer to Luka to make his voice heard above the hubbub. "Now you have had enough liquor, I can tell you that a man in a suit of many colours was seen in Kaliso."

"How does that concern me? There are some who like to put their money on their bodies. That is their business."

The noise nearly drowned Ogwang's voice. "It might be your business too. The many-coloured cloth was stolen from a train. My Bwana Inspector knows of this. He sent me here to find out about it."

"And what will you tell him you have found out?"

Ogwang thought for a moment. How could he milk the most from this? "It could be that I say I have found out nothing."

Luka watched him from the corners of his eyes. "Are you going to tell me who or do I have to wait until it floats out from you on the beer – my beer – you have drunk?"

Ogwang waited again. The liquor was taking its toll. He could not think of a way of making more of this and so he leant close to Luka and whispered. Luka's eyes opened wide.

"He sold it to that idiot watchman?" He beckoned to one of the drinkers and talked quietly to him. "We will find out."

After some time – Ogwang had no idea how long – Hamisi, the Railway night-watchman, appeared in the compound. Ogwang pulled his chair back into the shadows.

Hamisi beamed. "They said you wanted to talk to me, Bwana Luka."

Luka offered him the chair by his side. In Swahili he said, "Come and sit, Askari wa Railway. I want to talk to you, but first you must have some beer."

A large pot of banana beer was brought and Hamisi smacked his lips in appreciation after the first draught. The conversation was light-hearted and Hamisi began to enjoy himself. To be invited to Luka's compound was an honour. To be given beer without having to pay for it was beyond words. *Make the most of this* and he gulped down more of the sweet-sour liquid and settled in the chair.

Luka leaned closer to the night-watchman. "You are a man of surprises, Hamisi. I never took you as one who dresses in suits of many colours."

"Is there anything wrong in that? You cannot deny a man the right to dress how he pleases, can you?"

"No, Hamisi, and why should I? All I want to know is where you got that wonderful cloth. They tell me it is stripes of green and red and black. I have never seen anything like it."

"I bought it in the market at Jayanja."

"Really? But it sounds like muzungu cloth. No market person will sell that for fear of the polisi."

Hamisi pulled himself up in his chair. He regurgitated the tart taste of the beer. Luka leant back in his chair. The light of the fire danced on his forehead.

'Well?"

Hamisi hung his head lower. He wanted another gulp of beer but couldn't get the mug to his lips.

"Well?" Harsher, menacing.

Hamisi shivered. Part of the truth might satisfy.

"I was coming back along the railway line. I wanted some kindling wood, so I went into the forest. It was still twilight and there were some old branches piled up. I pulled these off and I saw the boxes and bales that had been opened."

Hamisi looked up to check how his story was being received. He could see no more than the glow of the firelight on Luka's face. He coughed a phlegmy cough, swallowed hard and continued.

"There was cloth wrapped up in a bundle and I took it out. It would make very nice clothes, I thought. It couldn't belong to anyone since it was in the forest and everyone knows, don't they, that no-one wants that land since the spirits live there."

Hamisi stopped and looked around for approval of his claim.

"So I wrapped it up in my shirt, and took it back to my quarters. I had it made into a suit by Benjamini the tailor. He took five shillings to make it."

"So you thought such a piece of cloth didn't belong to anyone?" asked Luka. "You must have seen someone there?"

Hamisi could still see Yowana appearing suddenly in the clearing and demanding payment for the cloth. He stammered. "No, Bwana Luka, I saw no-one." Even to himself this sounded unconvincing.

"Do you think I am as stupid as you? You saw someone. Who was it?"

The watchman hung his head. It was swimming, drowning, in the beer he had drunk. He didn't speak the words; they just spilled from his mouth.

"Yowana was there. I paid him ten shillings."

He peered from under his eyelids without raising his head. Luka didn't look angry so what had he, the Askari wa Railway, to worry about?

"Hamisi, you will burn the suit. You will go to Benjamini and see if he kept any of the cloth and you will burn that too? And you will say nothing of this to anyone."

"Yes, Bwana Luka."

Ogwang looked at the watchman who had now sunk into his chair. He seemed much smaller than when he arrived. What next? And wouldn't Carver, the Muzungu who knew nothing, like to be here to witness all this.

Luka reached out toward Hamisi who shrank back as far as he could. But not far enough. Luka's arm embraced him round the shoulders and he squeezed like a python.

"And when that is done, I will give you the ten shillings you paid for the cloth and the five shillings you paid Benjamini." Luka released his grip. "Now go and do it."

Hamisi fell backwards from the chair, scrambled to his feet and scuttled from the compound, tripping, sprawling. The sound of laughter taunted him as he ran. Despite the amount of beer he had drunk and his humiliation in front of so many of the Nyangule people, Hamisi's mind hardened. The vision of the body of Manassi was spinning in his mind. The watchman stopped once he had left the compound and squatted in the darkness behind the woven bamboo fence. He could watch Luka clearly from there. The drumming and chanting began again.

And who was this? Yowana was stepping into the light from the shadows and flung himself into the chair Hamisi had vacated. The watchman could see Luka bending towards his half-brother, flicking the fly switch in his direction. His voice was raised.

"You are a fool, Mulefu," using the nickname he knew Yowana hated. "You do not sell without my permission. Did you not hear what the Muhindi said about that cloth?"

The effect of liquor and the cannabis he had smoked had built Yowana up to seven feet tall. He shrieked, "Hamisi lies, he lies, that is not what happened! He stole the cloth from the forest. I did not sell it to him!"

Yowana stopped. *Why was he making excuses? Wasn't he an important member of the gang now that he was the climber? He had shown them all that he was better than Samwiri. The best.* He got up and danced a few shuffling steps. He swung his body, he was invincible, a giant, untouchable. He should be respected, not spoken to as a child. The dance tired him and he sat down again. People craned forward to get a better view.

Yowana stuck out his chest and leant forward until his face was close to Luka's. "Yes I did sell it. And why not? I do the job that needs skill." He rose from the chair and danced a few more steps in front of his half-brother. "It is me, Yowana, who is looking after our village's interests. They took our land for the station. And you should thank me."

"Eh...h...h...ehhh." The traditional murmur of agreement came from the crowd at the beer party even though there was no apparent logic in what he was saying. But that was Yowana. There must be more. It egged Yowana on. "I have taken steps to keep you safe, brother. The Muzungu policeman came three nights ago, so I put a snake into his car."

Ogwang leant towards Luka and whispered in his ear. Luka roared with laughter. "So you have hurt the Muzngu, have you, Mulefu? We will have no trouble from him now."

Yowana sat up straight. "That's right. He won't worry us."

Luka turned to him. "I have just received the news that the snake bit his messenger. So now we won't have any more trouble." He spread his arms to those around him in mock praise.

Everyone was looking at him. He felt small and insignificant after Luka's performance.

"Alright. So it didn't bite the Muzungu, but he'll know it's a warning."

He was aware of the sniggers. He had to save the situation. He pushed out his chest and beat on it with his fists.

"You may all laugh, you who do not try, but I have something more to tell you, brother."

He paused and peered around. The sniggering stopped and Luka was looking at him.

"I will tell you another thing, my big brother, it was me, Yowana, your Mulefu, who stopped the Muhindi station master from seeing what we do. Not so little then, was I? What do you think of that Luka, high-and-mighty, Japani?"

Luka's mouth dropped open and closed again just as suddenly. "You? You did that? You killed the Muhindi? Why?"

"I had ordered him not to come to the station at night and he disobeyed. So I showed him who is the bwana mkubwa – *the boss*."

"You are a bigger fool than I thought, Mulefu." There was that hated nickname again, the mockery of one so short being called 'the tall one'.

Yowana leapt to his feet. He danced a twirling, wheeling, spinning dance of triumph. He stopped suddenly, his face within inches of Luka's.

"Asante ya punda ni mashuti," – *the only way a donkey can say thanks is to fart*. He spat the old Swahili aphorism at Luka. His energy now completely spent, he sank onto the chair.

Luka was used to the petulance, the drunkenness and the loss of control, but he never expected open defiance and insults. All this in front of the people of Nyangule. Still seated, Yowana threw his head back and bellowed with laughter.

Luka's anger was a storm bursting. His fingers felt beside his chair and his touch told him what he had found. His half-brother never saw the long fish arrow with the array of tiny barbs that was plunged deep into his body through the soft outstretched throat. Down it went ripping through the diaphragm and into the pancreas.

Little Mulefu fell to the floor and rolled in the red dust. A long, wailing moan came from deep in his body but already the blood was flooding into his lungs, drowning the life from him.

Events had taken Ogwang by surprise. All he could see was Yowana writhing on the ground with the shaft of the fish arrow protruding from the wound in his throat, and blood darkening the red soil. Luka stood up slowly, flicking his fly switch.

"The jackal always perishes if it defies the lion."

Then he turned to Ogwang. "We can't leave this here. It must be moved."

He called quietly but in a high-pitched tone that carried through the night. "Mamayangu!" He put his foot on Yowana's face and tugged hard at the shaft of the arrow. There was a ripping sound and the arrow was pulled free, pieces of his step-brother's inner body spiked on its barbs. He went over to the fire and thrust the arrow deep into the embers.

Luka's step-mother appeared at the edge of the compound, rubbing the sleep from her eyes. Luka beckoned and she walked slowly over. He whispered to her. She went and returned with a roll of bark cloth and within seconds she was wrapping the barely-dead body. Ogwang's thoughts were only of self-protection. Word must not get out that he, a policeman, was witness to a murder.

"What now, Luka?"

"You will see," and he disappeared into the darkness. He returned, driving the Austin pick-up, which he backed to the edge of the deserted compound. Between them they pulled the wrapped body up over the tailboard of the truck. No-one saw them take the track to the lake edge. After four miles Luka stopped at a clearing by the edge where the thick papyrus had been hacked back to make way for canoes. Silver fish scales on the ground glinted in the moonlight. Together the two men dumped the parcel in one of the moored boats. A few strokes of the paddle slid the canoe easily through the oily-looking waters of the lake. Forty yards out, the bark-cloth shroud was removed; an old lorry brake drum was tied to a leg and the body was tipped into the swampy water. Two hours later a catfish, eight feet long and massive in girth, started to feast.

Hamisi peered round the bamboo fence. The fires were dying out. There was no-one left. It was all over. He slipped away back to his cotton bale nest at the goods shed.

Chapter 23

Matamu station. The train slowed to a halt. Ogwang stepped down into the swarm of people on the platform. All the way from Kaliso he had fretted over his part in the disposal of Yowana's body. His knowledge of the law was weak, yet he knew what an accessory was. He had kept out of sight until early morning when the train left. Then, oh then, he recalled with sharp clarity, that stupid performance. That would be remembered by anyone there. And Luka, his old army comrade could be trusted, couldn't he? Yes, but only if it suited Luka.

The detective had been so absorbed with his own troubles he had almost forgotten why he went to Kaliso. Soon he would have to report to Carver and he knew that just to say he had no success wouldn't hold up under questioning. Carver was good at questioning. Try this, yes – *a man had been seen near Kaliso wearing a suit of such cloth but no one knew who he was. He was not from the area and he had not come back.* That would have to do. And then his instinct for survival reminded him that the matter of Yowana's murder was more threatening and his mind switched to that.

He spotted his inspector on the platform talking to the Station Master. He tried to use the crowd to shield him from view but the tall European could see over the heads and turned as Ogwang made for the steps. Now it was too late; he would have no time to embellish his story with tit-bits of misinformation.

He stood in front of Carver's desk.

"Right, what's the good news from Kaliso, then?"

He went into the story he had rehearsed, padding it out as much as he dared. Carver leant back in his chair, head cocked on one side, the straw-coloured hair bristling. The detective could feel the gaze penetrate to his heart.

"All those words to say you got nothing? That was damned good information and you couldn't do anything with it?"

"I did all I could…"

"And what was that?"

"I saw informers. I went to beer parties."

"And…" The inspector was wanting more. It was just as Ogwang thought.

"Kaliso police didn't know anything about the man. He must have been visiting from somewhere else."

"You're not even good at lying, Ogwang. Go away, man. Get out of my sight. Go and catch some pickpockets, that's all you're good for."

Carver's hopes had been high, but now that hope had evaporated.

*

Ogwang was not the only one agonising. As he hid in the darkness outside Luka's compound, Hamisi had heard Yowana boast about killing the Station Master. Then there was the death of Yowana himself. At first he had thought he was hallucinating. Was it all the beer he drank? No. He really had heard and seen all this. So, it was Yowana he had seen entering the office on the night of the Station Master's death. He suspected it but until now he had not been sure. This was valuable knowledge; there must be some way of using it.

He sat in front of his quarters on a low wooden chair waiting for the water to boil to make tea. While he waited he unwound the police puttees from his legs. They gave more substance to his Railway uniform of drab khaki. He had bought them for one shilling and fifty cents from a Kaliso constable. The police wore them with boots, but he could not afford such additional luxury. He still didn't know what to do. He missed Manassi badly and sat dreaming of vengeance. Suddenly, his private world was invaded. Two men stood in front of him, Luka's men.

"Hamisi, come with us."

He started to stammer.

"Stop your noise. You come with us. At once."

There was no option but to comply. They walked quickly from the Railway quarters towards Nyangule. He stumbled. He opened his mouth to speak but a fist hit his back.

"Keep walking and don't ask questions. Mamayangu wants to see you."

The old woman sat on a low carved stool in a glade near the house. Hamisi stood in front of her while she explored a goatskin bag and produced bones, feathers, coloured stones, rams' horns, and dried articles which none but she could identify. She spread these on the ground and made and re-made patterns, all the while chanting quietly. The old woman uncurled herself until she was standing. She turned away from Hamisi who had not seen the near-dead jackal hanging from the branches of the tree behind the old woman. She ripped open the creature's under-belly with a knife, catching the blood in a wide necked gourd. Shaking some dark powder from a small bag into this she stirred it with a long bony forefinger. She reached up and daubed the compound onto Hamisi's cheeks and forehead. The smell was vile; the sensation of his own urine on his leg disgusted him.

Mamayangu was gone; one of the men who had brought him had taken her place.

"It is Mamayangu's curse. It will kill you if you say anything about the cloth to anyone. Do you understand?"

His tongue wouldn't move. He just nodded.

"Go back to your house now."

Hamisi walked slowly away from the glade. He felt ashamed. Angry. Above all else, impotent, frightened.

He slept a little in the sun in front of his quarters, the image of Mamayangu still invading his mind. He repeated to himself, "Her magic cannot affect me as I'm not of her people," but he didn't convince himself. So it was that Jomu's intrusion into his reveries was welcome. Jomu worked in the Permanent Way Inspector's gang and often passed the time of day with Hamisi. As he strolled by, gnawing on a hunk of sugar cane, he called out, "You still look sad, Hamisi. Manassi was our good friend."

"He was more than that. What really happened to him? That's what I want to know."

Jomu sat down beside the watchman, producing another length of sugar cane from his shorts pocket. He handed this to Hamisi and together they gnawed and sucked the sweet juice.

"I will tell you something, Hamisi. Keep it to yourself. I was on duty at dawn that morning, checking the track. I saw Manassi's body."

Hamisi listened intently. Jomu was from a tribe whose boast was that they were the people who 'witnessed the elephants copulating'. Trackers and hunters of all kinds of animals.

"He died six hours earlier. His tracks were too far from the line for him to be hit by a train. Three men had stood near him. But he was killed by something heavy dropping on him. Many more things, heavy things, had dropped along the line and were dragged away. One box had landed near where Manassi was lying. It had come from the direction of the line. I think he was hit by that box."

"You can tell all that from the marks you saw?"

"Of course. And I can tell you something more. One of the men who stood by Manassi stood by this house earlier today."

Jomu pointed to faint marks on the red earth. He gnawed again on the last remnant of sugar cane and threw it away.

"I must go. Good health until we see each other again."

Six hours before dawn. This put Manassi's death around the time of the 119up, The Long Train. So, there had been a truck breaking. One of Luka's men had been there. Luka led the truck breakers. That was enough for Hamisi. Luka had been responsible for the death of Manassi, but if he tried to take Luka on directly it would mean certain death. There had to be other ways.

It was Hanisi's rest day. He caught the mail train to Jayanja, walked through the market place, watching to see if anyone knew him and then continued on to the township. Inside the low whitewashed building of the police station was a counter with a sergeant and two constables busying themselves with prisoners, books, papers, anything but paying attention to Hamisi. After a fourth attempt to gain their notice one of the constables asked his business.

"I want to see the Singa Singa Inspector"

"Inspector Gurbachan Singh? Why do you want to see him?"

"Tell him I have important news from Kaliso. He will want to see me, I know."

"You know nothing, little man," said the constable but he went off through the rear door of the charge office, shortly to emerge.

"Inspector Singh is busy. He will send for you."

Hamisi joined the dozen others squatting on their haunches along the wall of the charge office.

Gurbachan was vexed. That damn place Kaliso again. *Has that name been sent to plague me?* He continued going through the pile of files on his desk, but his curiosity overcame him and he sent for this man who thought he had news for him.

He was just like so many other Africans. Khaki drill shorts which had seen better days, white shirt worn loosely. But he knew him. Yes he knew him. Now where was it? Yes, he was the Railway watchman.

"Important news is it? You are Railway. I remember you. What is it you are going to tell me?"

The Singa Singa looked fierce with the nose of a hawk, his beard neatly set and his bulky body planted firmly in the armchair. Hamisi's confidence ebbed. He must collect his thoughts. Where should he start?

That sixth sense, which all good investigators have, said this watchman was worth humouring. The Inspector's voice softened. "Come now, Hamisi. Sit down in the chair and tell me what you came for."

"I have news of Kaliso. I can tell you many things if you promise no one will know it was me who told you. I have to live there."

Gurbachan recalled the man. What did he remember about him? Of course, he was ignored by most at the station, a figure of fun and hungry for recognition, oh yes, hungry for recognition most of all.

"Go on, Hamisi. You are a good watchman. It is the next best thing to being a policeman. You have some standing. You are a man who knows his duty and I respect that."

Make him feel important but don't forget there is always greed lurking inside.

"Now, let's see what you have to tell. If you really know something worth telling I can find you some money."

"There is a man at Kaliso known as Luka. He leads thieves. They break into trains and steal."

"Is this Luka Wamala you are talking about?"

The watchman nodded.

"Have you seen him doing all this?"

Hamisi skirted the question. "It is not well known but I know it to be true, Bwana Inspector. This is not just beer party talk."

Gurbachan tried different approaches to get more from Hamisi, but nothing was forthcoming – just the same thing said in different ways. He began to lose his patience and the watchman could see the strings of the bag of money being tightened in front of his eyes. Time for the prize item?

"Bwana Inspector, there is something more you might like to know."

Gurbachan waited. What was it now? Not much if the rest was anything to go by.

"I can tell you something about the death of the Station Master."

Gurbachan started to twirl his moustache with his right hand while the fingers of his left drummed lightly on the desktop. Now he was excited. There were times when you just kept quiet. The other person feels compelled to fill the void sooner or later. He drummed on. Hamisi looked for a cue. There was none.

"Did you hear me, Bwana Inspector?"

Gurbachan continued his drumming, looking all the time at Hamisi with unblinking eyes. It's coming, any moment now, it's coming.

"Yowana killed him." Hamisi had intended to be more subtle, but the Sikh's way had drawn the words from him.

"Yowana? Who is Yowana?"

"He is Luka's brother – same father different mother. He is short, not like Luka."

Gurbachan didn't know Yowana. He nodded encouragement.

"I overheard Yowana saying he had killed the Station Master. Now he had gone away in fear of being arrested."

"You have done well to tell me of this. Go back to Kaliso and keep your ears and eyes open."

Taking a bunch of keys from his shorts pocket, he opened the green-painted safe which stood in the corner of the office. He took out a notebook, wrote in it and slowly unfolded two ten shilling notes and placed them on the desk.

"There you are, my friend. Twenty shillings. I am generous to those who have good information. You have given me a little and in the future I shall expect better than this. But this will do for a start."

Hamisi had not anticipated such a windfall. Backing out of the office babbling his thanks, he scuttled out into the street and found his way to the railway station where the guard of a goods train allowed him to travel back in his van. In the gloom of his quarters he prepared to go on duty. Had he told the inspector enough to be able to snare Luka? Would Luka know he, Hamisi, had gone to the police? The anxiety was becoming too much to bear.

*

This was the first glimmer of light on the Kaliso murder. Gurbachan had a name for the killer, even if he wasn't sure how far he could trust the informant. No matter. Some progress to report, at least, but the railway thefts were of no consequence to him. He did not hold any case files for them, so it was not his responsibility. In fact, he recalled, they had given the railway thefts to that young European at

Matamu. Carver. Let him get on with it. He called his sergeant in.

"Find out all you can about Yowana Wamala of Kaliso. Tread softly; we don't want to scare him off."

What Gurbachan wanted was something with which to prod this Yowana. And then, aided by Singh's infamous 'hot cup of tea', a confession would certainly follow. That wonderful thrill of the chase was starting to stir his blood.

With the murder enquiry under way again, Gurbachan's spirits lifted. He thought once more about the thefts. He could afford to be magnanimous. He ought to talk to Carver about this. Luka, eh? A villain if ever there was one. And his brother coming into the frame for the killing. Float some bread on the water, as the Europeans say. Maybe Carver might be lucky and find something. He picked up the phone.

They met the following day half way between Matamu and Jayanja where the road passed through a small glade of wattle trees.

"I have an informant who tells me that he knows who is breaking into the railway trucks. He says it is near Kaliso."

"So who is it, Mr. Singh? Has your informant given a name?"

"He gave the name of Luka Wamala. I could get no more than that from him."

"And of course you're not going to tell me who your informant is?"

Gurbachan smiled. "Would you? I have only one thing more to say. I advise caution. Luka is a big man in Kaliso. A dangerous man, too. He has been suspected of many things, murder among them, but never convicted. He has ears in all kinds of places. In some police stations, naturally."

The two policemen continued to talk for a while and then went their ways.

Carver drove back to Matamu thinking about Gurbachan. He had a reputation for being a wily old soldier with some direct ways of investigating. But he knew the area and the people well. It was worth heeding his advice.

Gurbachan did his own weighing up. Carver? Not long enough in the country to know all that much but he listened and that was more than he could say about some of the officers he knew. He was keen; just hope he won't jump in too quickly. He even felt a little guilty for thinking of not telling him about Luka in the first place.

*

Rod Stern's car was still outside the Administration Offices as Carver drove into Matamu Township. With what Gurbachan had told him he wanted as much information about Kaliso as he could get and a soak in the bath would have to wait. He parked under an acacia tree.

"The tea's still fresh enough if you fancy a cup," Stern offered as Carver entered his office.

After a few welcome mouthfuls Carver asked, "How well do you know the Kaliso area?"

"I doubt if I know it well enough. It's years since I was there. Why do you ask?"

"I've got a name. I want to find out more about the man, but I'm not ready yet to go into the area asking around."

"There is a possible avenue. Father Joe was at the Kaliso mission. Although it was some time ago, he knows everything that goes on in his parish and outside it too. It might be worth seeing him. But watch out, you're likely to get landed with something and no-one says no to Father Joe."

Chapter 24

St. Benedict's College nestled in a forest five miles from Matamu. After the dusty bush roads flanked by elephant grass, the college with its neat buildings, church tower, and well-cut lawns was another world for Carver, now accustomed to Africa's raw untidiness. He parked his van by a row of motorcycles and walked along the paved footpath under the arches of vivid orange and purple bougainvillaea. Tables lined the verandah of the main building and at one of these, Father Joe Higgs worked steadily at a pile of exam papers. The sound of the Peugeot van lifted his head from his work.

His greying hair was cut closely to his head and the army style round-rimmed spectacles perched on his long nose were completely at one with the man. He peered up over the rims and waved as he recognised Carver.

"Not the best road in the District," called the priest as Carver walked over from his van. "But it's passable in most weathers. First time here?"

"Yes, it's like an oasis after the heat and dust down in the township."

"They said you wanted a word with me. Didn't say whether this was social or business. But let's take refreshment before we talk. A glass of beer?" and Father Joe re-appeared with two glasses and bottles of the European styled lager.

"You realise you are doubly welcome," he said with a twinkle in his eye. "One – I want to ask a favour of you. Two – we aren't allowed to partake of such refreshment unless we have a guest."

With that, he sat alongside Carver at the table facing out towards the eucalyptus lined avenue and gently, lovingly, poured the lager. "Cheers," and he sipped a little of the frothy liquid. #

"Now, what was it you wanted to talk about?"

"It's a long shot. I am trying to find out about a man from the Kaliso area. I'm told you were at the mission there."

"Yes, I was at Kaliso before St. Benedict's."

"My information says that the man is probably breaking into railway trucks. And maybe he's involved in worse than that. I've heard a few things about him and I need to know a lot more before I start to tackle him."

"Go on. Who is he?" Father Joe took his glasses off and rubbed his eyes.

"He's called Luka Wamala. I'm told he's well known in the Kaliso area."

"It's not such a long shot," said the priest replacing his glasses. "I was thinking about Luka just the other day."

"And what made you do that?"

"In an idle moment I was thinking about that handful of special pupils. Most of the boys who come to our schools want to learn to read and write English, do some sums and wear nice shirts and shorts and a pair of shoes. Then become clerks somewhere. He wasn't like that. He was good academically, but he could also use his hands. I used to think that Luka could have become whatever he wanted."

The priest paused for another sip, leaving a thin line of froth along his upper lip. "Luka's is an interesting story. A long one, too. Have you got the time?"

Carver nodded. How many times had he found gems of information when he expected very little, and indeed he had come to St. Benedict's more in hope than in expectation.

"Mind if I smoke? It'll help to keep the mosquitoes at bay while you tell me."

He took a cigarette from the box he had put on the table as he arrived. He offered it to Father Joe, who shook his head and resumed his narrative.

"Luka joined the army. The war was spreading into Africa and the recruiting people came round and off he went into the King's African Rifles. Funnily enough it was my turn next, as a padre. They gave me three pips on my shoulders and a motor bike to get around on. They called us 'sky pilots'."

"What happened then?"

"It wasn't long before we were off to Ethiopia. Most of the action at that stage was fighting off the Shifta – you know, a brutal lot of bandits. Guerrilla war is second nature to them. They had taken a terrible revenge on the Italians who had occupied their country – and some Germans too. Those they took alive they crucified along the roadside. The main duties of the unit I was with became protecting the Italians and Germans. Luka was part of that unit.

"I think I will have one of those after all," and he reached over and took a cigarette. He lit it and continued.

"He was a good soldier, they all said. He was involved in some act of bravery when he was given the job of escorting an officer from the Judge Advocate General's Branch and I think he got some form of official recognition for it."

The priest leant back against the wall, savoured his cigarette and continued. "From there it was on to Eritrea. I became ill with dysentery and was invalided to Britain. Do you know, I hadn't been there since 1935. The unit went to Madagascar and then on to the war in Burma." He leant forward. "When we were in Eritrea, Luka came to talk to me. Someone had brought news that his mother had been killed. She was going back to her own area for a visit, travelling on a lighter – one of those huge steel barges. There was a fire and she was killed."

"How did this affect him?"

"The mother holds a special place in his people. He was distraught and kept blaming the Railway Authority who operates the boats. Until then he had been an easy-going fellow – except to the Italians and Germans. Then he changed. He became harder, brutal at times, difficult to approach. He took to drinking, heavily – they always seemed to manage to stew up something. I went off with my dysentery and that was the last I saw of him. Yes, it is a big coincidence you should come here asking about Luka."

He reached for another cigarette.

"Oh, yes, I nearly forgot. He saw so many British killed by the Japanese in Burma during the jungle fighting, he began to admire them, so he adopted the name Japani. That's what I was told by an officer who was there. It angered a lot of his fellow soldiers, but he didn't care about that."

They continued to sit in the dark with the occasional flash of lightning cleaving the sky. They talked a little though both were relishing that time when day became night and a soothing coolness replaced the heat.

"Now I want a favour. I'm told you've been in the ring a few times. I want a referee for our boxing match with Kisigi College two weeks on Saturday. Will you help?"

Boxing, Kipchai. That feeling again. But as Rod Stern had said, no-one says no to Father Joe.

"Well, yes, if you'll tell me what I have to do."

"Good man, good man. I'm sure Kipchai will help you brush up on the rules. It's always a great event. We set up a ring on that football pitch near the hotel. We bring a lorry load of benches down and we charge all the Europeans five shillings to sit on them – Africans free of course."

Carver stubbed out his cigarette. Darkness covered him as he made his way to his van. Luka Wamala, alias Japani. Father Joe had given him some solid information and he needed to share this with someone, Before Maggie went away he would have sought her out to tell her all about this. He wondered if there might be a letter from her and he felt in the glove compartment for the key to the police station's Post Office Box.

Chapter 25

"I know it is Kaliso, sir, but I've got no evidence."

Ngirenga was back. Carver smiled as the corporal made his report.

"We both have the same idea and I've got information that clinches it."

He told the corporal about Luka Wamala.

"It's strange, though; there haven't been any thefts for ten days or so. What's happened? I can't think they've just given up after all this time. It will start again and when it does I want to be ready. What chance do you think you have of getting information at Kaliso?"

"With all we know now the chances are good. I will go tonight as a herdsman again. I have been seen around there. I won't be suspected."

"Where will you start?"

"Why not the horse's mouth?" and he looked at Carver for reassurance that he had got the right phrase. He went out wondering what a horse was like. He had never seen one in the flesh but the cowboys rode them in the movies.

*

Why, why, why had he lost his temper and killed Yowana? It was not remorse that brought the question. Since Yowana's death they had been unable to open a railway wagon quickly enough. Nor reseal it while it was moving. None of his gang could do it. Boastfully, he himself had tried and failed. It irked him; he was not used to failure. Grudgingly, he had to admit that piece of hyena dropping was good at something. But now there was no Yowana. His anger with the railway had made him forget how much he had become accustomed to the income the thefts gave him. Unless he solved this problem, his standing in Nyangule would plummet and that was another matter for concern.

Yet, was he not outwitting the Railway authorities? Resealing the wagons after goods had been taken had kept them off the scent. Despite his bravado with the Station Master, he wondered if the Muzungu Inspector from Matamu had really discovered something. He could tell that he was like some of the officers he had served under in the army, persistent and determined. Yowana had been right. He could mean trouble. But that was the *future*. What was he going to do *now*?

A skinny looking African appeared in the compound, wheeling a bicycle. The brightly coloured cloth across one shoulder, held in place by a belt round his waist.

"I am told you are Luka, the Bwana Mkubwa here."

He stood, holding his bicycle.

Luka watched the man. Skinny he might be, but there were muscles and strength in this man. This tribe had a reputation for fearlessness. It was said that some killed lions with their spears while tending cattle. Not that there were many lions about these days. Luka nodded.

"I am Tadeo. I am looking for work. They said you employ people."

"I have no need of a cattleman. What brings you here? You are a long way from your own area."

The man put his cycle on its stand and squatted in the shade by Luka.

"I came to find work at the cattle pens at Muganga. There wasn't any work so I have followed the railway to see what else there is."

Luka knew that there had been no cattle movement at Muganga for some months.

"What work can you do?"

"Anything. I need the money badly. I must find enough for a bride price. There is no work at home that will give me what I need soon enough."

Bride price. That custom was well known for driving their young bucks to any lengths to raise enough money.

"How much do you need for this bride of yours?"

"Five hundred shillings. Her father is a very hard man. My father's cattle have nearly all died of sleeping sickness and so he can give me little."

"Mmm... I might have some work. Come back tomorrow at the same time."

The man mounted his bicycle and rode slowly out of the compound.

Luka sent one of his men into the township of Kaliso to check on the cattleman. Three hours later he reported back.

"He has been here two days. People say he rode along the railway track from Muganga. He has been asking for work. He has tried all the Muhindis but they were scared of his spear. He has been begging food wherever he can get it. He smells of cattle dung."

Tadeo reappeared at Luka's compound the following day. Luka threw a piece of thick wire and a hacksaw in front of him.

"Can you cut that?"

He was impressed with the way Tadeo handled the tool to cut through the metal.

"Are you any good at climbing?"

"Show me what to climb, I will climb it."

Luka pointed to a tall straight trunk of a eucalyptus tree with no lower branches to give purchase. "There. That tree over there."

Tadeo unwound the cloth from his body, twisted it tightly like a rope and holding it round the trunk of the tree climbed easily to a height of thirty feet. Luka had seen enough. "All right, come down."

Without leaving his chair, Luka called for tea and bread.

"If you are to work for me, you must keep your strength up."

They talked, with the stranger saying little but nodding his head from time to time. Luka's last words were, "Go and practice. Try it out on a train and tell me when you are ready."

Luka could not believe his luck.

Now he had wormed his way in, Ngirenga began to feel anxious. How do I get a message to the Inspector without Luka knowing. The man had a network of informers and this would certainly extend into the Kaliso police post. Then he remembered the sergeant there. They had worked together in the Capital. He could trust him.

Chapter 26

Carver had taken to visiting the Post Office himself rather than leaving the task to the office messenger, but each time he unlocked the box there was nothing from Maggie. There had been one or two short notes which had seemed distant. He just wanted to forget that night before she went. His insensitivity was unpardonable. Still, she should be back soon. He must enquire at the hospital; they would know. Wouldn't it be wonderful to surprise her at the airport?

He also had other things on his mind. He was worried about Ngirenga. He had been away for six days and there was nothing from him. The sharp brringg… brringg of the telephone bell interrupted his thoughts.

"Sergeant Bugiri at Kaliso Police Post. I have a message from Ngirenga. He said you would know what that means. One one nine tomorrow night."

An American Covered Bogie wagon, with big sliding doors was marshalled as close as possible to the petrol tankers and just before the time for departure Carver counted his ten men aboard. Each, including Carver, clutched a heavy riot baton. His last act before the train left was to send the Landrover driver to Kaliso, to keep out of sight there until 119up had passed.

Although the wagon's bodywork was wooden rather than steel, it was sweltering and the anticipation of action brought its own pungency. The wagon swayed and bounced where the track needed levelling. One of the policemen retched with travel sickness.

The shrill of the locomotive's whistle. The regular clacking of the wheels over the rail joints and then another long whistle blast. The brakes were beginning to bite, steel on steel hissing harshly and slowing the train. Though he couldn't see their features he could feel the pent-up anticipation of his men.

He glanced through the partially open door. Entering Kaliso station. The rumble as they crossed the points. The slower beat of the locomotive. Walking pace. Stopping, stopped, with the lightest of squeals as the wheels slid the last inches on the smooth rails. He could just make out the shape of the goods shed fifty yards behind them. Ahead of them was the water column. The moon broke through the clouds. The cicadas fiddled, far away a hyena howled, an owl screeched, a long way off a human shrieked, distant laughter, drums, and the faintest sound of voices singing.

After being in the wagon so long the darkness seemed impenetrable. He shut his eyes and opened them quickly several times and his night vision sharpened. He thought he saw figures moving from the shadows of the station outhouses. Now he was sure. Keep looking. There were men and they were moving along the train from the direction of the locomotive. So close now. They had reached the Covered Goods Bogie, the travelling Aladdin's cave, prized by thieves. They were just forms in the darkness but there was no mistaking the clink of metal and the squeaking of the bottom door as it was lowered. Every instinct said go for them now but if he did they would melt into the night.

He could hear water splashing as the locomotive was filled. How far ahead was that? Sixty yards? There were no other noises that he could identify. Were they removing goods here? All his plans were based on the thieves opening the wagon here and then throwing the goods out by the track as the Long Train dragged itself up the gradient. But what if he had misjudged? He couldn't chance that and silently he slipped to the ground. He could see both doors of the goods wagon. They were open but there was no one visible. They could only be inside. He was startled as someone in shoes walked along on the other side of the train, scrunching on the loose, gravelly soil. That must be the Assistant Station Master returning to the office. The train wasn't due to leave for another twenty minutes. The sound of one of his men scraping a boot on the wagon's floor. *Quiet damn you.* He motioned to the constables to climb out. Five on the station side and five on the goods shed side. *Slowly, no noise. There must be no noise.*

Although there had been little time in which to prepare for the ambush, Carver and his men had rehearsed enough for each to know what was expected. Seconds later the fighting exploded. Four raiders leapt out onto the policemen. Wearing only shorts, their upper bodies were smeared with mutton fat to slip any grasp. But fat was no protection against the heavy riot batons. Carver heard the thud alongside him and a howl of pain. Then another. Bodies rolled on the ground. He heard a shriek and one of the constables screaming, "He has bitten my ear off!" More screams, grunts, groans, and then pleading.

Carver noticed the form slip away from the affray. It was not one of his policemen, of that he was sure. He moved as quietly as he could towards the man shape. The moon slid from behind the clouds. There would be a glimmering light only for seconds and soon he wouldn't be able to see him. For a second he tasted the onion soup again. Would he…? But he sprang forward. The tackle was instinctive. Both men crashed to the ground, but the grease did its job and the bare torso slipped through his clutching fingers. The smell of the mutton fat was nauseating.

The man was groping around on the ground. Something glinted in what remained of the moonlight. He stood feet wide apart, arms spread, a long-bladed weapon in his right hand. In the dive to make the tackle Carver had lost his baton and they were far enough from the melée by the train that none of the policemen would see them. Carver dived for the man's legs. They weren't greased and as he caught the man's calf he felt the thud of the weapon across his shoulder. There was no pain. *No harm done.* He urged himself on, yelling out loud, but all he could do was stagger a few more yards. There were more blows. On his head. On his back. Across his shoulders. Another blow and then another as he lay prone. *The pain set in. I won't scream. I won't.* He bit into his lip. He moaned. He was swamped in total darkness.

Kipchai had led the arrest of one of the thieves. He hadn't needed a riot baton. The body punch had piled the man into a limp heap. Three thieves were now secured. Kipchai quickly scanned the scene.

Where was the Inspector? He had been by the wagon when the fighting started. A cloud broke for a few seconds. Carver lying on the ground thirty yards away, not moving. The man raising a weapon to strike again. Kipchai was as fast over the ground as a cheetah. The depth of his massive lungs threw out a murderous roar.

A moonbeam picked out the man's features, lips curled back, snarling. Kipchai dodged the thrust of the weapon. He punched; the hardest punch he had ever swung. The grease did its work again. The blow had stopped the man but skidded on with no real damage. Kipchai hesitated. He glanced back to see the Inspector. In that half second the man was gone. He may have lost him, but he would never forget that face.

There was a rustle beside him.

"Steady, Kipchai, it's me, Ngirenga. I was with the gang. On top of the wagon. How is the Inspector?"

"I think he's badly hurt but I can't see properly."

Ngirenga bent over Carver's body. If ever he was to earn his First Aider allowance of two shillings a month it was now.

The fighting was over. Five men had been subdued and were being taken to the station buildings. The short journey carrying the Inspector was difficult, with the hazards of rails and trackside signal wires to be avoided in the dark. Twice the policemen carrying him all but dropped Carver but eventually he was placed on the office table.

Ngirenga began his examination by the light of the Tilley lamp. Blood covered the upper part of the khaki drill tunic and he slit the cloth and gently removed it. He saw deeply hacked cuts on the shoulders and chest. The wounds on the head had exposed the white of the skull and the right shoulder lay at an awkward angle. The upper body was drenched with blood.

He searched the station's first aid box and found it held only a few bandages, scissors, and iodine. He did what he could with the limited equipment, wiping away blood, gently applying the brightly coloured antiseptic where he thought it might be of value and using bandages as pads to cover the worst of the wounds. He had experienced enough injuries caused by animals to know that this was serious. For the first time since he had left his home Ngirenga uttered a prayer. *"Please, don't let him die."*

Three hours later, still unconscious, he was taken into Jayanja hospital. The surgeon examined him. He shook his head.

"His condition is critical. We haven't the facilities here for such a case. He'll have to go to the Capital as soon as he's ready to be moved."

Chapter 27

The police had lost him, Luka was sure of that, even though they might have taken the rest of his gang. In their clumsy boots he would have heard them. The area was so familiar that he didn't have to think about where he was going.

He moved fast but quietly in through the back door of his house. He swept up his more valuable possessions and piled them into the back of the pick-up truck. He went back to gather clothing in his arms and threw these onto the passenger seat. Finally, he collected all the large tins of Mamayangu's waragi he could carry. This would be as good as any currency where he was going.

His last act before he drove off was to push the two feet nine inches of Italian serrated bayonet under the passenger's seat. He drove as quietly as he could to the lake where what was left of Yowana now mingled with the decaying matter at the bottom. Standing in the shallow water at the edge, he started to wash the grease away from his upper body. It clung to him and he had to use handfuls of sand to scour it off. With the last trace cleaned off he dressed and set off towards Jayanja using the bumpy tracks through the forest.

As he drove he cursed himself out loud. His troubles had all started with that thin-nosed, copper-coloured cattle man who wasn't a cattle man. He cried out loud. "How could I be such a fool to be taken in by him?" In an involuntary movement he felt under his seat and touched the bayonet as he would touch his lover.

His fury rose. Now he was hacking, hacking, hacking at the body just as he had hacked the policeman's Muzungu master. In his imagination he could see the blood, not as he had seen it earlier that night on the European's body, but spurting rich and thick from gaping wounds. At least there was the consolation that the European was dead. He screamed at the top of his voice as he drove, the same word over and again – "Fisi, fisi, fisi" (*hyena*). His anger was still bubbling as he pulled into the track alongside his rented house near Jayanja market. He pounded on the door.

"Bulandina. Bulandina, open up!"

The noise reached the consciousness of the sleeping girl.

Chapter 28

Immigration. Then the officious fussing of the Customs man. But she was back at Ndubi airport. Now where was her posting to be? The letter from her department had said she would be told of this on her arrival. At last she saw the Medical Department's Administrative Officer. He took her case and loaded it into the car and they were soon on the road to the Capital. He drove in silence but at last he said, "Do you know where you've been posted, Miss Baird?"

"The letter said I would be told on arrival."

"Of course. You've been assigned to Mbarali…"

Her lips tightened. Mbarali was right over the other side of the country from Matamu. So maybe fate was taking over. Paul. Their last evening together. It was months ago and yet she still had that feeling in the pit of her stomach when she thought about it. How had he really taken the news she had given him? He had written letters to her while she was on leave, but they never gave away how he really felt. And hadn't she asked herself a thousand times how she felt about his reaction on that awful evening?

Her reverie was broken by the voice of the AO.

"You'll love it there. Nice little township. The game park's not far away… the District MO is easy to get on with."

He swerved to miss a gaping pothole in the tarmac.

"PWD are getting worse. That's been there weeks."

They drove on. After a while he said, "You'll have tomorrow to sort yourself out and then you can drive up there on Tuesday."

Maggie was lost in her thoughts. *I'll leave phoning Matamu until I get to Mbarali… He might have made the effort to meet me; it is the week-end... but what if he didn't want to... he's had all this time to stew on it.*

*

Inspector Carver had been killed. That was the news that reached the Capital. A disgruntled Superintendent Glennon of the CID was ordered to Jayanja at once to take charge of the investigation.

It was four thirty in the morning when he received the message from the Assistant Commissioner and Glennon liked his bed. The night mists of the forest hugged the road and threw his headlight glare back at him and he drove gingerly for the forty miles. His first reaction on hearing the news had been that Carver had got his comeuppance. Too many remembered their row in Central Police Station, even though it was a long time ago. Now he couldn't go anywhere without people talking behind his back. And then a pang of conscience told him that this was taking his hatred too far. The poor sod is dead and that's the end of it.

Glennon arrived at Jayanja Police Station. He was met by Inspector Gurbachan Singh. Ah, yes, he of the untidy paperwork.

"Well, Singh, where is the body?"

"Body, sir?"

"Inspector Carver. How was he killed?"

"Mr Glennon, sir, he is not dead yet, but by how much I don't know."

Gurbachan related what he knew of the incident. "Two of Inspector Carver's men are still at the hospital. They can give you the first-hand story. I will drive you there."

It is comforting, sometimes, to find that the big men from the Capital can get it so wrong. His Chevrolet nosed into the hospital drive.

Constable Kipchai stood in front of the table in the office that Glennon had requisitioned. The Superintendent's Swahili was poor and to his disgust he had to depend on Gurbachan as an interpreter. Kipchai gave his account, straightforward and unembellished.

"Why did you not arrest this man who nearly killed your Inspector?" was Glennon's last question.

"Either I chased him or I went to help my injured OC," was Kipchai's answer.

"You're lucky you are not on a charge for dereliction of duty, Constable," muttered Glennon as he scribbled the last of his notes. The mischievous thought crossed Gurbachan's mind that if he translated this to Kipchai he would be picking the Superintendent up from the floor. But there would be too much trouble, and Kipchai did not deserve the inevitable consequences.

"Get me the other man, the corporal."

Ngirenga entered the room. He was still clothed as he had been for the raid on the train – shorts, no shoes, and a dark, ragged shirt.

"Who the hell is this, Singh? I thought we were seeing a uniform corporal. This man is scruffy and he stinks. What are you playing at?"

"With great respect, sir, this is Corporal Ngirenga. He has the information that will help us catch the man who did this."

Ngirenga's account was clear. He related the events leading up to his joining the gang, showing that Luka Wamala led the raid. And what was more, Kipchai and Ngirenga could both positively identify Luka as Carver's assailant.

"We shall have to be very careful that Ngirenga is not seen as an agent provocateur, Singh. The defence could make a meal of that."

The corporal had no idea what the Superintendent was talking about.

"Right Singh, now that we are sure who attacked Inspector Carver, get some men out to that village near Kaliso and arrest this man Wamala."

"I radioed Kaliso police post at 2.30am, Mr Glennon, sir. They are on the spot and they will know Luka Wamala."

A pause. Gurbachan looked at the Headquarters man expectantly.

"When will you be going out there, sir?"

Glennon's face showed his distaste for going 'into the bush', as he would put it.

"Get those statements completed, Singh. Must keep the file up to date at all times. Where can I get some breakfast?"

*

A torch beam shone on Mamayangu as she stood in the middle of the compound, a slight figure wrapped in a goatskin. Chanting in a high-pitched voice, she shook a bunch of kite's feathers at the policemen. The Sub-Inspector shuddered. Even though a devout Christian, he found the old hag's curses chilling. He had brought ten men and searched Luka's house. The bed was cold. They searched the compound and the area surrounding it. The pick-up truck was gone. Certain that Luka was not present, he led his men away and was glad not to have to remain there any longer. He sent a radio message to Inspector Gurbachan Singh.

Rumour said that Yowana was dead, though no-one would say how or where or when. Luka had just disappeared. So much for wrapping up the killing of the Station Master. Gurbachan was in his office, hoping to escape any more attention from Glennon. He drummed his fingers on the table, scratched his beard and slowly rose from the table. He had had enough of sitting.

What took him to the Exhibits Store where all the pieces of material evidence were kept, he would never know. There on a shelf at eye level was Carver's bloodstained khaki uniform jacket. He could see the hard outline of something in one of the pockets. It was an official pocket book. He thumbed through it. Carver had kept notes of various meetings. *Here's that priest Father Higgs.* He summoned Ngirenga and Kipchai.

"I see Inspector Carver talked with the priest Higgs about Wamala. He made some notes. Did he tell you about this?"

There were blank looks from the two men.

"Well let's see what else there is. He wrote here that Wamala hated the Railway." Still no response. "There's the word 'Japani' against Wamala's name. I don't suppose that means anything?"

He was surprised when Ngirenga's face lit up.

"He is a man who rents a house in Jayanja market. A woman from my tribe looks after it for him. He must have gone there. It is a good place to be lost."

*

Luka pointed to the cloth and hardware piled on his bed.

"You are done with dealing in vegetables. Get into the market and make sure you sell all this. I need money, quickly."

Bulandina pouted. "But there is too much for me to carry on my own."

A stinging blow caught her across the face. She struggled off to the familiar stall hauling everything in a blanket. Now alone in the house, he could think of nothing other than the image of the cattle man who was a policeman. He had been duped and that skinny brown man was not going to get the better of him. He weighed the bayonet in his hand. It felt good. But the market place was buzzing with stories that the Muzungu policeman was not dead.

The bayonet had not finished him off. It must be sharper. He spat on the stone in his hand and worked away at the weapon. The edge of the serrated blade was now a thin sparkling silver ribbon.

Chapter 29

The surgeon and the doctor stood watching him. There was no discernible movement, no rise and fall of the chest. After a week in Mbuli Hill hospital in the Capital he was still unconscious. He lay immobile on the bed, the dressings and bandaging around his shoulders, head and chest obscuring his identity. From its stand a drip released nourishment into his arm.

"There's a pulse; the very faintest. I can't pick up any breathing, though."

He touched the stethoscope dangling from his neck. The doctor bent over the bed and put the instrument to the chest. He shook his head.

"Has he gone?"

"Not yet, but I don't know how much longer we'll have him."

*

There was a voice so faint he could not distinguish who it was or what it was saying. And then it became stronger, more distinct. "It wasn't your fault, son." It sounded like his father's voice. Even though it was so long ago that he last heard him he couldn't forget the way he talked. "Don't let yourself fret about it, Paul." That was one of his words, 'fret', he often said fret.

Did this mean he was going to meet him? *But you don't believe all that stuff – life after death – do you? Whether you do or don't, you're not going yet.* It was even darker now. The voice was gone. He longed to hear it again. If he concentrated hard maybe it would come back.

"Paul, son, it's me." Here it was again. Faint. He would have to concentrate hard to catch the words. "It wasn't your fault, Paul, what happened to Robert. You're not in the same boat as he was. You can fight it, boy. Fight it." The words trailed off into an echo.

*

The District Hospital at Mbarali was even smaller than the one at Matamu but was just as busy, and Maggie was drawn into its work even before she had unpacked. Her first attempts to phone Paul were frustrated by heavy storms having uprooted the telephone lines. Two days – with a bit of luck – before the service would be reinstated, said the Post and Telegraphs engineer.

On the second day, the District Medical Officer called her to his office.

"Is it just the problems of settling in to a new place or is there something else on your mind? You look as though you've been somewhere else all day."

"Oh, I didn't realise. I desperately want to telephone someone in Matamu and the lines are down."

"It must be an important call if it distracts you so much."

"I thought it was important…" She found she couldn't explain any more. *Could I have made a worse start in a new posting?*

As she was going off duty the DMO called out from his office, "There's a hop in the club tonight. Only records, of course. It starts at eight. It'll be a good way of meeting everyone." After a day like that how could she refuse?

In every up-country station 'The Club' was the focal point for the local Europeans and any passing through. Mbarali's was a thirty-foot square shed, whitewashed inside and out, with a small bar at one end and tables and chairs grouped round a space for dancing.

"You were in Matamu, weren't you?"

She looked round to see who was asking the question. It was the vet. She had been introduced to him earlier.

"I was at Mbuli Hill on Saturday for some jabs. It may be a bit antiquated but it's a good hospital…"

"I don't follow you. What' this got to do with Matamu?'

'Hold on, I'm coming to that. There was a patient from Matamu. Sad case really."

"And?"

"He's been in a coma for a week or more…'"

"That's serious. Who is it? I'll probably know him."

"They said it was the policeman."

It didn't have to be Paul. He could have been posted and it was someone else. Her voice quivered. "Did you get his name? Was it Carver, Paul Carver?"

The MO heard the conversation. She hadn't spoken to her boy friend since coming back off leave. That explained her distraction all day.

"You'll want to know more."

She nodded.

"The phone lines are still down but the police radio isn't affected. Let's see the OC Police. He's at the bar now."

"Don't need to radio. I know who it is. It's the talk of the force. Paul Carver ran into some trouble on the railway."

The policeman turned his head to look at Maggie.

"Catch her, someone. She's passed out."

It had been a sleepless night. Now at seven thirty she sat in the DMO's office.

"What are we going to do about it? You're not going to be much use like this."

"I don't know. What can I do? I want to be near Paul."

"Why don't you get on with the job while I think of something?"

Two hours later the doctor met her at the dispensary.

"I've got an answer. One of your colleagues in the Capital will do a swap with you – even for a short time. You can get down there as soon as she arrives."

Being in the same hospital as Paul was harder than she had anticipated. Even though she was busy, she wanted to keep going to his bedside, to be the first to see any signs of change. The worst part of it was knowing she was unable to do anything to help him. Going and looking at the immobile body just made her feel despair. Every time she asked she was told, "Too early to say. He might pull through, but we don't know."

It was late morning. She stood at the door once again willing signs of movement to appear. Her mind drifted back to the evenings together they spent in Matamu. Yes, perhaps there *was* something she could do. Her luck was in. Get to a phone, girl.

"Morley. Who's calling? ...Yes, of course. Everyone here's worried sick. You were quite right to call me, Maggie. Sounds a bit far fetched, but if that's what you want, I'll drop everything and come."

*

Only the subdued movement of his chest as he breathed showed he was still alive. No sounds other than the whirr-whirr-whirr of the overhead fan as it moved the hot air from one place to another. The sheet was peeled back to allow air to circulate, the white linen stretching like a barrier across his pelvis. She stood, arms folded across her chest. She felt that shiver, that same excited shiver as when they had first met. She smiled at the memory of her righteous indignation about the arrest of one of the hospital staff.

Paul had been right, though she still felt a soft spot for Justin, the orderly who pretended he was a doctor.

*

"I've got what you wanted. When do you want to use it? God, this place stinks of disinfectant."

Jonathan set up the gramophone on the table by the bed and carefully took the record from its cardboard sleeve. It was that awful record that Paul and Maggie had billed and cooed over so often. He put the disc on the turntable and lowered the needle arm. "Eartha Kitt therapy," he muttered.

They played the piece again, and then once more. No reaction. "It's no use." She had banked on the music working, to bring some reaction, however slight, but what did she know about these things? It was a stupid idea after all. Jonathan saw her shoulders sag and even though he had little faith himself in what they were doing, he said, "Look, Maggie, we haven't even started yet. He's been like this for days. Give it time. You go and have a rest. Then you can take over from me."

As she returned he looked up, winding the handle again. "Nothing yet. I'll go and stretch my legs. You keep on trying. It'll hit the spot sooner or later."

Taking turns, they continued throughout the night.

> *He was at home.*
> *Mum, can we go to the fair tonight? Robert and me, can we? I'll look after him Mum. He'll be alright with me. I'm thirteen now, you know.*
>
> *I can hear the music, it's faint. Judy Garland. It always is, at the fair. It's louder now. The lights are flashing, people laughing and yelling.*

It's eight o'clock. Promised Mum we'd be home for half past nine. Come on Robert, race you. I'll give you a start. Count to ten. Cor, look at the roundabouts. Galloping horses. We'll save them to the last. What about the coconut shy. Ginger said they're glued on and any way they were mouldy, and it wasn't worth a tanner.

*"Clang, clang, clang went the trolley..." Judy Garland again. The dodgems are wizard, those kids from George Street gunning for us. Robert was scared but he loved it really. What's the time please, mister? Five past nine. Still time for the roundabout. Where **is** Robert? He's a nuisance. Too little to be here really but I promised Mum.*

Come on, Robert. They're not real rifles, only air guns shooting darts. You don't want the ghost train. You'd be scared. Come on, we've just got enough for a ride on the big roundabout. That's where all the music's coming from. I know it's whizzing round. That's why you'll love it.

I know it's going to happen but if I keep my eyes shut tight I won't see it.

Carver passed again into the depth of his own personal night.

Jonathan was asleep in the chair but the sound of the door opening wakened Maggie. It was light. A doctor stepped into the room.

"What are you doing here at this hour? It's only just six."

"I had this idea that if we could stir some good memories though this music it might… I don't know… wake him up, pull him out of where he is. I know it sounds a bit far-fetched…"

The sound of voices woke Jonathan in time for him to hear the doctor say, "Sounds a bit like mumbo jumbo to me…"

"Come on Doc. Nothing else has worked has it? What have we got to lose?"

"Ok. It's not a standard procedure, I'll grant you. Maybe a different winding hand will work the magic."

The doctor wound the machine and he gently lowered the needle onto the first groove.

> *Wait till it stops. What are you going on? The horses? They're a bit big for you. You'd be better in the fire engine. You can ring the bell. No, it's not for babies. Ok, if you want the horse then you can sit on it with me. You've got to hold on tight. Promise.*
>
> *It's getting up speed. The horse is going up and down. Robert's clinging on. He's looking back, laughing. How does the man stay on when it's going so fast and he's coming round taking your money? Here's a shilling for me and Robert. He's alright, mister. I am holding him tight. I know it goes fast. I've been on this one before, you know. Yes, I am over fourteen.*
>
> *The horse is going up higher. And faster. I'm going to be sick. Robert cling on, I can't hold you. Oh my God. He's gone. Mister. Mister. Mister…*

It's stopped. Where is he? They're all looking down inside. There's blood near his head. He's gone and got hurt. Is he bad, mister? Leave me alone that's my brother. What's wrong with him? An ambulance? They're bringing a red blanket. I want to go. I can't stay...

Maggie hardly dare say anything in case it had been her imagination. She brushed her hair from her eyes with the back of her hand. She peered more closely. There was movement. Both his eyelids flickered and opened to slits.

The doctor's excitement showed. "He's breathing more deeply. I do believe something's happening after all this time."

The eyelids continued to flicker for what seemed an age. Maggie clutched Jonathan Morley. Was it going to remain as this? Then as they watched, both eyes together opened and stared up at them. Unblinking. Inspector Paul Carver returned to this world after an absence of fifteen days.

Chapter 30

Now natural sleep had replaced the coma, a sleep full of dreams, healing dreams. And while Carver slept, Gurbachan Singh, Ngirenga and Kipchai went to Jayanja Police Station.

"There is good news. Inspector Carver has woken up. Now I want you to find this man Wamala, or Japani, or whatever he calls himself. Be careful, he's a wily man and we can't afford to lose him now."

Anyone seeing Ngirenga, dressed in shorts, knee length plaid socks and a clean white shirt, would not see the cattle man, but a typical clerk pushing his cycle round the market, looking at the fruit and vegetables.

Kipchai moved slowly from one shaded area to another. He wore old shorts and a singlet. To hide his long-looped ear lobes he had covered his head with a coloured cloth with a broad-brimmed straw hat over this.

It was mid-day and although trade was dwindling, Bulandina was still at her stall. Today there were no vegetables, no cooking bananas. In fact there was little on display – a few aluminium ladles, some enamelled mugs and a roll of coloured cloth. Tomasi observed her for a few minutes from a distance and then he wheeled his bicycle closer. He greeted her in their own language and then, "I hope trade is good today, market lady."

Still bending over her stall with her back to him she answered, "Tadeo, it's you?" Smiling at the prospect of once again seeing him she gasped at what she saw. "You're not a cattle man. You've changed. I wouldn't have known you if you hadn't spoken."

"I couldn't find my kind of work so I got a job as a clerk with an Indian." The lie did not come easily to Tomasi's lips but what else could he do. "Aren't you going to offer me something to drink? Even a clerk gets thirsty."

Bulandina looked at him. She was still puzzled that Tadeo could have changed so much.

"I must be careful. Japani has been staying here longer than he usually does. He has been here several days. He can be very jealous and if he found you at his house I don't know what he would do... to you... and to me. His temper is very bad now."

"Where is he, then?"

"He went out early in the morning to collect some more things to sell. He keeps a store of them in the house. He hasn't brought any vegetables this time and I'm glad because I like selling these things better."

Bulandina continued to chatter as she cleared the stall, wrapping the unsold goods in a coloured blanket.

"I must take this lot back to the house until tomorrow's market."

"Here, I'll carry the bundle on my bicycle."

Bulandina was happy. She liked this man with the familiar coppery-brown skin and the finely chiselled features of their people. They reached the house and Tomasi leant on his bicycle. He wanted badly to see what other goods there in were the house. On his previous visit he must have been looking at loot from Kaliso and didn't realise it. But it was too risky at the moment to try to enter. He continued to make small talk.

And then he realised his instinct was crying danger as it did in his days as a herd boy. He pulled his bicycle back into the shade of the roof overhang just as the faded blue Austin pick up pushed its way through the tall elephant grass which bordered the earth track. He leant back as flat against the house as he could.

The vehicle stopped ten yards or so from him. There was no doubt. The man they wanted was the driver and he watched as Luka turned the ignition key. The engine ran on lumpily and then died with a thump. Bulandina skipped over to greet her man. Japani. He talked to her as he opened the door which groaned on its unlubricated hinges. He set one foot on the ground, the other still in the car, as he talked with the girl. It was then he noticed the stranger. A man in a white shirt. He sneered dismissively. Obviously, a mere clerk, yet there was something familiar about the bicycle. Bicycles took on their owners' characteristics. A vivid flash of recognition and his left hand felt the reassurance of the bayonet handle under the seat.

Tomasi Ngirenga saw the tightening of his calf muscle. *He has recognised me.* He saw the jaws clench. He had no spear, not even a club or a baton. Nothing. He moved onto the balls of his feet, reflexes sharpened. Here he comes. Bulandina was in the way of the headlong rush but Luka brushed her aside as if striding through her.

"Cattle man. I'll show you real butchering," screamed Luka, swinging the Italian bayonet above his head.

Now Tomasi Ngirenga did feel fear. The shining edge of the weapon, honed with murderous skill, came arcing down straight at his head. The policeman felt as rooted as a tree. As if by witchcraft his bicycle was flung up in front of his head. The bayonet bit deep into the crossbar of the machine, born in the cold climate of Nottingham, now here in the heat of an African marketplace. The weapon was firmly embedded. No act of sorcery was responsible, Kipchai had flipped it into the air as the bayonet swung down. As the bicycle crashed to the ground, the big policeman flung his whole weight at the thief. There was no grease now to help Luka slip the blows. The struggle was fierce and the three men, each physically powerful in his own way, rolled in the red dust, locked together.

Bulandina tore savagely at Tomasi. She screamed abuse.

"Shut up. This is police business. Keep out or you will be in trouble," the corporal shouted over his shoulder.

She fell on her knees in the dust of the track, sobbing. Over and again she cried out, "You deceived me. You should not have told lies, Tadeo."

Luka managed to free one arm from Kipchai's grip. With his forefinger in his mouth he made the ululating cry of alarm, a cry that anyone of the tribe is duty bound to answer. Faces began to appear through the long grass and from the track.

"Thieves! They are robbing me. You must help me. It is your duty!"

Thief beatings were a common form of summary justice. There were no rules of procedure, no questioning of the evidence and no hope of appeal, with the death of the person nominated as the thief a near certainty. The chanting had begun. "Beat them. Beat them. Beat the thieves…"

Kipchai hit Luka as hard as he could on the point of his chin and then the policeman sprang to his feet. Cloth and hat had long since been swept away. He towered over the closing villagers, ear loops swinging.

"I am Kipchai," he thundered. "If anyone wants to see me fight he must come to the Capital and pay his money."

The movement of the crowd had stopped. He swivelled his head slowly round, eyeballing each of the crowd in turn. He swung his glare onto a man who had been leading the mob. "Do you want to fight me?" Silence. "Well, do you?"

"Eeeee… eeeh, truly it is Kipchai. I have seen him fight." A thin man at the back of the mob pointed. Another man spoke, shaking his head to and fro. "Also, he is polisi. I don't want that sort of trouble."

Kipchai saw a man with a bicycle among the crowd which was now easing back. "You! Go to the police station. Tell the Singa Singa inspector we need him."

The man fumbled with the bicycle. Kipchai's voice boomed. "Get on that bicycle and ride fast!" The man was gone.

Gurbachan took no chances. He brought five constables, but the leader of the railway thieves was unconscious. The corporal's cycle with the bayonet still embedded in the cross bar was hoisted into the back of the tender.

Gurbachan sat at his desk. It was well past office hours, but he didn't care. He felt the glow of success. He was the hunter and the chase was won. He would celebrate that evening with a little brandy, no less.

Tomasi Ngirenga and Kipchai walked together back to the police barracks.

"I think we can celebrate, Kipchai. Lots of strong liquor tonight."

Kipchai stopped dead and turned to Ngirenga. Angrily he said, "I do not drink strong liquor. You must know that."

The grin was all over Tomasi's face. "Nor do I, but a stew of cow meat will be fine. I will even pay for it."

"I thought you people loved your cows too much to eat them," said the big man, shaking his head in puzzlement.

Chapter 31

Mbuli Hill was swathed in a mist, the low clouds drifting over the pudding basin shape. Ten past eight and the doctor had completed his first round of the morning.

Carver was alive. Since the time he opened his eyes to the sound of the record three days ago, he had gained a new awareness. Now his dreams were different. Instead of his sleep being troubled by the visions of his brother he was back at Kaliso, a dark night, moonlight cutting through the clouds, the bayonet raining down on his head, neck and shoulders.

Maggie stayed with him as much as her duties allowed and, when she was off duty, sleeping in the chair in the corner of the small ward. Often her rest collapsed when his dreams forced groans and shrieks from deep inside him. None of the medical staff would say much but she sensed a general pessimism. She hardly dared to go in the ward in case… in case of what? She had seen dead people before, even helped to lay them out. They made you do that as a young nurse. *Stop it, stop it. He won't, he can't.* She wouldn't even think the word.

Eight-thirty. The ward orderlies were well into their tasks of cleaning the floors, furniture, and equipment, with cloths smelling of disinfectant. It was a time Maggie liked. The hospital's routines were in hand and she had a clear view of the day ahead. She sat at the roll-top desk on the verandah writing notes, when she was conscious of someone approaching. Ngirenga and Kipchai appeared, uniforms pressed, boots shining, puttees perfectly wound.

"Can we greet our Inspector?"

Their smiles were the password.

"Just a few minutes. You will have to go when I tell you."

The two policemen entered the ward.

"Jambo effendi."

Their presence stirred Carver and he turned his head slowly. For the first time, he pulled himself up on the pillows. There they were, the lithe corporal dwarfed by the forest tree of a constable. There was no better sight for his well being.

"We come to bring you good news, sir. We have caught Luka Wamala. He will be tried. Inspector Singa says for attempted murder. And for stealing from the railway. Four more have been charged with theft also."

They talked a little more and then, seeing Carver tire, they left.

After their visit, Carver's progress was remarkable. Later that day he took his first few steps across the ward, and then he walked a few more on each succeeding day. He sat talking with Maggie, clutching her hand with both of his. The nightmares abated.

In the following week the Commissioner visited Carver. When the he had left, his Staff Officer stayed behind.

"A date has been set for Wamala's trial. 30th September. The medics think you will be fit enough… Are you alright?"

"Sure. I was just thinking how I've got to go all through that night again. Got to be done, I know."

"Cheer up, the good news is that arrangements will be made for you to fly out on home leave as soon as possible after the trial."

Chapter 32

The African stood in front of the building on the Capital's main street. He walked by, waited, and then eyed it up and down. He moved towards the door with its brass plates:

> Gideon Ochieno,
> Barrister at Law

> African Union for
> Freedom Party
> Registered Office

Gathering up his courage in his khanzu skirts he opened the door, dragging himself up the long flight of wooden stairs. He paused only to rehearse what he had to say. Gideon Ochieno's Goan office manager looked silently at the man, weighing him up. This was not the usual type of affluent client and was probably in the wrong building. A muttered "Jambo" – then, "Wewe utaka nini?" *what do you want?*

"I must see Mr. Ochieno."

"You can't just walk in here and see him. He is an important man. He's busy. What is your business?"

"Tell him it is about Luka Wamala. He will see me."

He left the man in his office, went along the corridor and knocked on Ochieno's door. The lawyer sat behind a vast desk, an overhead fan rippling the papers spread on it.

He continued his writing without looking up from behind the stack of law books, the only part of him visible his balding head.

"There is a man here who wants to see you. He's a villager. I told him to go away, but he said it was about a man named Luka Wamala. He thinks that's enough for you to see him."

The reaction surprised the office manager. Ochieno put his pen down. "Show him in at once."

The man sat on the edge of the armchair, uncomfortable in such surroundings. What he saw put him even more in awe. As he took in all the office paraphernalia, the Muzungu suit and tie, and the squat, solid figure of the lawyer, he told himself that this was no ordinary chief. The barrister looked at him for several minutes.

"You come from Luka Wamala. Why hasn't he come himself?"

The man stammered, and at last managed to say, "Luka is in Lubrika."

"Why is he in prison?"

"They say he tried to kill policemen. He says you must save him."

The barrister was silent. It was a long time since he had dealt with a criminal case and it would mean a lot of revision. He should say no.

He's not going to say anything more, thought the man. *I shouldn't have come.* The silence was intimidating. At last it was broken.

"You can tell him I will see him." And then remembering Luka's tendency to say as little to those in authority as possible, he added, "Make sure he knows I shall want him to tell me all that happened."

"I will tell him today," and the man bowed himself out of the office, walking backwards, as if ending an audience with royalty. How could Luka have influence with such an important man?

After making several phone calls, the office manager briefed Ochieno.

"The hearing will be in that dingy hut at Jayanja, I suppose, with its iron roof. You can't hear yourself speak when it rains there. Find out the strength of the case."

Two days later he drove his Mercedes to the prison. The buildings, with their high brick wall topped by coiled barbed wire, seemed to vibrate in the heat on the top of Lubrika Hill, six miles outside the Capital.

A warder led him to the visiting room. The only furniture was a small wooden table and four chairs, and these were lined up against the wall. The barred window high up admitted little natural light and the electric bulb hanging from a cord high out of reach barely gave sufficient illumination for writing and reading. After civil litigation he found this repugnant. He settled on the chair, which he had pulled to the table, his body overflowing the flimsy piece of furniture. There was the noise of people in the passage outside and the heavy door was thrust open.

"Kwenda ndani" *get inside*, the warder pushed, and Luka stumbled in.

He surveyed the man who asked for his help. He was dressed in the standard prison garb of coarse khaki drill smock and shorts and wooden sandals with a peg between the big toe and the next. The growth of beard gave him a piratical look. But it was the eyes, dark brown, boring in on him. There was arrogance about the man, a swagger. This was the same man he once knew and yet such a different man.

"It's been a long time, my friend, a very long time."

"Yes, a long time. Now that you are so big, I wondered if you would want to help a humble man from a village like me."

He looked at the prisoner. Too much alcohol had left the whites of his eyes bloodshot and his face still bore the marks from the bruising during his arrest. With his knowledge of Luka, he knew how fierce that the fight would have been. Luka took a chair and placed it by the table and sat down.

"You are in trouble, deep trouble. Trying to kill policemen."

"I had no choice. I was forced to. I have a right to vengeance and the polisi were stopping me."

"Vengeance? I know about your mother's death, but the court will say that doesn't justify what you did. You will need a better defence than this."

"To avenge a mother is our custom. What more do I need." Luka crossed his arms defiantly.

"A Chief's court might accept it as a defence, but these are serious matters and the case will be before a Resident Magistrate."

"The magistrate will be a Muzungu?"

"Yes, a European. These are charges of attempted murder, and of policemen. This is not just a case of stealing a goat or brewing illegal liquor."

"I will not be tried by a Muzungu."

"It will not matter whether you like this or not. The Resident Magistrate will still go ahead and try you. Have you nothing better we can offer in your defence?"

"Something better? Why is it you people will not understand?"

"Then you had better plead guilty."

The instant glare from Luka brought Ochieno an involuntary shiver.

"No. I will not submit to the Railway."

The interview ended there. The lawyer sighed. If that's what he wanted, the only approach he could use was one that had worked for him occasionally in the past – manoeuvre so that there were procedural errors during the trial and win on appeal. But the success of that approach would depend on who was the magistrate. Aloud he said, "All right, my friend, I will do my best but don't expect miracles."

"I do not need miracles with Mamayangu."

"I don't want that old woman in court. She will do more harm than good."

The prisoner glared. "She will be there."

Gideon Ochieno drove slowly back to the city. *Maybe I can twist some of this around. Agent provocateur is about the only possibility. Raise doubt, though there's little to work on. Crown Counsel will be prosecuting and he will stick like glue to the Criminal Procedure Code. This is one I am going to lose.*

Chapter 33

The surgeon looked at his notes. "You've made remarkable progress. You have the use of your arm again and you've got your balance back. I think you're ready for discharge. You will need to take it steady. After all it's only just eight weeks since…"

"Since someone tried to kill me. And now I have to relive it all at the trial."

"You've shown remarkable determination. Someone with less – what shall I say – bloody-mindedness would not have pulled through."

Maggie drove him to the hostel. Her Morris Minor was so cramped that fitting his long frame into it was obviously painful. She just wished he would yell, scream – be human for Heaven's sake, but there was no sound from him. She helped him through to his bedroom. She sat on the edge of the bed hoping they would be able to talk. This was the first opportunity they had had to be alone and she was desperate to know how he now felt about her after what she had confessed the night before she went away, but his head had dropped, and he was asleep. He was oblivious to her.

Will things ever get better? How much more of this can I take? She made her way to her car and drove back to the hospital.

*

It was now a month since he left hospital and he had recovered well, at least physically. His hair was growing again but the scars still showed through it. The wounds on his back only hurt occasionally. But deep inside he did not feel he had recovered. His moodiness disturbed him. Surely, he was strong enough to manage this without upsetting people all the time. And particularly Maggie. He parked his van.

The court building was a relic of earlier times when any hearing was an occasion for a crowd of curious onlookers to gather. It was no more than a corrugated-iron roof on tall brick pillars which were linked by a three-feet-high block wall, open to the elements and public gaze. A large wooden table had been placed at one end, with two smaller tables a short distance in front of it. Benches lined the rest of the floor space. A pair of fruit bats hung motionless from the high rafters.

The place was filling, and people were elbowing for places to lean on the wall and look in. There was the air of a market place, the anticipation of rich entertainment to come, something to fuel the conversation around late night fires.

The Resident Magistrate's light green Ford Consul drew up alongside Carver's van. Roland Pound slipped out from behind the driving wheel and busied himself with his black linen jacket. An African clerk came from the passenger's side, pushing his way through the gathering throng to lay out papers from a briefcase. Carver studied the magistrate. Pound had a reputation for being punctilious, testy, and bitingly sarcastic. But above all, he was a penetrating observer.

A scarlet Mercedes arrived. Gideon Ochieno made his entrance. This was the first time Carver had seen the barrister, who was more notable to the police as a politician than as a lawyer. He would have stood out anywhere even if he were not wearing the pearl grey Savile Row tailored suit. For a man of bulk he stepped lightly into the building, the crowd parting before him, twittering like weaver birds.

A noisy Bedford truck, with bodywork of expanded metal, slid to a halt on the loose soil fifty yards from the court building, raising a cloud of red dust. There was Luka, in prison khaki now, standing alongside the truck. Carver's only memory of the man was as a moonlit figure crouching to attack. He looked different to his vision of him, but the sight still sent a sensation through his entrails.

The last character about to strut this stage arrived, the prosecuting Crown Counsel. Realising he was late, he struggled to pull his jacket on as he strode into the court. Nine o'clock. The clerk rapped on the table. "Everyone stand." There was a rustling and shuffling and Resident Magistrate Pound took his place behind the magisterial table. One leg of this ancient piece of furniture had been eaten by termites to be replaced by concrete blocks. Luka Wamala was led by the two warders, one bearing a large-bore shotgun slung over a shoulder.

And so the trial began. The clerk read the charges, two of attempted murder and three of theft of goods in transit on the railway. The magistrate looked at the lawyer.

"How does your client plead, Mr. Ochieno?"

"Not guilty to all the charges."

The clerk wrote meticulously on some blue legal file covers.

"I am going to hear the evidence in the two attempted murder cases first. Some of the same witnesses are involved in each and it will save recalling them. Have you any objections to this, Mr. Ochieno?"

The lawyer shook his head.

"I take it that means you have no objections? Good. I shall record that."

Carver chuckled to himself. The old man was laying it down the line from the beginning.

Carver was the first witness. Ochieno's cross-examination was brief. Ngirenga was next. He related the story of his time at Kaliso and produced the rogue seal press given to him by Luka for resealing the wagon. Ochieno moved towards the corporal, a presence that would have intimidated many.

"It is obvious that you lured the accused and his friends into trying to steal from the train that night."

Ngirenga shook his head. "No. What I said was the truth."

"You engaged in blatant entrapment. Short of having any evidence against my client, you got him to go to the railway where it was you who opened the truck."

He was used to witnesses wilting under the force of his personality but Ngirenga still shook his head. He continued with twenty more minutes of blustering trying all he knew, as lawyers do, to twist the words and defile the truth but the corporal remained firm and credible.

Now came the drama the onlookers were awaiting. Kipchai stood facing the magistrate. He gave his evidence in Swahili. With no delaying translation the crowd could understand immediately the words of this man, now a folk hero. Kipchai described the man standing over Carver slashing with the bayonet. His clear voice penetrated the mind of each member of the crowd. A collective gasp was like the waves lightly breaking on the lake shore. Private translations and interpretations were whispered.

A bigger gasp rose when Kipchai described the bayonet cleaving down towards Ngirenga's head and the protecting bicycle flung into the air. Spontaneous applause. A loud chattering flitted round the court building. Pound looked up magisterially over his half moon glasses.

"Silence! Will you all be silent, or I shall clear the court? I need to hear what is being said."

Ochieno rose, one big man challenging another, but it was a mismatch. The lawyer's tongue could not get inside Kipchai's guard. Though his face was impassive Magistrate

Pound inwardly chuckled. *This beats hands down the prostitutes' parade at Bow Street on a wet November Monday morning.*

Unhurriedly the trial progressed, the to and fro of the interpretation of the evidence from one language to another slowing the proceedings down. The technical terms taxed the skills of the interpreter and, as always with such evidence, approximation had to do. Nevertheless, by the end of the first day Pound was pleased with the progress. He adjourned the court until ten the following day.

*

The Lakeside Hotel where Carver was staying was a short distance from the court. Having seen the Mercedes in the car park he was not surprised to find Gideon Ochieno in the tiny dining room. The barrister had changed into casual clothes and had shed the pomp of the courtroom with his suit.

He turned his head, smiled and said, "Mr Carver, I am truly sorry about those horrific injuries described in court, however and by whomever they were caused, of course." There was laughter in his voice. "I hate dining alone. Won't you join me?"

In a welcoming gesture, he pulled back one of the chairs. Seeing Carver's apprehension he confirmed, "I can assure you it won't be a miscarriage of justice if you do."

At first Carver's conversation was guarded, but as the meal progressed he couldn't curb his curiosity.

"I was surprised to find you defending Wamala today."

"And you would like to know why?"

Carver relaxed.

"Now we have finished eating, let me get you a brandy with the coffee. We'll go to that miserable little alcove they call a lounge and I'll tell you a story.

"My father sent me to a public school in England. Then I went to Oxford to read law. I became a barrister in chambers in London."

He took out a pipe and worked on it.

"They treated me well even though I was of a darker hue to them. My father's wealth induced colour blindness. Then the war. I was commissioned into the Judge Advocate General's department."

Carver listened, intrigued, wondering what was to come.

"I was sent to Eritrea to look into alleged war crimes. I suppose they thought that being an African I would know my way around there, though I really was much more at home in Soho."

Suddenly Ochieno's story sprang so vividly to life that Carver felt he was there witnessing what was happening.

"I was sitting in a jeep driven by an African private. A corporal was in the back. The day was hot, the road was smooth tarmac, and I was dozing off, when there was the hammering of a machine gun. The jeep was hit. Its front tyre burst, and it careered off the road into a ditch. Italians and a few of their African troops were dug in, a perfect ambush.

"I found myself lying on the edge of the road, bullets flicking up dust round me. The driver was hanging over the steering wheel, the top of his head blown off. I thought this was the end. Then I saw the corporal calmly removing the Bren gun from its mounting. He was charging head-on at them, firing bursts from the hip, screaming at the top of his voice. Those of the enemy who weren't falling were running for their lives."

The vivid narrative stopped.

"You must have guessed that Luka Wamala was the corporal. He took a trophy from one of the dead. It was an ancient Italian bayonet. But you know more about this than I do." The arcane smile again.

"That's a remarkable story. I heard Wamala was in the army, but I didn't know about this."

"We were rescued by a patrol and I finished off my enquiries. I don't know where he went from Eritrea. So, you see I owe him a debt I can never fully repay. I shall defend him the best I can."

After this there was little room for other conversation and Carver went to bed astonished by what Ochieno had told him. There were new dimensions to the man who had tried to kill him and, indeed, to the lawyer. In their own ways, each was a formidable opponent. He hoped he would never have to oppose them again.

At 10am the following day, the trial was resumed. The rest of the evidence was routine – a medical report, details from railway officials about missing goods, Indian traders producing documents. Those spectators who had missed the first day felt cheated.

Throughout the hearing, the magistrate had noticed the small space around the old woman in an otherwise crowded area. Dressed in a goatskin cloak she had spread out horns, bones, feathers and powders on the bench. From time to time she swayed and appeared to be mouthing words to herself. The magistrate eventually called a recess. He asked his African clerk about her.

"She is the defendant's step-mother."

"But what is she doing with all that paraphernalia?"

"She's a witch. She is making spells to affect your decisions, sir."

"Go and tell her that I have greater powers than she has. Mine have been given to me by the Queen of England."

A court usher removed her, but not before she had collected her bits and pieces. He led her outside the court building where she reconstituted her patterns on the trampled earth. All gave her a wide berth.

The evidence was complete. Defence submissions and the final prosecution summary had been heard by late afternoon. Roland Pound closed the file in which he had made notes.

"I shall adjourn to consider my verdict. I will announce my findings at five-thirty," and with that the clerk followed the magistrate to the Administration offices.

The crowd started to drift away, believing the entertainment was over. Those in the know held back. Knots of spectators debated what they had seen and heard. The defendant was taken back to the Prison Services tender to remain in the cage. Mamayangu continued to chant, rocking backwards and forwards.

When Pound reappeared, Carver watched his face to see if the verdict was written there. There were no tell-tale signs. The prosecuting counsel wriggled his backside on the hard wooden bench, leant forward and shuffled his papers. Luka was brought from the prison tender. Throughout the trial he had said nothing nor shown any emotion.

Pound cleared his throat. "I have listened to all the evidence. I was impressed with what Corporal Ngirenga and Constable Kipchai had to say and the way they said it. They were well supported by other evidence. In respect of the charges of theft from the railway, the fingerprint evidence clearly connects the implement used for resealing the trucks with the defendant. The forensic expert, with his enlarged photographs, showed that this implement was used to reseal trucks from which goods were stolen. Property from three or more instances of theft was found in the house rented by the defendant at Jayanja market. The only defence offered by Mr. Ochieno was that corporal Ngirenga acted as an agent provocateur. I dismiss this as fanciful.

With regard to the attempted murder charges the eye-witness accounts of the police officers were graphic and consistent. The medical evidence describing Inspector Carver's injuries leaves me in no doubt whatsoever that the defendant was trying to kill this police officer. It was only the prompt action of PC Kipchai that saved him. Having seen the bayonet embedded in the bicycle's cross bar, I am certain that had this been allowed to strike home, Corporal Ngirenga would have been killed. I therefore find the defendant guilty of attempting to murder Inspector Carver and of attempting to murder corporal Ngirenga and on each of the counts of theft of goods in transit on the Railway."

A babble of voices broke out inside and around the building. Mamayangu continued her rocking. The magistrate waited for the noise to subside.

"On each of the charges of attempted murder I am sentencing you to ten years imprisonment. On each of the theft charges I am sentencing you to three years imprisonment, all of these sentences to run consecutively."

The quietness, which had fallen around the court, was shattered by the shrill, ululating voice of the old witch. She stood up shaking a bunch of feathers at Pound. Luka's demeanour changed. His head was thrust back, his eyes narrowed. His contempt for the court was emphatic as he spat, the unpleasant fluid landing on the table in front of the Magistrate. Before he could move he was seized by the warders, secured in handcuffs and led away through the crowd. The warder unslung the shotgun from his shoulder pointing it at the prisoner. Luka Wamala, also known as Japani, was about to start his sentence.

Ochieno stood up and walked over to Carver.

"I suppose justice has been done. Pound is a wily old bird. He hasn't left any room for an appeal. I wish you well and I am sorry for your ordeal. I look forward to our meeting again, preferably not in court."

Tomasi Ngirenga straightened his tarbush, pulled his black leather uniform belt tighter and started to walk away. It was then he noticed the elfin face peering round the brick column.

"Now that you have taken my man away, who will look after me? Only someone from my own people will do now."

Ngirenga beckoned to her. She picked up a heavy bundle and hoisted it onto her head as she walked off beside him.

Late that night Mamayangu's messenger delivered a small packet of powder wrapped in a banana leaf to the servants' quarters at the rear of a house in Jayanja.

Pound started vomiting late in the evening. Then the diarrhoea. Then the blood. At 2am a neighbour found him lying by the back door and drove him to the hospital. Amoebic dysentery said the nursing sister. An injection stopped the vomiting but for two days it was touch and go. It must have been the fish he had for supper they said or perhaps the lettuce had not been washed sufficiently. On the third day he was a little better, though all that kept coming to his mind was that old crone shaking feathers at him.

Chapter 34

With Luka's trial ending, Maggie tried to recreate the world they had known, the world that had started in the cool water of the mountain stream. They played the same records, they sat on the verandah and talked as they used to, but the intimacy of the up-country station wouldn't return. Just when she thought he had recovered he would throw out self accusations.

"Kaliso was a cock-up, a failure. I made a mess of it."

"Look, Luka's in prison, his gang is broken, for ever. That isn't failure."

"I don't see it that way," and the subject was closed.

They stretched back on the blanket on the grass on the low cliff. Below them lake flies collected in a cloud. She rolled over awkwardly, turning towards him, and propped her chin on her hand. For a minute she watched the thin trail of sugar ants marching off with the remnants of their picnic while she thought about what she wanted to say. She used to know how to get inside the protective shell but since his discharge from hospital it seemed impenetrable.

"No sooner are you well enough to be interesting again than you'll be on the plane to England."

Carver remained stretched out. "You mean that you didn't find the lump of meat in the hospital bed interesting? What sort of a professional are you?"

"You always twist words round. Don't you understand I want to be serious? I don't want you to go away just now – or ever, for that matter. Can't you say no to leave. Put it off or something? Give us time to…"

"It's the same as when you left Matamu. I've tried, and they referred me to the Conditions of Service. You take leave when you're told, in a temperate climate with no mosquitoes, it said." On cue he slapped the buzzing insect sucking blood from his neck. "Your own department says I've got to go as soon as possible."

"That's unfair. Don't blame all this on the Medical Department."

"The fact is, I've no choice."

"And when you come back, what then?"

"Before I go I'll plead with the Staff Officer for a posting back to the Capital."

"Can't you do better than that? Something more positive?" Without realising it, her voice was rising.

"There's no need to shout. Do you want the whole world to hear?"

"You are the most infuriating person!" Now she was shouting. "It's been long enough since you left hospital and all you do is feel sorry for yourself!"

"That's not what I'm feeling…"

She cut him off before he could finish.

"I've had enough. I can't go on like this. I want more than just seeing you each night and goodbye until the next time."

"If Kaliso had never happened, things would be different, but after all that I can't think much beyond next week."

"Well you've got to start looking ahead more than you do now. What are you going to do with your life? And my life too?"

She sat up and hugged her knees. What more could she say? Now, that very afternoon, had been the perfect occasion to move things along, but that was all gone. She jumped to her feet, tugged at the blanket, shook the grass and dust from it, and folded it.

"We should be going, it will be dark soon."

She flung the blanket into the back of the car and slammed the passenger door so hard it shook the vehicle.

Chapter 35

A police driver drove him to the airport. Soon he would have to make his way to the BOAC Britannia plane shimmering in the heat. He turned and looked at the terminal building. The world was closing in on him; that dark cloud that took over his feelings was back again. Failure – it hurt so much, more than the injuries. First Kaliso and now with Maggie. All he had to do was offer commitment and he couldn't do it.

The loudspeaker system shut off his thoughts with its last call for boarding. He reached the platform at the top of the steps, stopped and looked back. There was no sign of her.

Her arms wrapped round, hugging herself, she peered from the shadows of the viewing gallery. After the row at the picnic she had made excuses not to be with him and only an impulse had brought her to the airport now. Blast, blast, blast the man for leaving her in such a mess.

"Fasten your seat belt for take off please."

The stewardess offered the basket of barley sugar, but he didn't notice it. She shrugged and moved on. It was a bumpy take off, then turbulence over the lake. He shut his eyes and eased the seat back. No comfort. He tried crosswords and then reading but he couldn't concentrate.

It's going to be a long journey.

He dozed. He woke. He dozed again. He watched through the window for any signs of light. The stops at Benghazi and Rome were just two more airports offering their luke-warm drinks and heat-soaked flagstones. Now getting to London was all that mattered. Off this damned plane and shedding these memories.

*

His leave was as he anticipated. Once family visits were over, he sought out a few of his former police colleagues and caught up with their news and the small comfort was that, listening to them, he had no regrets that he had gone to Africa. The hours hung heavily, and he found himself wishing the days away so that he could return to where he belonged. At least he felt fully recovered. The nightmares were but an unpleasant memory. And yet one shining event from that dark period still puzzled him.

Was it really dad's voice? Was that what pushed him to survive?

*

"Telephone for you," called a voice along the corridor. Maggie hurried to the reception area.

"Hello, Baird. Who is it? …Jonathan! Where are you calling from… you're here in the Capital? …Of course I'd like to see you. I'm off at five this evening… You'll be round about seven?"

Jonathan Morley picked her up and they drove to L'Escargot, a bar and restaurant run by an expatriate Frenchman. They talked about old times in Matamu and her spirits were lifted by Jonathan's stories and mimicry of some of the characters there. With Gallic flare the proprietor managed to conjure up a delightful meal from the limited ingredients available and Maggie found herself laughing for the first time in months.

"The company has posted me to the UK," announced Jonathan late in the evening. "They've promoted me to Head Office. I'm here in the Capital for a while before I go to London. We'll be able to see each other quite often since I shan't be travelling about so much."

"Well done. You deserve the promotion."

"Have you heard from Paul? How's he getting on?"

"I've had a couple of letters from him. I don't think he is enjoying his leave all that much, though he says he has recovered completely from the attack."

"I'm glad about that. It was a nasty business. When does his leave end?"

"He has another six weeks. He still doesn't know where he will be posted when he gets back."

They changed the subject, talked a little more, and around midnight left the restaurant. From then on he met her every evening. She found his constant attention flattering but, more than that, it was fun. He had a company house high on a hill just outside the city and in the evenings it was heaven to sit on the balcony high on the second storey and catch the cool breeze coming in off the lake. They often watched the sparkle of the city's lights spread out below them, a Fats Waller record playing in the background.

It was Sunday, dinner was over and they took their coffee onto the balcony. Even though there was an uninterrupted electricity supply here Jonathan still used his wind-up gramophone and he slipped 'Just Squeeze Me' onto the turntable. He came over to the settee and sat beside Maggie.

"It's not long now until I have to pack up and go. These past few weeks have been the most wonderful of my life. I don't suppose you realise it but I've wanted you from the time we met in Matamu."

Maggie looked at Jonathan and as she looked, she found the two men's faces merged – the serious, quiet policeman and the ebullient, unpredictable tobacco salesman. She shook her head slowly. "I never realised."

"I didn't push things since you were obviously attached to Paul. But I'm going to now. I want us to get married.

And then we can go to England together and start a wonderful life there."

The suddenness of his proposal startled her.

He persisted. He was on one knee in front of her, an old-fashioned proposal. "It's a shame your father isn't here and then I could formally ask for your hand. But since he isn't, just saying 'I will' will do."

I could say let me have time to think about it, but time and timing always seems to be the problem with me. The memory of that evening by the lake haunted her and reminded her how angry she was at Paul's lack of response.

"Yes I will, Jonathan."

Jonathan obtained a marriage licence and with his blend of charm and skill in negotiating he managed to arrange the ceremony at the Anglican Church two days before the flight to England. "All a bit rushed, but at least we shan't have time to worry about what might go wrong, shall we? It will make it all the more fun."

*

Carver had been summoned to the Crown Agents offices on Millbank in London for a medical examination. The postman arrived as he was leaving to make his way to the station so he tucked Maggie's letter into his inside pocket. Reading it would lighten the journey. But then the fist in the guts –

> Dear Paul,
> This is the hardest letter I have ever written. Where do I begin? By getting to the point, I suppose. Jonathan and I were married two days ago. We leave for London soon since he

> has been posted to his company's Head Office there.
> There was so much I want to say to you but I don't know how to put this down in cold print so it will all have to be left unsaid. I would much rather have told you this in person, but since this is not possible please forgive me. I hope you will understand.
> With deep affection,
> Maggie

He had read it and re-read it a dozen times before the train had reached Harrow. By the time he entered the Crown Agents offices he didn't care what the medical examination showed.

"I've seen the notes they sent me about your injuries and your treatment."

The doctor packed his instruments away while Carver buttoned his shirt and put on his tie.

"You've come through it well. You're A1 now. Fully fit for duty."

He picked up the fat brown envelope before he left. It contained a ticket for his return flight and details of his posting. He was going to take over Eastern Road Police Station in the Capital. It didn't matter, anywhere would do.

Chapter 36

Eastern Road police station was run down. Discipline was slack and crime was high. All Carver's waking hours were spent on duty. Political parties were now flexing their muscles publicly with rallies held frequently. These grew bigger and more militant. *'Uhuru'* – Freedom – was the word of the day. The wide-open spaces of the market and bus station were within Carver's area and these were the places favoured for assemblies.

There was no doubt that the skirmish at Kaliso had been a turning point for him. After that what more had he to fear? Six months had gone by since his return from leave. He still had the letter from Maggie and some nights in his quieter moments he would look at it and fill himself with regrets. If he'd had any sense, Maggie and he would be together now.

Mid-day Saturday. He put down his pen and closed the last of the files he had been reading. He hoisted his uniform tunic over his shoulder and climbed the stairs to his flat. His house-boy had laid the table and a plate of salad with corned beef was ready under a gauze cloth. It had been a heavy week, early mornings and late nights. Thank God for Saturday afternoon. First a cup of coffee and then lunch, a nap and finish off the Simenon.

He became aware of the distant noise. When he looked out of window towards the market area he could just make out a crowd assembling. Of course, it was an AUFP rally. There were so many of these now and what he heard gave no cause for alarm.

Several hundred people had gathered for the African Union for Freedom Party rally. The warming-up had gone well and there was a carnival spirit for the arrival of the party's leader, Gideon Ochieno. He sat in the back of his Mercedes as it inched through the crowd, smiling broadly, waving regally. Willing aides helped him onto the platform. As he raised his hands high, the crowd quietened. His first attempt to speak through the public-address system was buried in crackles, then with a loud spluttering his voice boomed out. Rapturous applause. Impromptu dancing. He started his address. 'Uhuru' featured regularly. This is what they all wanted to hear. The membership of the AUFP was drawn almost exclusively from the local tribe, the biggest in the country. Their main rival was the Peoples Party who looked elsewhere for its membership. Violent conflict was inevitable.

The Peoples Party had organised fifty of their supporters in small sections. They all wore khanzus, but underneath these long loose garments were an assortment of weapons. They started to infiltrate the crowd.

Carver had just begun to eat when the distant sound changed. Although it was too far to see what was happening, the shift in the sound was ominous. He wasn't to know one of Ochieno's strong arm men had recognised a member of the Peoples Party. He had challenged him and the man pulled out a panga. The phone rang.

"What, sergeant? ...The Markets area? I'll be down right away. Parade everyone. Shields and batons."

The assembly was quick and efficient, thirty men, each holding a wickerwork riot shield and a three feet long wooden baton.

Two police trucks and Carver's Landrover pulled up at the edge of the market place and his men were out of the vehicles and lined up in seconds. Carver climbed onto the top of the cab of the nearest truck, from where he could see over the tightly packed crowd. There were struggles taking place in various parts but what took his attention was a file of seven or eight men snaking through the back of the crowd. Not rushing, gently easing people aside, looking around to see if they were observed. Now they were working their way towards the rear of the platform.

He gave the order and a section of his men formed a wedge of shields. He jumped down to the ground. The crowd looked different from here, tight, more difficult to penetrate but he memorised the scene he had observed from the top of his vehicle, took up his shield and baton and positioned himself at the front of the wedge. The crowd parted as the police thrust through the heaving bodies. The loudspeakers were out of control. Voices babbled. The noise was deafening.

Ochieno was exposed. He stood in the centre of the dais holding the microphone stand, desperately trying to speak through the ailing PA system. As his squad closed on the platform, Carver spotted a man struggling to remove an article from the folds of his long robe. A heavy-bore game rifle was about to be pointed at Ochieno. Carver swept aside all in his way and with the long riot baton swung the gun's barrel into the air. The echo as it fired boomed round the enclosed space stunning the crowd into silence. Now the only noise was that of the unpredictable public address system. The crowd wrenched away the gun and the man was pounded by hands and feet before he was carried away to the police trucks. Carver stood in a space that had cleared at the rear of the platform and wiped his forehead with the back of his hand.

"Mr. Carver, Paul, the last time we met I said I would be pleased to see you again. I didn't think these would be the circumstances."

The politician was helped down from the platform and edged towards Carver with his hand extended.

"A bit like Eritrea, though the consequences of me being shot there would have been nothing compared to what would have happened here. It looks like you have given a service to us all. To the country. I will be in touch with you. You can count on it."

Ochieno motioned to one of his aides to close the meeting. He eased himself into the back seat of his car and the crowd parted, lining the car's route out of the market place. A ripple of applause flowed along the line.

"What's your last day here in Matamu feel like? Are you ready for life in the big city?"

The Provincial Commissioner lowered himself into the chair opposite Rod Stern's desk.

"I'm darned if I know. I don't like the Capital, but it's where all the action is these days."

"Working for the Governor will keep you busy. He needs a man of your experience. The politicos are starting to stir things up. Not surprising, though. Sudan got independence a couple of years ago, the same time as France and Spain gave it to Morocco. Then there's Ghana of course. My guess is Nigeria next."

"How long before we get independence here do you think?"

"If we are to believe the Deputy Governor, not for a long time. He met the prison officers a few months ago when they were all muttering about low morale due to the uncertainty. He told them not to worry, they would all make their pensions here. Can't see it myself. Maybe someone in London is holding out on him."

"He has to play a cagey game. But what do *you* think?"

"Best guess, within the next five years. It's started and nothing's going to stop it." Suddenly his passion burst through. "God knows the scramble to get into Africa in the last century was bad enough. It's the current wisdom that we shouldn't be here in the first place, but we are and we have done and are still doing a damn good job. I know, the way the borders of these countries were drawn up was a nonsense and the country isn't a nation at all. And, yes, we've pushed them to a cash economy, displacing what has worked for them for centuries. It would have happened, one way or another. If we had another twenty years before independence – fifty would be more like it – there would be a chance of this country developing nicely. With the way it is now going, the opportunists will take over and feather their nests at the expense of the ordinary people."

"Why the rush?"

"It's no secret that the Americans and the Soviets are pushing our government to get out of our colonies. It's amazing how many American Peace Corps people looking like crew-cut marines I have met in the past few months. Who knows what threats are being made, what deals are being struck, how many politicians' careers are being held to ransom? It looks as though we are going to make a mass scamper out all over Africa. This will be immoral – worse, criminal. Let's change the subject. I get quite angry when I think about it too much. How's Donna feel about the move? I haven't seen her lately."

"The timing's right. She's bored with up-country life." *And that's not all she's bored with*, thought Stern.

Chapter 37

Mubindi Prison Farm was fifty miles from the Capital, approached from the main road by a causeway track through a swamp. The Prison Services tender bumped over the corrugations, puffing up dust with each bounce. It pulled up outside the offices, a row of rooms made of concrete blocks, thatched with papyrus. The prisoner accommodation and that of the warders stretched out in long lines like spokes of a wheel with the offices as the hub. Everything was whitewashed – the buildings, the stones lining the pathways and roads, the flagpole bearing the Union Jack, dazzling in the bright sunlight. In the distance were the fields of vegetables and the cattle and pig farm and beyond them the fish-farm ponds.

Mubindi was the showpiece of the Prison Service. Harry Box, the Superintendent in charge, was proud that the farm supported itself and even more proud that when the inmates left his charge they were cheerful and better informed. Harry encouraged local chiefs to come and see what the prisoners had achieved. Some held the view that the cattle on the prison farm were so fat and sleek they had been blown up with bicycle pumps. The carp in the ponds, fed regularly with the manure from the pigs, were gargantuan. He stood by the office door and wondered about the new batch of four prisoners, transferred from Lubrika. He would see each of them personally tomorrow. Time to go up the hill. He whistled for Barney, his ridgeback pup, and set off to climb the track leading to his single-storied house overlooking the farm.

"Go and tell her I'm coming, Barney."

The spiky hair along the animal's back stood up and it

raced off towards the house. Liz Box appeared, waving.

Luka had begun his sentence in the cells of Lubrika prison. The appeal against conviction and sentence had been lodged and when he was called to the Superintendent's office one morning it was to be told that the appeal had failed. He said nothing and went back to the cells to consider how he would handle this. There were few escapes from Lubrika but the time will come, Luka, the time will come. Now he stood in front of the table. Harry had already read his file but even so he was surprised that the man's English was so developed. A corporal in the KAR, with an interesting war record.

"Your report from Lubrika is good, Wamala, and I am pleased to have you at Mubindi. You were convicted of attacking a police inspector. I hope you have put this behind you now."

"Sir, I have. I have come to know it was wrong, but I had been smoking bhangi and I had drunk much beer. I am truly sorry for what I did. Jesus has saved me."

Each evening, sitting on the verandah, over a gin and tonic, Harry re-ran the day's happenings to Liz.

"One of the new ones is interesting. He's the chap who tried to do for young Carver at Matamu. Unless he was like it before, and I doubt it, he's the picture of humility. It seems that a spell in Lubrika has shown him the error of his ways. He says a lot of that is due to finding religion."

Liz tidied the bun of greying hair with one hand. "I've yet to meet a really bad prisoner. Treat them with respect and they'll return it."

Luka was allocated work with the cattle. With the smell of cow in his nostrils he could think only of the copper-coloured face of Ngirenga who had made such a fool of him. And but for that Muzungu policeman, Carver, he would have got clean away. Inside him the anger gnawed like rats at a maize bag but to the outside world he remained the picture of contrition.

Working at the cattle farm at Mubindi made Luka more determined to get away from prison life. He wasn't sure how he was going to achieve this, but he knew the opportunity would arise and he would have to be ready to take it when it came. The regime at the prison farm was lax and most of the prisoners, including those with sentences as long as his, seemed content. They called it the King Georgi Hotel, even though the monarch was Elizabeth. His crimes caused him to be viewed with awe by most other prisoners and few attempted to get close to him. The only people he really associated with was a small group who ran a lucrative business growing cannabis under the cover of the long rows of king sized cabbages produced on the farm. With the help of some of the warders, this bhangi was taken to the Capital and sold there. It was taken out of the farm on prison vehicles in small bundles packed into mattress covers. Such was his faith in his prisoners and staff that Harry was completely oblivious of this enterprise.

The pile of eucalyptus logs was nearly exhausted. With Mubindi having no electricity supply Liz depended upon the firewood for cooking and water heating. Whenever her stock was depleted Harry sent the nearest available prisoner to the plantation to chop wood and bring it to the house.

"Wamala, I've a job for you. Mrs Box needs firewood. You'll need to cut enough to fill the shed by the back door. Mrs Box will show you where to put it."

Luka resented play-acting subservience, but it paid off. His demeanour had bought him privileges and an amazing amount of freedom. He saluted as he had been taught in the army and he could see the Superintendent's pleasure at this.

Harry left the house at 6.30am for a meeting in the Capital soon after he had given his instructions. Luka cut the wood and filled the handcart. He returned the axe to the store before manhandling the cart up the long hill. He was still busy stacking the logs in the shed when Liz went to pick vegetables.

He needed to change from the conspicuous prison garb of khaki smock and shorts. He waited until the Superintendent's wife was in her garden and slipped into the laundry room. As he picked through the pile of clothes he heard the sound of the outside door. It was Liz coming into the kitchen carrying a loaded basket. A pot of coffee, that was to be her next move. Then she thought she heard movement in the laundry.

"Barney." There was the noise again. "Barney, come out of there."

She put the bag on the kitchen table and moved to the laundry. An African in prison khaki was bending over the clothes stack.

"What on earth are you doing in here?"

He turned his head and she found herself caught in the smouldering glare of prisoner No. 1113 Wamala. She saw disdain, hate, anger. She wanted to yell but this was something she never did with prisoners. She mustered as much normal tone as she could.

"What are you doing with those clothes? You're not thinking of walking out of here, are you?"

No woman other than Mamayangu had ever questioned his actions or told him what to do. There in front of him stood the heavy charcoal iron. He reached forward slowly, still watching over his shoulder. He swung round so quickly that Liz did not realise what was happening. The flatiron crashed into the side of her face. As she staggered forward, Luka hammered the improvised weapon into the base of her skull. The bun of hair was no protection and it was instantly soaked in thick, rich head blood. She fell to the floor, face down, motionless.

He changed clothes quickly. Now what? He saw her Austin A30 car standing under a thatched awning barely fifty yards away. His eyes alighted on the keys on a hook inside the kitchen. No-one anywhere in sight. He squeezed himself into the car, cramped for lack of space in the small vehicle. His lack of control of the clutch and the gears brought protesting noises which were like shouts for help on Liz's behalf, but he managed to drive along the back road from the Superintendent's house down the hill, out of sight of the offices. There would be no other security until the warder at the causeway but, as Luka knew, they seldom remained where they should be. He revved the car as hard as he could and sped across the narrow swamp crossing. No shouts, no shotgun fire. Luka Wamala was free.

He turned onto the main road leading to the Capital, heading for the outskirts of the city. He stopped in an area where there were no Indian shops and no sign of Europeans. But there would be police. A clean car in such good condition stood out from the other vehicles and would be suspicious. He abandoned it at the edge of a banana thicket leaving the keys in the ignition. It wouldn't be there long.

It was only then that he considered what he should do. To lose himself in the suburbs of the city should not be difficult. He was not known anywhere there. And then he would decide what to do after that. Surviving would be no problem since he had sufficient money from his earnings from the cannabis trade. And by the time it ran out he took it for granted he would have worked out a fresh way of getting money. It was not a long wait for the local bus and this took him several miles away. He started his search for a room.

Liz's body was discovered an hour after Luka had fled. The Head Warder had not seen Luka after his first trip to the plantation and came to look for him. He liked the Superintendent's wife, but she was too soft. She was probably giving this man Wamala food and drink. He knocked on the back door which was open. There was no answer and he was about to turn away when he heard Barney. Liz was lying between the laundry and the kitchen. The young dog stood by her growling defiance.

The Assistant Commissioner CID called Superintendent Glennon to his office. "No stone unturned. I want this man caught."

Glennon had much to prove. The spotlight wasn't going to be switched off and he knew he would need a lot of help to crack this one.

"Inspector Singh must know his haunts and Carver might be able to help. I'll get things moving straight away."

He met Carver at Eastern Road police station.

"Not Wamala again," were Carver's opening words. "He won't go back to Kaliso or Jayanja and I can't see him getting a job. He'll need money, so he'll be into some racket, something that won't draw too much attention to him. He'll be somewhere here in the Capital."

Now he needed someone who knew about Luka. More than that. Someone who knew how to hunt him down. There was one man for this job.

Monday morning and Carver came down to the charge office from his flat to find a kit bag with the number 1436 stencilled across it, dumped where it shouldn't be. He was just about to berate the Charge Office constable for untidiness when a familiar figure appeared. Ngirenga was now wearing sergeant's stripes.

"Good to see you sergeant. I've got a very special assignment for you."

The area was favoured by itinerants and Luka was inconspicuous among the comings and goings of the many people there. He rented accommodation but inevitably his money ran out. He had made it his business to know the layout of the city. particularly the areas in which Europeans lived. Breaking into these houses carried limited risks but he could not afford to be captured. Murder still carried the death penalty and for killing a Muzungu woman he would certainly hang.

He cut a long bamboo pole from a thicket and fashioned a hook for its end. When the nights were hot most of the Europeans left their bedroom windows open. With bars protecting these it was impossible to break in without making a noise but there was little risk in slitting the fly netting and reaching in with the pole. Most Europeans were stupid enough to leave wallets and watches on their bedside tables and there were always clothes strewn around. He stuck razor blades into slits in the pole as a safeguard against anyone grabbing it, in the unlikely event of their waking. The gardens of the Europeans' houses were large and the hedges were high and perfect cover.

It was two o'clock in the morning and Carver had just completed a check of his uniform patrols. It was a pleasant night and the sweet scent of the frangipani and hibiscus had made being out at that time a pleasure. He stood talking to the Charge Office corporal before turning in. The phone rang. The corporal put his hand over the mouthpiece as he said, "It is a European lady, sir, on Queen's Drive. She has disturbed a thief."

The corporal was still standing with the phone poised. Carver sighed. Why hadn't he gone to bed straight away?

"There's no-one else is there? What number Queen's Road? Twenty. Right, tell her I'm on my way."

The headlights picked out the number on a board by the road and he pulled into the driveway. The front door opened and a woman, silhouetted against the light, stood at the top of the steps.

"Good Lord, it's you, Paul. What service. The boss turning out in the middle of the night."

"Donna. Donna Stern. I didn't know you were in the Capital. What's happened?"

"Someone tried to get in to the house. At least he stuck a pole with a hook on the end of it through the window and tried to take things."

The light was still on and Carver could see that the fine mosquito netting had been cut and neatly turned back. He went outside and searched the surrounding area with his torch. There was no sign of anyone. He returned to the house to find Donna sitting on the edge of her bed.

"What did you do?"

"I screamed like hell and before I could grab the pole, he dropped it."

"It was just as well you didn't grab it. Look at those."

He pointed to the razor blades embedded in the pole. Donna shuddered as she realised what would have happened.

"Did you get a look at him?"

She shook her head. "I only caught a glimpse of a face." She was starting to shudder. "I was all right earlier but now I'm falling to bits."

The dressing gown fell open, exposing her knees. She looked directly at Carver. "I could do with some company until I feel better. Stay and have a coffee or something. Besides, I haven't seen you since we were in Matamu and there must be lots to talk about."

She was shaking too much for her to light the cigarette he offered. He held her hand still and struck the match.

"You'd better sit down and I'll make some coffee."

"I'd rather have a brandy," and she pointed to the decanter on the sideboard. "I don't like drinking alone. Have one with me."

"So how do you come to be in the Capital?"

"We were posted here when Rod was appointed Special Assistant to the Governor. He didn't want to leave Matamu but the job looked too interesting to pass up."

"Where is he now?"

"Oh, H.E. is always travelling these days. Rod has to go with him. He's away for the rest of the week. It's quaint the way they call it 'going on safari'. Sounds like trekking off with porters carrying their stuff on their heads. Not driving everywhere in Landrovers and a baggage lorry full of enough gear to set up a tented village."

He found his eyes being drawn to her bare knee. "How are you feeling now?"

"A lot better for the company. And what about you?"

"Busier than ever. Work and lots of it. Eastern Road covers a lot of the city."

"I didn't mean work. What about your love life?"

He didn't answer.

"I heard about Maggie getting married. Have you heard from her?"

"No, I don't expect to. She'll have other things to think about now."

His eyes didn't meet hers as he spoke.

"God, you were an insensitive clod, Paul Carver. The only thing that girl wanted was for you to ask her. Jonathan just picked her up when you knocked her flat."

"When I did *what*? I didn't do anything to Maggie!"

"That's just the point. You didn't do *anything*. You can trample all over someone's emotions without doing anything. Didn't you want her?"

"Want her? Of course I did. More than you'll ever know. I should have settled things with her before I went on leave. I had the chance and I…"

"No good crying over spilt milk. Everything's moved on. After what happened tonight I'd feel a lot better if I had someone who can show… say… lots of sensitivity. I'm sure it would make both of us feel better…"

The bamboo pole still had traces of the black fingerprint powder on it when Carver went to collect it from Police HQ. The forensic expert looked up from the stack of forms.

"You're in luck. There are some really good prints. Palms as well as digits."

"Having prints is one thing. Knowing who they're from is another."

"I said you're in luck and I mean luck. The right thumb has a scar across the middle. I knew I had seen it somewhere recently. I checked back and found it belongs to a man named Wamala who is wanted for the murder of Mrs Box. And escape from Mubindi. I don't suppose you know him?"

"I know him alright. You might say he left his mark on me." Carver's fingers had started the involuntary search of his neck again.

Chapter 38

After he had run from the house on Queen's Drive, Luka didn't leave the rooms he rented for two days. His ego had been shattered. As he sat drinking some of the stinging liquor from a tin mug he took stock. He was making enough money from stealing from Europeans' houses for his present way of life, but this is not what he wanted. What was he now? He was a common thief with no standing in the world. Now the fear of informers selling him to the police stopped him experiencing that sense of power he gained when he was telling the circle around him about his exploits. He had been stopped in his tracks by a woman. A scrawny European woman.

On the third day he could take the solitude no longer. He waited until dusk and then went to a quiet bar where he was barely known. He wanted a drink, lots of drink, and a woman. He wanted the European-styled beer that he was used to drinking, but prudence made him settle for the local banana brew at a fifth of the price.

He moved to the gloom of a corner, only to find another man sitting at the one available table. As his eyes became accustomed to the darkness he saw the man more clearly. He was dressed in an old Railway Authority khaki drill uniform, patched and dirty, with parts of the Railway Authority's initials still visible. The man fixed on Luka's beer mug with rheumy eyes, licking his lips pleadingly.

"Where are you from, friend?"

The answer was better than he expected. The man came from a place near enough to Luka's own area to know his language. His offer of banana beer was readily accepted. They drank and talked.

"So you work for the Railway do you?"

"I did, until they threw me out. I haven't been able to get any other work."

"That's bad luck. And why did they throw you out?"

"They said I was drunk on duty. I wasn't of course. I'd had a little drop of beer but that was all."

"What did you do when you worked for the Railway?"

"Permanent Way gang. Keeping the track strong enough for the trains to run over it and the points working."

Now Luka was really interested. A shilling or so more might prove a worthwhile investment. More beer.

"With all your expert knowledge you must know how to make a train fall from the rails, then?"

"A man of my experience can do that."

"Just suppose, just suppose, mind you, that someone wanted to make a train fall over, what would be the best way to do this?"

The man started to explain, warming to the task. "The best way is to take a piece of rail away."

"Could one man do that on his own?"

"No. Six men minimum. And you'd need the right spanners for the fishplates."

"What could one man on his own do?"

The man looked knowingly over the rim of his mug. "Ah, here's a special one. Not many know how to do this, but I do. I've seen it…"

"What is it then?" Luka called for more beer.

The man explained. He demonstrated with gestures and even with a diagram of railway points drawn in spittle on the table. The man was still preoccupied drinking the last dregs from his mug when Luka left.

*

It was not normally within Ngirenga to hate. He did not hate the lions who tried to take his cattle. He did not hate the wild dogs that he speared when they were attacking his charges. They did what was natural for their survival. But he hated Luka. Luka killed because he liked hurting others.

He spent his days walking or cycling slowly through the shanty towns and markets which made up the suburbs of the Capital. Gradually the word was spreading that he was looking for information about the 'pole fisher' and delivering this could be worth a lot of money.

With his hair grown long and wearing a beard, Luka stayed in his rooms during the day time, emerging an hour before dusk. He no longer spent his night times roving the residential areas looking for open windows. Instead each evening he went to the railway track. He walked by the side of the line until he came to where the Quarry siding branched off, a mile from the main station. There he squatted near the points under cover of the long grass and watched as the porter removed the padlock and heaved on the weighted lever to change the direction of the line ready for the Quarry Special to leave. When the train had passed through the points from the siding, the porter reset them for the main line traffic, replaced the padlock and walked back to the station.

He made a habit of meeting the porter on his way back to the station. "What trains tonight?" he always asked.

"Up Goods Special tonight. It's a big one from Jayanja. Petrol and gas oil tankers and mixed goods wagons. It will come through this section in two hours time."

Luka looked along the track in the direction of Jayanja. The main line was a long, straight down-gradient coming out of the Muvuli forest and passing over a steep embankment, forming a causeway immediately after the siding line points. Swampy water fed by a stream spread out from the foot of the embankment.

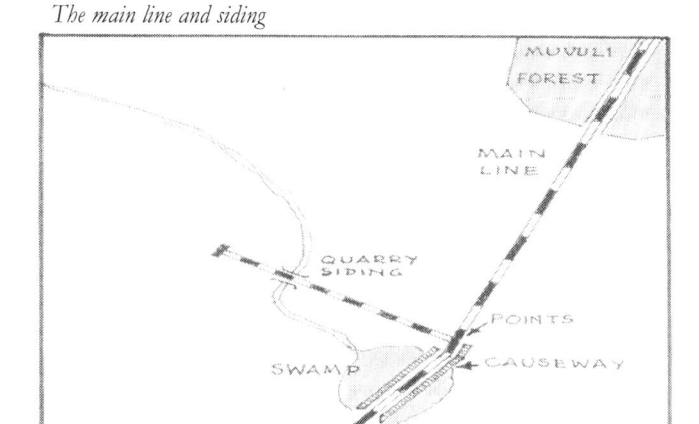

The main line and siding

[Map showing MUVULI FOREST, MAIN LINE, QUARRY SIDING, SWAMP, POINTS, CAUSEWAY, and CAPITAL STATION]

*

5901 was steaming gently in the sidings at Jayanja. For this night's work she was to pull the Up Goods Special. Driver Farnie de Hoek and Fireman Ben Kagwa made their usual inspections and gave the shining brass work in the cab a special rub.

"He'll be here, Ben, don't you worry."

As Farnie spoke, the portly figure of the District Motive Power Inspector appeared. He carried a small leather attaché case and despite his bulk he swung himself with accustomed ease up the ladder onto the locomotive's footplate.

"The last hurdle, Ben. I've got the forms in here ready to sign when we reach the Capital." The Inspector tapped the attaché case. "The final practical tonight. Pass this and you'll be the first African Garratt driver. You ready?"

Ben nodded, and smiled, though this didn't mask his anxiety.

"Course he's ready. He's right on top of it."

The inspector smiled. "You can belt up, Farnie. You're just the fireman tonight. Ok. Ben, here comes line clear."

Ben wound the gear handle, eased the regulator arm, and released the brakes. 5901 snorted gently, very gently, passed steam through the piston casings and moved forward.

*

The porter had already made his way back to the station when Luka emerged from the long grass near the siding points. He stood listening, pulling the hacksaw from under his loose shirt. Another moment of listening with all his being and then he started to saw through the hasp of the siding points padlock. The squeal of the blade seemed to cut the night as well as the metal. He spat on it to lubricate it and continued. It was quieter now. At least the metal was mild steel not the hardened kind. And then the blade was through. The lock fell off. He didn't bother to look for it; it would soon be lost in the mess of metal.

Now he was recalling the words of the disgraced Railwayman who had told him the secrets of the points. He pulled on the weighted lever and eased the points fully over until they were directed to the siding. Now any train coming from Jayanja direction would divert into the siding. But that was not what Luka intended. He eased the points back until from the footplate of an approaching train they would appear to be set, as they should be, for passage along the main line and on into the Capital's station. He had to trust that the railway man was right when he said that with vibration from a train, points set in this way would flick back towards the sidings.

The Up Goods Special had passed uneventfully through Ngoma and Mango stations. There were no trains to cross, no water to be taken on, no delays. Ben Kagwa had travelled these sections of the line so many times. Not long to go and the assessment for his promotion to driver would be over.

And then Kibanda. There were flat wagons loaded with logs from the sawmills to be picked up here. Only one section of line to go. Muvuli forest. Ben could feel the foliage close in on him and the sound of the train bounced back from the leafy walls. They passed the four-mile track marker. Four miles to the Capital's station. Ben wiped his hands on a wad of cotton waste more out of habit than necessity. Out of the forest and the long incline before the embankment, straight, downhill and the last opportunity to give the old girl her head. He moved the regulator up a touch and then a touch more. 5901 responded and the tramping beat of her engines echoed in the cutting. Ben kept his eyes on the track. The quarry siding was coming up.

Some drivers would take the points for granted but not Ben. Not tonight. He peered down the long beam of the headlight. Yes, the points were straight ahead for the main line.

From his vantage point Luka could see the train. He listened to the familiar clackety-clack as the wheels of the front bogie went over the points and along the main line. Then the rumbling vibration created by the weight of the locomotive flicked the points back to the siding line just as the man said they would. He screamed in exultation. With a screeching of steel on steel the rear bogie travelled up the siding line. 5901 was trying to go in two directions at the same time.

Two hundred and fifty two tons of metal were out of control. Two hundred and fifty two tons of metal were being heaved from behind at first by wagons loaded with tree trunks and then by a string of tankers. 5901 was sliding from the track, her headlight pointing straight at the swampy water. The lines buckled. The track ballast was flung into the air. One of the tree trunks broke its chains and flew up high, crashing down on the rear engine. The rails were ripping apart and the tankers were no longer balancing on the metre-wide track. Another log broke loose. The leading tanker ran into this and smashed open. Thousands of gallons of petrol sprayed onto the embankment, along the track under the locomotive and down onto the swamp. The goods wagons further back hammered on, flinging tankers off the line. In slow motion they toppled over, one by one and slid down the embankment. Only the guard's van at the very back of the train and a few trucks in front of it remained standing on the line. The guard watched the disaster unfold along the line in front of him.

Farnie de Hoek hit his head on the regulator handle and was flung, unconscious, onto the floor. His red check shirt was spattered with fuel oil from a feed line that had broken, and the driver's hat with the oilskin cover had disappeared, leaving the blond curls uncovered to soak up the fuel now washing freely around the cab. When the locomotive's first bogie derailed, the Motive Power Inspector was standing close to the footplate's entrance and the impact knocked him off balance. He fell through the gap onto a grassy bank. He broke two ribs and his left shin bone as he hit the metal stairway. He was still clutching his attaché case.

Ben was flung clear into a bed of reeds on the edge of the swamp. He could feel himself sinking into the slimy water. Breathing was difficult. His legs hurt. As the foul water swilled around him he could only watch the tableau above, a detached spectator. He could smell the petrol and the fuel oil. And the heat, the heat, the heat.

The locomotive's fuel burst into flames. Ben was unable to move as he watched 5901 in silhouette. He felt the heat as the whoosh of roasting air swept over him. The petrol spread out over the swamp and after the initial fireball, flames were dancing over an area of fifty square yards. All the fire was on the other side of the embankment and while he felt singed he could move a little. He was going to survive.

Luka danced as the first fire started and screamed out loud as the tanker's load ignited. Never had he expected such devastation. Now the Railway was really suffering. All the goods stolen in the past were as nothing compared to this. His revenge was complete.

Chapter 39

The sound of the crash had echoed into the City and the fire rose like a massive beacon. The noise brought Carver to the window of his flat. He could see the fire. It reminded him of the time when, as a small boy, he had stood in the garden at home and watched the flames as the Germans bombed London. But this time it was in an area where dealing with law and catastrophe was his responsibility. He phoned the fire station. They knew no more than something had happened to a train. He picked up two of his constables and set off in his car.

The Chief Fire Officer didn't hear the noise of the train crash. He was playing bridge in the Capital Club, a haunt of senior people from government and the commercial world. A club servant waited for an opportune moment and laid the envelope on the card table beside him. Suspecting it was a reminder about his unpaid bar bills he left it until another hand was completed. When he opened the envelope his fellow players were startled at the speed with which he left the building. The city's two fire engines were ready to go when he arrived at the fire station and he led the cavalcade with the big silver bell under the bonnet of his car pealing continuously.

As there was no direct road access to the site of the crash, the fire engines went to the quarry and from there a small team explored on foot. The senior management of the Railway were finding their way along the track by the light of torches and storm lanterns. None really knew what he was going to see, but each had already started thinking about how he could safeguard the interests of his own department. They were not prepared for the sight that met them as they rounded a bend in the track. The vivid inferno had burnt itself into widespread smouldering and despite the heavy pall of smoke they could see the immensity of what had happened.

!My God!" was all the District Traffic Superintendent could say as he put his hand to his mouth. The Motive Power Superintendent was assessing the lifting gear required to start making order from this gigantic mess. The Locomotive foreman had already sent a messenger back to the station to arrange for flood lights to be sent and the heavy mobile crane to be prepared.

The first fireman at the crash scene reached the cab of 5901. He found Ben Kagwa kneeling on the ground by the body of Farnie de Hoek. At least, that's who Ben said it was. The red check lumberjack shirt, the blonde hair, the blue jeans were no more. The body was charred and the flesh on his left arm had pulled away from the bone when Ben had levered him out of the cab.

The African guard had found the Motive Power Inspector lying by the embankment and had run back to his van for the big leather first aid satchel. Another fireman found the guard sitting dazed alongside the Inspector. His application of the splint to the Inspector's leg was a work of art, to quote the doctor who came to the scene.

Knowing that this was the most serious incident he was likely to deal with, Carver fought against being overwhelmed as he parked his car in the quarry. He picked his way through the rough ground to the branch line. The going was much easier then as he stepped from sleeper to sleeper. He could see the tangle of steel that was once the points. The locomotive had slipped down the embankment and only its rear bogie remained near the track. Its headlight was touching the water of the swamp, its beam long since extinguished. Wherever he moved he felt the searing heat of hot metal.

How could this smash have happened – unstable track, faulty rail, something like that. Driver speeding perhaps. If it was an accident, what could he contribute to the investigation? Only the railway men could make sense of the confusion. But here was that gut reaction again; what if it wasn't an accident? He sought out the Locomotive Foreman and the Permanent Way Inspector. If any railwaymen knew anything it would be these two. They agreed there was nothing more he could do that night. They arranged to meet at first light.

Dizzy with emotion and drained of physical energy, Luka had seen and experienced enough. He had heard the fire engines arriving in the quarry and listened to the people coming along the main line from the station and now he should get as far away from the smash as he could. He followed the narrow track between the six-feet-tall grass, now well away from the quarry siding and walking towards the city's edge. In the darkness he didn't notice the puff adder asleep in the dust of the path. His right foot landed squarely on it. Sluggish in all its movements except attacking an enemy or prey, the reptile puffed itself up and struck. It sank its hollowed venom-bearing fangs deep into Luka's calf. He resisted the natural inclination to yell out, reached into his pocket and pulled out one of the razor blades that used to adorn his bamboo pole. He slashed at the holes made by the fangs and his blood poured out taking some of the poison with it. Crawling around he sniffed among the grass and found the wild herbs he wanted. He chewed the leaves to a pulp and pushed this into the wound, binding it round with strands of the long grass. He lay back on the ground breathing deeply. The wound hurt fiercely and he could feel the venom moving in his veins. How he wished that Mamayangu was here to ply her healing craft.

He must have dozed, since he was now looking up at the milky light of pre-dawn. He dragged himself to his feet and hobbled along the path, now well away from the railway track. The injured limb throbbed and pains were shooting throughout his legs and arms. An hour later he staggered into his rooms and collapsed on the bed.

6am. Early as he was, Carver found the Locomotive Foreman was there before him. A lean, intense Yorkshireman with a shining bald head, he had learned his trade at the LNER locomotive sheds at Doncaster. The skin between mid-thigh, where his shorts ended, and mid calf, where his boots began, was mahogany. His chief responsibility was maintaining the locomotives and repairing them when they broke down but there was little he didn't know about how the rest of the railway worked.

"Have you had time yet to see what happened?" asked Carver.

"Not really, though most of it started around the points. Shan't be really sure until the wreckage is cleared away and that's going to take a lot of time. 5901 was in good shape. She had only just been in for a major inspection. I drove her myself a few days ago. Can't believe it was down to her." He prodded a piece of metal with the stick he was carrying. "I wanted to get here before the other departments turned up."

"Why is that?"

"There was a serious derailment a few years ago – not as bad as this one. At the official enquiry, the Permanent Way department said the track was perfect, the Traffic people said all the trucks were properly loaded and the guard had done what he should, the Mechanicals said there was nothing wrong with any of the wagons, their brakes and couplings and so on, and the Motive Power people said the locomotive was all in order and being driven at the right speed. The magistrate said he only had one course left to him; the official verdict was 'Gremlins on the line'."

He looked up at Carver with a wry grimace. "In Yorkshire we call a spade a spade. Departmental investigations seldom get at what's really happened. They're about whitewashing your own. Come on, let's have a scout around."

The Locomotive Foreman wandered off towards the wreckage of the points, now thirty yards away from their original location. The lever mechanism's concrete mounting had been torn up and borne along with the tangled steel. The railway man carried on to the wreck of 5901, looked up at the blackened paint work which had been a sparkling claret and gold and shook his head wistfully.

"I could weep. It'll take a long time to get her back on the rails, if ever."

They walked round both sides of the locomotive, the foreman poking here and there with the stick. Eventually he turned to Carver. "I think we'll have to wait until there's some lifting gear. It's going to be a long business."

The policeman leant on the handle of the wrecked points. He looked down. And then it struck him that there was something wrong. "Shouldn't there be a padlock on these points?" he called out to the Foreman. He bent down to take a closer look. "It's missing. It couldn't have been torn off during the impact, could it?"

"I don't see how it could. The metal around the locking holes shows no signs of stress."

Carver bent down and ran his finger along the concrete mounting block. He held up his hand to show a few specks of silver metal. "Aren't these iron filings?"

The Foreman brushed a mixture of sand and metal dust gently into the palm of his hand.

"They're filings alright. Mild steel, they're fresh, too. Haven't had time to rust. There's no reason for them to be here unless someone cut the padlock off. If this is so, this wasn't an accident."

"Let's see if we can find that padlock and confirm what we think."

With his constables he started an inch-by-inch search of the area around the original site of the points. Sixteen minutes later his patience paid off when he found the padlock almost buried in the churned earth and coarse ballast. There was no doubt that the hasp had been cut through.

"You're right, it wasn't an accident," said Carver. "Farnie de Hoek died in the crash. It's homicide."

Chapter 40

The crash was the centre of public excitement. The Railway Authority spokesman kept reporters at arms length by daily bulletins saying investigations were in hand and that when the causes were known all the media would be informed, which, of course, led to instant speculation by the press. Photographs of the scene appeared daily, and the heavy crane lifting 5901 provided the drama needed for the front page of both the Clarion and Habari ya Leo, an African language paper. Visiting the scene was a popular outing, with yards of film being shot daily. Hawkers claimed their pitches for selling charcoal, roasted corncobs, and peanuts.

Tributes were paid in the press to Farnie de Hoek and there was a story about the guard who gave first aid to the Motive Power Inspector. Then, as is the way of the media everywhere, the news which was launched with such a splash died like an evaporating raindrop. It was just another 'story', a tale to entertain a voyeuristic public. World news headlines re-established themselves on the front pages with particular emphasis on the impending independence of colonial territories. On the middle page of the Clarion, sandwiched between the review of the Capital Players production of the Gondoliers and the shipping reports from the Coast, was an item about police promotions. Among these was Chief Inspector P. Carver's elevation to the rank of Superintendent.

*

That the crash was due to sabotage was confirmed. Carver took charge of the investigation himself. He called the

Locomotive Foreman and Permanent Way Inspector to his office. Ngirenga joined the meeting.

"Only a railway man is likely to know how to play that trick with the points?"

The railway men agreed.

Carver continued, "Anyone who rigged the points would know what would happen?"

Again there was agreement.

"So, it would need a strong reason – a very big grudge, say – to make someone do it. Who's likely to have both the reason and knowledge?"

The Loco Foreman scratched his head and looked up at the Permanent Way man. "I'd have to say someone from either of our departments."

The railway men left, leaving Carver and Ngirenga to consider what had been said.

"We've got little to work on, so we'll find out who have been dismissed from those two departments and who have had disciplinary action taken against them. Find them and talk to them. Make enquiries among those they worked with to see if there are any rumours."

"It may not be easy to trace those dismissed if they are not from local people. They will have gone back to their own areas."

"So it may mean it will take you longer."

As Ngirenga rose to leave, Carver said, "By the way, were you getting anywhere with finding Luka Wamala? We haven't talked about him recently."

"No-one has seen him. Maybe his step-mother has made him vanish," and he smiled his broad smile. "We shall see him again. Luka is not a man to be hiding all the time."

One by one Ngirenga and his men tracked down the possible suspects. They were given lists of former Railway employees and those against whom disciplinary action had been taken. One by one their stories were checked, and they were crossed off the lists. It's often said that five per cent of the success of an investigation is due to inspiration and ninety-five per cent to perspiration. Carver never fully believed this. To him intuition, insight, inspiration, premonition, sixth sense – call it what you will – was the all-important factor. All this meticulous work put in by Ngirenga wasn't going to solve this case. The sergeant, on the other hand, believed you gained little success if you didn't work for it. Hard graft and the application of the mind were the driving forces in his work and in the way he lived.

*

Staying within his room was misery for Luka. For three days he had tossed and turned on his bed, wracked with fever. A woman had looked in and prepared some gruel which she spooned into his mouth.

Then the fever was over. He ate more substantial food and felt his strength growing. Everywhere except in his leg. It was badly scarred from the slashes he had made to purge the snake's poison and the calf muscle had begun to waste. When he began to walk more than a few steps, he was unable to do so without limping. At these times, when he was below par physically and mentally, he recalled the splendour of the smash. The fireball, the wagons upending, the locomotive sinking down the embankment. His aches and pains were as nothing when he re-lived this triumph.

This euphoria sustained him for a while, but then he began to take stock of his position. He had little money, but stealing by poking a pole through windows was petty for a man of his calibre. He asked himself, to whom did he turn when he was last in difficulties? Well, one man was the powerful lawyer, a man destined for great things – *Ochieno*.

*Ochieno might know what to do. No, **I** will tell Ochieno what to do. **I** will make him listen.*

*

Gideon Ochieno's house stood on a hill overlooking one of the shanty towns that made up the suburbs of the Capital. The red pan tiles capping the double-storied house rose above the sea of corrugated iron of the houses around it. The building was surrounded by three acres of garden, given to growing bananas and plantains for cooking. At one side was a tennis court. The entire area was enclosed by an eight-feet-high fence of sturdy bamboo poles tightly laced together, a barrier both to entry and to prying eyes. The tall double wooden gates were tended night and day by a uniformed watchman.

Luka was high up a mango tree from which the flight of bats, like a fleet of marauding aircraft, had headed off to the valley for their nightly feast. This was his third night watching for patterns in Ochieno's household. Earlier the Mercedes had glided through the gateway and the watchman had settled down in the sentry box. Once Ochieno was inside the house, a servant locked the tall carved hardwood front doors. Now he could see the lawyer through the window, lying back in an armchair, holding a glass up as though toasting someone.

It was time to act. He slid out along a branch towards the fence and swung his body up and over, dropping inside the compound. Here was the same feeling he experienced when breaking into railway trucks, but then his leg didn't hurt. He could smell the appetising aroma of meat cooking. In the dim light from a window he straightened his clothes. He had bought a dark suit in the market and it fitted him well. He had black shoes which did not. He even wore a shirt and tie, something he had not done since he was in the mission school in Kaliso.

Front doors were always locked, but cooks liked their back doors open to savour the cool air. The kitchen boy was cleaning pans under a running tap well away from the house. Luka slipped inside the kitchen and stood by the door surveying the room. The cook was nowhere to be seen. And then he heard him. He was fetching provisions from the store. Luka reached inside his jacket, pulled out sunglasses and put these on and cleared his throat loudly. The cook, who was just entering the room with a tray of vegetables and a piece of meat resting on a banana leaf, stopped in his tracks and looked at the tall suited man whose eyes he couldn't see. *Trouble. People looking like that were always trouble nowadays.* His tongue dried up.

"I am making a security check," said Luka and strutted importantly round the room, trying to hide his limp. The cook stood still as though engaged in a juvenile game of statues. A minute of this charade and Luka said, "You are lucky. Everything is all right. You can get on with your work or your master's dinner will be late."

He walked through the passageway which he knew must lead to the room where he had seen Ochieno. He knocked gently on the door. A muffled voice commanded him to enter.

With his back towards the door, Ochieno could not see who had entered, but the woman sitting opposite him looked up, mouth open, in alarm. Ochieno turned slowly, put his glass on a low table and stood up. Who did he expect to see? The woman's husband, perhaps. His initial feeling of relief swung instantly to anxiety, fear. He was facing a man he didn't know in a dark suit, with a beard, and all he could manage was, "Who are you? How did you get in here?"

"You don't recognise me?"

Ochieno shook his head.

"That's good."

No other voice was like that. The arrogance. It can't be... He's too thin. He wouldn't dare to come here. But yes he would. It's him. It could only be... Ochieno's internal churning stopped as suddenly as it had started. He turned to the woman.

"It would be as well if you left us for a while. Go and tell the cook to start dinner for you."

The woman left, shutting the door.

"Now, what are you doing here?"

"I am testing your security. It is not very good. A man in your position ought to be better protected than this."

"I didn't ask you to test my security. Who gave you instructions...?"

"No-one. I thought it needed checking. And wasn't I right?"

"Sit down. This needs considering. What do you want from this?"

"I need work. I need money. You need protection. Like you needed me once before."

"That was a long time ago. The Italians aren't shooting at me now. In any case I can't afford to be associated with you. It is well known that the police are looking for you."

Ochieno realised that he was actually afraid of Luka, but it would never do to have him recognise this. It would be as well to have some control over him. To have him working covertly for him was a possibility.

"I have an offer for you. You will be the man who watches over me. I have other guards, but they will not know about you. I will pay you and you can have a house which I own at Muzinga. If you're found there by the wrong people it will not be connected with me. That is the best I can offer... for now."

"As you say, it will do for now. I will expect more when the time is right."

"I can't continue calling you Luka Wamala. What name will you be known by?"

"Musa Mulangi." He gave the name of a fellow soldier killed in Eritrea. "Yes, I will be known as Musa Mulangi."

"Right, I want you to make checks of my security here and for the public meetings I shall hold. There will be many more of these now. I will keep in touch with you at Muzinga."

As he left Ochieno's compound he could not resist padding quietly to the watchman's box and shaking the man physically into wakefulness. "You will be seeing more of me. You had better be awake then."

*

It was now a month since the train had crashed. Now there was only one of the dismissed railwaymen to interrogate. Records showed that he had been dismissed for persistent drunkenness when he was working in the Permanent Way Inspector's gang and had all the qualifications to be a suspect. He had been seen locally still wearing his old railway uniform. A detective found him sleeping in an alleyway outside a bar and brought him for questioning by Ngirenga. It took twenty minutes of interrogation before he told the sergeant of the stranger who was interested in ways of making a train fall off the line.

"No, of course I didn't tell him how to do it. That would have been wrong, wouldn't it? And does the sergeant have a little money for some bread?"

There was a ring of truth in what the drunkard said. This witless individual hadn't the courage or energy to do anything like that himself and yet his description could have fitted so many people. They couldn't pull in everyone wearing a beard. But the man said that the stranger spoke a language he knew, and this might narrow the hunt down. With a few shillings in his hand as he left the police station, he had promised to keep his eyes open for the man and to tell Ngirenga if he saw him again.

"So much for our theories," said Carver when Ngirenga reported to him. "It's not a railway man after all."

Who else has the sort of grudge against the railway that he would want to wreck a train? Or was the target Farnie de Hoek or Ben Kagwa or the District Motive Power Inspector? He frowned at the range of possibilities. The day staff had long since left and he sat at his desk.

For some reason he thought of this time of the evening in Matamu with Maggie. Still that was then, and this was now. He set off for Twenty Queen's Drive.

Chapter 41

The monthly meeting of the officials of Matamu District was nearly finished. The District Commisioner tapped the table.

"A few words before we go. We all know we face a period of unrest until Independence arrives. With the timetable published you might have thought things would settle down, but among the political parties there are those who want Independence to come even faster…"

"Less than two years is a ridiculously short time," interrupted the District Forestry Officer.

"That's because your occupation is watching trees grow," quipped the Medical Officer.

The D.C coughed. "As I was saying, gentlemen, some local chiefs think there will be agitation under any pretence. With four main parties and half a dozen lesser ones, there's potential for a real conflagration. The front runner is Gideon Ochieno and his AUFP, but The Peoples Party has a greater following around here."

"What's this leading up to?" The Medical Officer leant forward, elbows on the table.

"In short, what I'm saying is these unsettled times mustn't stop us pushing on with our jobs."

The Forestry Officer continued. "Well it would be a bit surprising if this didn't affect us. I was in the Capital last week and there is an air of unreality. The only topic of conversation of every expatriate I met is how much compensation will be paid and what sort of jobs we might get when we have to leave. Everyone I met said they will be off as soon as they can."

"Well that's as it may be, but we've got plenty to be done up here and I'm sure that despite all the uncertainties we shall all get on with what we have to do."

The OC Police stopped twisting his pencil between his finger and thumb. "What does this mean for me in particular? Is there anything specific that I ought to get cracking with? I'm stretched as it is. Two more gang robberies this week, attacks on Asian dukas out in the country. They say the robbers were shouting political slogans. Hard to know whether they are party agitators or just thieves. Both, probably."

"I don't know there is much any of us can actually do, other than be aware. You might, of course, make sure that you double check what your Special Branch chappies bring in. I'm sure we shall get some distorted messages. It's already happening, of course. One or two of the chiefs are being fed lines by the parties who want them to pass these on to us."

"I think I'll bring the annual range practice forward. The sound of rifle fire is a useful reminder to everyone."

The DC looked up quickly. "I'll leave that to your professional judgement, Arthur. Any other points? No? Well thank you all for coming."

Political party rallies in the Capital increased in number and size. Weekends were the most popular times for these. For each of these Carver went to the area with a party of his policemen, keeping them out of sight in a covered vehicle. Ochieno addressed fewer meetings himself, leaving all but the largest to other members of his party's leadership. When he did appear, Carver marvelled how he held the mass with his oratory. But even the 'moderate' politicians were now making immoderate promises. 'Running water for everyone if you vote for us' became an often-repeated slogan.

In contrast, the People's Party rallies were more militant and each time he watched these he wondered how long it would be before he had to deal with a serious riot. One speaker took as his theme, "All the European and Asian houses will be handed over to you," with the insinuation that all that was in these houses, animate or inanimate, would be theirs.

*

Rasak left his hut on the outskirts of the forest at sunrise to look for wild honey. He was hitching his climbing rope around his waist, about to climb the tree where the bees were swarming, when the breeze brought the smell to him. There was no mistaking it. He dropped the rope and it took him little time to find the source of what was now deep and pungent. With his stick he uncovered three bodies, barely covered with the loose leafy soil. As a young buck he had seen enough bloodshed when his people fought a local tribe who were trying to push them from their land. He could see that each had been killed in the same way, by blows to the head which had pounded their skulls into bloody disarray. The bodies wore suits. It wasn't a sense of duty that took him to the police. Suits. Important people. This must be worth a few shillings.

Although the place where bodies were found was twenty miles from the Capital, it was just on the edge of Carver's area of jurisdiction. Once the initial enquiries had been made, the Assistant Commissioner CID called in to see Carver at his police station.

"What do we know so far?" he asked.

"The Medical Officer says the bodies had been there for two days. They were starting to decompose. The cause of death in each case was severe head injuries inflicted at the scene. It is probable that something as crude as a sledgehammer had been used."

"Do we know who they were?"

"The injuries were so bad that identification was impossible in one case, but we know the other two were both members of the Congress Party, Ochieno's rivals."

"Then we have political assassinations?"

"I'm sure we do, though it's going to be hard to get evidence. There were tyre marks near the clearing where the bodies were found, but they weren't distinct enough to make plaster casts. No witnesses, no murder weapons. I just hope this isn't the start of a trend."

His fears were realised. As the weeks went by, other human remains were found in different parts of this forest. Each time the bodies were of opponents to the AUFP. In some cases shallow graves had been dug, but the bodies had not been covered sufficiently to stop animals unearthing them. Carver had no doubt that these were intended to be found.

Rasak eventually told them he had seen a vehicle come several times to the clearings where the corpses were found. He was shown photographs of various makes of car and eventually he pointed out a black Peugeot estate car, the type favoured as taxis. There were many hundreds of these in the country, most operating illegally, and nearly all were black.

Inspiration hasn't done much so far, Carver said to himself. Now it's the perspiration. He set up an incident room and from the intelligence gathering one name kept recurring – Musa Mulangi. No-one seemed to know who he was or where he came from. Tall, well-built, beard, slight limp, well dressed, always wearing sunglasses, was all that appeared on the suspect card. The intelligence said that he had assembled a vicious and ruthless gang, though there was nothing to link him with Ochieno's party.

Chapter 42

It was dusk when the Peugeot taxi bumped down the rutted track leading to the old airstrip, its sidelights flickering, one bulb more powerful than the other. It pulled up alongside Ochieno's car.

Mulangi lowered his window. Once they had gone through the customary greetings, treating them as the ritual they were, he said "I got your message. It sounded as though you have something urgent to tell me."

"You are right. I have. There have been killings. Do you know who has been doing them?"

"Who do you think? I'm doing what you wanted, I am watching over your interests. You said you wanted to make sure you won the elections. I am doing that."

The barrister thought for a moment. Luka – Mulangi – whatever he called him, was not a man with whom you could argue. And he knew he would need his services in the future. For a long time, no doubt.

"I appreciate what you have done. But now I am becoming known as a man who disposes of his opposition by killing them. People are talking about it."

"Of course they are. What I have done has persuaded a lot of people to vote for you. It won't be good to stop but if that's what you want…."

"I need more than that. I hear the police have got your name and sooner or later they will connect you to me. You will have to disappear until the elections are over. I can't afford to be seen to associated with you."

Luka remained expressionless. Silent. Ochieno knew he had few options. He would have to make a promise that he wanted to hold back until much later. "I promise that when I am president I will find you a special position."

Luka shrugged. "I will not let you forget that. But for now, I know places to go. I shall need money."

"I will give you enough money to live well. I do not want to know where you are until the elections are over. Come back to me then."

The taxi left the airstrip first. Ochieno sat a little longer. He hardly dare admit to himself how much he had benefited from the deaths of his opponents. There was no doubt about it, Luka had his uses. He left fifteen minutes later when he was certain that no-one was watching.

Sergeant Ngirenga was in fine spirits as he entered Carver's office.

"I have good news, sir. The Permanent Way porter who told us about the points has seen the man he told how to make the train fall. He knows where he lives."

"Do you trust what he says?"

"Yes. He is angry someone destroys a train."

Carver had thought the railway case was dead and here was the possibility of opening it up again.

"Let's see the man. Bring him in."

The man shambled into Carver's office. He was more forthcoming than the policeman expected.

"I was at Kintu market, effendi. I had heard there was cheap posho flour there and I was looking around the market. I saw the man. The sergeant had told me there was money for information about him. I followed him and he went into a house."

"And where was this house?"

"Very near the market, a long house with a white painted door in the front and a compound at the back with chickens and goats."

Carver was satisfied he was telling the truth. With Ngirenga in plain clothes and the informer sandwiched between two detectives on the back seat, Carver drove off. At last here was a good lead. As they neared Kintu market, the single-storied corrugated-iron-roofed African shops, bars, and houses took over from the Asian buildings, the tarmac road became narrower, and the roads leading off were of red earth. The informant pointed to a house standing fifty yards back from the road. Banana trees were to one side of the building and a small plot of maize stretched along the other side. The compound at the rear wasn't visible from the car but they could hear the goats.

Carver couldn't see anyone. He drove the car away from the house and parked.

"Take a walk around. Find out who's there."

A detective slipped out of the car and blended with the throng. Ten minutes passed. Carver peered at his watch and scanned the scene. Another ten minutes and the detective returned.

"There are six men at the back of the house. One was putting things into a taxi. Some people said the men come and go a lot in the night-time. They are afraid of them. They think they are bakondo – *gang robbers*."

He could go in and try to get the man now. There were six of them, who might be armed too if they were in fact what the local people thought. Too risky. He would need more men. He called the city's Central Police Station on the car radio. The best they could promise was back-up arriving in thirty minutes.

"Get out now and get away from here," he said to the informer. "If your information is good you'll get a reward." The former railwayman was delighted. He would not have to confront the man now and tomorrow he would be well off. He faded into the local scene.

"Jambo Muzungu." A man had appeared by the side of the vehicle close to Carver's window. Carver returned the greeting.

The man continued, "What do you want here? We don't see many Wazungu at Kintu market. Have you come looking for our women?"

Carver looked carefully at the man. He was well-built, very black, and his cheeks and forehead were etched with the tribal scarring from a long-ago circumcision ceremony. There was a mocking leer about his face. His Swahili was coarse but there was no doubt about its intent.

"We don't like Wazungu coming for our women. You must go or we will beat you."

Carver swung the driver's door open with all his might, hitting the man's midriff as he sprang from the car.

"Those are the words of a piece of animal dung!"

This Muzungu was different. Such a command of Swahili. He took a step back. Ngirenga came from the other side. He saw the two detectives closing in. He spun round and ran. The incident was over, but with this diversion Carver missed the black Peugeot racing away from the back of the house into the maze of tracks.

With the arrival of reinforcements, he was ready to search the house. But what were they looking for? What might connect anyone with the train crash? The results were disappointing, a few pieces of clothing including an Indian sari, but even if they were stolen, identification would be impossible. They turned their attention to the compound. Twenty minutes of digging, prodding and probing and still nothing. Carver's frustration was turning to anger when Ngirenga pointed to the thatched grain store in the corner in the compound.

"One more place to look," and he smashed the lock from the door. All that faced them was a mound of maize.

The sergeant plunged his arms into the grain and with big sweeping movements felt into its heart. As he straightened his back, Carver could see he was holding a khaki military metal ammunition box. When it was opened the only contents were a service revolver and a club hammer, the kind used by masons, a short handle with a two-pound metal head.

Despite finding the box, Carver was in a bad mood. The bird had flown the coop and what he really wanted was the arrest. He should have known better. He should have brought more men in the first place.

Enquiries round the shops, bars, market stalls, and houses discovered a name. Not just any name, but Mulangi. The descriptions of the man they were given tallied with what Carver knew of this shadowy figure. His mood changed. Was it possible that the man who had caused the rail crash was also responsible for the brutal slaying of the bodies found in the forest?

Later, forensic tests on the hammer found traces of blood. In fact, two different blood groups, and these were matched to two of the bodies found in the forest.

"Not conclusive evidence," said the government pathologist, "but a pretty good start, I'd say."

"This man Musa Mulangi is our top priority. Now we want him for the forest murders and for the train crash," Carver told the Assistant Commissioner. The hunt was on. Radio messages were sent to every police unit in the country and to neighbouring territories. Luka Wamala would have to be put on hold for a while, he thought, unless we happen to come across him by chance.

The months passed and the day-to-day events in the busy Capital overtook those enquiries. Though the files were still kept on the active list, Carver knew in his heart each time he reviewed them they were as good as closed. There was no more information about either Mulangi or Wamala. Both men had disappeared into thin air. And around the corner loomed Independence, changing the emphasis of every Government official's work.

Chapter 43

The inevitability of Independence touched everyone and everything in the territory. The build-up dominated the conversations of all expatriates. In their work, normally conscientious people skirted the difficult decisions since it was hard to foresee what would happen once the 'Uhuru' celebrations were over.

Carver, now promoted to Senior Superintendent, was in charge of the planning for policing the Capital during the weeks of transition to Independence. Immersing himself in this helped to distance himself from past failures that still hurt whenever he thought of them – the crashed train and the unsolved political murders, and particularly his inability to catch Luka Wamala and Mulangi. After all the waiting, the time for the official celebrations arrived. All the planning that had consumed his waking hours steered the Capital's police with clarity and in this, at least, he tasted success.

*

In her regular letter to her sister in England, Donna Stern described the celebrations.

22nd May 1962

My dear Beth,

No doubt you will have read about our Independence but you might like to have some inside stories that the papers won't have carried. Rod was in the Capital for special duties. We were invited to a party at Government House for the first wave of visiting dignitaries. It gave H.E. the opportunity to introduce us to the new High Commissioner. It is said his staff, all rather green young men straight out from England, had already started apologising for the oppressive colonial rule that was now ending. They said they were unlike the people who were leaving since they wanted to be friends! This had all the African staff who know Rod rolling in the aisles. One of them asked him, "What sort of people are the British government sending out here now?"

Then the pageant on the sports field. Lots of marching by massed bands. The boy scouts and brownies did some exhibitions and Indian school children performed colourful dances. The finale was the police band playing some Beethoven. It was excruciating. The poor man must have been turning in his grave, though his deafness would have been an asset, of course.

The first really big occasion was the arrival of the Duke and Duchess at the airport. Although they call it 'International' it is not very big really and you can generally walk wherever you like, even out on the apron in front of the buildings. For this event though it was restricted. We had seats in the rows of chairs on the tarmac. The Duchess looked lovely in a turquoise-green dress with a full skirt. She stood with the Governor, who was in all his plumage, while the Duke inspected the guard of honour. Then we were presented, very quickly of course. Once this was over the British government representatives filed out of the plane. They all looked hot and sticky, undignified, really. One of them was visibly the worse for wear and I heard later he was hardly out of his cups throughout the whole celebrations.

The crowning event was the Independence Ceremony. This was held in the Capital's football stadium. There were massed bands again and lots of tribal dancing. By now the atmosphere was electric, all building up to the ceremony of the flags. A spotlight picked out the Union Jack. The massed bands played our national anthem. The spotlight went out and then the country's new flag appeared. The police band played the new anthem of the country but it was drowned out by the cheering. It was most good humoured and many local people came up to us to wish Rod and myself well. They actually queued to shake our hands, and you know Rod, he always wants to give time for a decent conversation. We were there hours, and I wouldn't have missed it for worlds.

> *We are not sure when we shall leave the country for good. I know Rod has been asked to put this off for as long as he feels he can, but he says it will be of little value for anyone if he were to remain. We shall miss it all, I must say.*
>
> *All my love, Beth dear, we shall soon see you in England.*
>
> *Donna*

*

For a while the spirit of this occasion held. Even crime rates dropped and Carver wondered if his decision to leave the territory was justified, but this state was short-lived. Violence, mainly inter-tribal, increased. Reluctantly he wrote his request for 'early retirement', the euphemism for redundancy, which would take effect in six months' time.

The telephone call was unexpected. Carver hadn't seen Gurbachan Singh, now a newly promoted superintendent, for a long time.

"How about coming round for a drink to wish you on your way? Mrs. Singh might even serve us supper."

Carver needed no more bidding. Nothing was more persuasive than the prospect of Mrs. Singh's curry.

The two men talked of old times but inevitably the conversation turned to the future. "You're going to stay on, of course, Gurbachan. There should be plenty of opportunity for you."

"If you think there will be opportunity for people like me you are very mistaken. For a start, do you know what happens when freedom – Uhuru as they call it – comes to a country? Of course you don't, so let me tell you. I have first hand experience, you see?"

"What do you mean? You can't have been through anything like this before."

"You've little grasp of history. Do you not recall that in 1947 in India we threw off the tyrannical and oppressive yoke of the British Raj?"

Gurbachan's eyes twinkled as he saw Carver rising to the bait.

"We were now free to do whatever we wished. So we slaughtered each other. By the train load. Hundreds at a time, vultures feasting off the corpses until, bloated, they could eat no more. We had gained freedom to do as we wished."

"I didn't know you were there then."

"Oh yes, I was still in the Army. My father and mother lived in a village in the Punjab. Houses were surrounded and the people fought like only people can fight when they know life is coming to an end. They were hacked to pieces."

Carver stared at the Sikh's face but there was nothing there to reflect the hideous memory.

"I left the army and came here where a relative had a business. Before I left I went to that village and the only thing I brought away was my father's sword. The old man died wielding it."

Gurbachan turned and pointed to the heavy weapon with the slightly curved blade hanging on the wall behind him. Carver's imagination saw the blood on the tassel hanging from the handle.

"So you see I know about what happens with independence. So many different peoples in one land, hating each others' guts and waiting for the chance to pay off grudges. Real or imagined, it doesn't matter. And if that is just among the Africans, how will they feel about us Asians who they see as foreigners hanging on the coat tails of the British, who have lived the life of... what do you say – the life of Old Mother Reilly?"

"Surely it won't come to that. I know we've had these political killings, but otherwise things have been pretty stable. The territory's doing all right economically."

"Assuredly it *will* come to that, once none of the promises made by the African politicians have been kept. Guns will be more available than piped water, education, and medicines. It's anyone's guess how soon such trouble will occur but occur it certainly will."

"What will you do?"

"Go to Canada or maybe England. I've got relatives in both those countries."

"Heaven help you. You'll never stand the climate."

"Never underestimate what a Sikh can tolerate, my friend. Now, what about that food?"

*

There was the inevitable round of farewells and then Carver was off. He loaded his car with a cabin trunk and two suitcases and started on his way to the coast and the Union Castle Line steamship to England. He stopped at the border, which was marked only with a signboard. He got out of the car to stand and look for a while out over the country where he had nearly died. Out over the dark greens of the forests and the washed-out colours of the small cultivated patches, the shimmer in the distance of sun on water. The stillness. The silence was barely broken by the faint wail of the whistle of a locomotive as it slid along the valley, announcing its arrival at Matamu. There was never again going to be anything like this in his life.

A car tore by on the dirt road, scattering gravel and raising a thick red choking plume behind it. Carver's reverie was buried deep in that dusty cloud. He drove on.

Chapter 44

Coming to terms with the change in his life took Carver several months. After the death of his mother, two years earlier, the house in Watford passed on to him. That was about all that was familiar in the England to which he had now returned. None of his ideas about work came to anything. He continued to feel a misfit and time was running out; he only had another month of paid leave.

He missed the company of people like him and to help fill that gap he arranged to meet the sergeant from his days at St. Albans. They met at the Old Fighting Cocks Inn in the lee of St. Albans Abbey.

"Can you see me in a helmet driving one of those little panda cars and visiting farmers about the Diseases of Animals Acts?" he replied, when he was asked why he didn't re-join the police.

"You're probably right. Besides which you're such an independent sod. Have you ever thought of running your own business? At least you won't fall out with the boss. There's a security firm up for sale in Hemel Hempstead."

"Security. You've got to be joking, that's like being a second-class bobby."

"You'd be surprised."

The more they talked, the more Carver was interested. He spent hours in the public library poring over back copies of newspapers. There was no doubt that the sergeant was on to something. While he was trying to make his mind up, not far from Hemel Hempstead, near a tiny hamlet called Cheddington, the Glasgow to London express was robbed and its driver viciously beaten. If the big boys will tackle that, lesser villains will tackle whatever is going and that decided it.

A helpful bank manager made the purchase of the company possible and with four vans and six employees, Carver was in business. Now the grind began. Equipment was needed, and all the vans had to be modified. When he wasn't driving or working on the vehicles, he was out in the industrial estates looking for clients. His business grew by the month and if he didn't get more staff it would be stretched beyond capacity. He was in his office thinking about this when his clerk shouted, "There's someone out here, says he knows you."

Expecting a client, he called "Send him through," and stood up ready to greet the visitor. In through the door came a familiar figure, looking a little older than when he had last seen him. with a few strands of grey just visible in his beard. Gurbachan. His story held few surprises.

"I left six months after you. I came to my uncle in Luton. He keeps a corner shop and I work for him. Hate every minute of it. I don't mind being up at four to investigate a murder but to sort out newspapers… I heard you were here…"

"Would working in security be more agreeable?"

"I could give it a try… if you would have me?"

"Can you start tomorrow morning? 7.00am?"

A May morning. The sun was high. Carver drove the Ford van, sparkling white with the company logo large on each side – a picture of the armoured ant eater that gave its name to his company, Armadillo Security. There were four cars behind the security van shortly after he left the town. He kept his eye on them in his rear-view mirror. It was the usual drill, nothing to worry about, but it's easy to get sloppy, he told himself. He went through the drill – *what's behind you now?* A green Hillman Minx, a white Ford Transit, a red Jaguar and VW. Now only two, the Beetle and the van have gone. Just the Jag and the Hillman. Watch the Jag.

Gurbachan was in the back of the van with £25,500, the payrolls for several companies in St Albans. Carver had never liked this route to the small cathedral city. The road was too narrow and while he used as many different routes as possible to avoid being predictable, the alternatives for this journey were all worse. But it was only a short stretch and the consolation was they would shortly pass the spread of bluebells at Prae Woods and this reminded him of the jacaranda flowers carpeting the red dirt road in Matamu where he used to walk in the evenings with Maggie.

Watch it, he said to himself, you're getting maudlin. That's all done with and it will take your mind off the job in hand. It very nearly had. The car in the rear-view mirror was closing. It was the Jaguar. There had been plenty of places for it to pass since Hemel Hempstead, but its driver had stuck behind the security van.

"We'll be in business in a minute, Gurbachan," yelled Carver into the intercom. *Overtaking now. Quite near the motorway, ideal spot for a getaway.* He felt under his seat and touched the handle. It was comfortingly handy.

"Here it comes."

The long low saloon slewed across in front of the security vehicle. Carver pushed the accelerator to the floor. The reinforced front end of the van crashed into the Jaguar, rocking it sideways. He reached under the seat for the old saw edged Italian bayonet.

Three men were out of the car, stocking masks over their faces. He could only see pick helves, no firearms. Then the fourth clambered out of the rear door, clutching a hand gun. Carver baulked in expectation of the shot, but the blast came from behind him. The raider dropped the weapon. Carver turned. Gurbachan was lowering a shotgun, one barrel smoking. Carver ran at the raiders slashing out with the bayonet, but the thick clothes and helmet slowed him down. They were over the fence and tumbling down the bank of the motorway. The gunman, blood streaming from him, was dragged to a Ford Zephyr standing on the hard shoulder. With a scream of tyres and an acrid smell of burnt rubber, it was gone, weaving crazily in and out of the other traffic.

"I don't know whether to sack you or pin a medal on you. You know we aren't supposed to carry firearms."

"And get killed. All I did was give him one of my hot cups of tea. It would have been Kaliso all over again if I hadn't brought my uncle's gun."

Gurbachan and a gun at Kaliso? How different things might have been. "The police won't see it that way. The sooner we report it the better but let's get the story straight. Shot accidentally by one of his own gang, I think."

Carver picked up the weapon from the ground where the thief had dropped it and fired it into the air. They delivered the payrolls, late but intact.

Armadillo Security went from strength to strength. Word spread about Carver's capability. Within two years he had a fleet of twenty vans, fitted with features of his own design. He was a name within the industry. Only occasionally did he get behind the wheel or ride shotgun, as he delighted to call it. The 'cowboy' epithet, with which the local police superintendent had labelled him, was a source of secret pleasure.

Gurbachan was now Carver's Operations Manager and his enthusiasm was infectious. During his Army service he had been trained in Special Forces combat methods and he passed his knowledge on to the Armadillo staff. "You're not escaping this if you're going to take a vehicle out even just once," he said to Carver and taught him techniques for evading criminals and for self-defence. He had a favourite saying. "You've got to have what the Americans call an 'Ace in the Hole'."

The usual Friday afternoon meeting for the next week's planning was over. "Time to go home, Paul." Gurbachan straightened up and put his jacket on.
"End of a long, hard week. Do you reckon you can do without me for ten days or so next month?"
"Why? Taking your holidays early this year?"
"In a way, I suppose. I've had an invitation this morning to go back for the country's fifth anniversary of Independence. It's from Ochieno himself. Listen to what he says, and Carver took a letter from his desk.

> *Without what you did when you tackled the man with the gun I wouldn't be president now. More than that, I wouldn't exist at all! I know I have never thanked you properly for your bravery on that day. I hope you will come and celebrate our first five years and take this as a deep expression of my gratitude. We are going to make this a very special occasion.*

"I'd very much like to go."
"Of course we can manage. You only get in the way most of the time, but we're too polite to tell you."
It was the answer Carver expected.
Gurbachan added, "But watch out, there will still be some who remember you and not too fondly. And the power is all in their hands."

His reply was in the post on Monday morning and the travel agent had booked his flights by mid-day.

Just keep reminding yourself you're a guest this time and you haven't got a crown in your shoulder and the backup of a whole police force.

Chapter 45

The landing at Ndubi took his mind back to the first occasion he had arrived in the Territory, when everything was new and exciting, though he had to admit a tremor of anticipation ran through his body even now. It was half past eight and the ground shimmered in the heat. The bump, the skid of rubber on hot concrete, the reverse thrust of the engines, and the plane was safely on the ground. And yet a pleasant sense of homecoming was leavened by a sense of foreboding. *Take a grip on yourself, man. This is an occasion to remember; you shouldn't feel as though someone is walking across your grave.*

In the minibus from the airport were journalists from London, an Eastern European agricultural machinery salesman, a Czech arms salesman loosely disguised as a tourism adviser, a professor from the London School of Economics, a member of the UK parliament who had earlier visited the country for three days and was now holding forth as an expert, an American who just styled himself as 'an observer', an economist from the World Bank, two Albanians who remained completely silent, and a Communist Chinese electrical engineer. Carver kept his former role in the country to himself.

*

The manager of the Orion Hotel gathered the guests round him in the lounge. He ended his welcome with, "To reassure you of our standards, anyone is welcome to inspect the kitchens and I will arrange a tour for those who would like it."

The following morning Carver joined the tour. Knives, sieves, jugs, pans, long meat skewers, everything used in the kitchen, were all laid out for inspection on a scrubbed wooden table. The cupboard doors were open and the cold stores were visited.

With some spare time in the programme, he took a stroll in the centre of the city. On the surface not much had changed. The Asians were still the main traders though there were more African-run shops. As he reached the central post office he saw a figure he recognised.

"Mohamed, Mohamed Ashraf." He was sure it was the station master from Kaliso.

The Asian looked around, taken aback to hear a voice he knew. "Mr Carver? It is Mr Carver, isn't it? This is indeed a surprise and a pleasure."

They stood by the post office steps.

"I am retired now, since two years. Life was difficult and I made way for an African. It was easier like that." Mohamed looked up, scanned the people nearby and carried on talking. "We have to be careful nowadays. A word taken the wrong way can lead to trouble."

"What sort of trouble?"

"It doesn't do to talk too much now about how things are. The Asian community have small troubles compared with the Africans. Many of them disappear." He looked around again. "I have said too much. It has been good to see you, Mr Carver."

As he turned to leave, he made a motion with his head towards a man some twenty yards away, dressed in a flowery shirt and dark flared trousers, his face masked by sunglasses. It was as much a uniform as the khaki drill of the army or police but inspiring more fear. Carver stood his ground and watched as he approached. The vague feeling of knowing but not being able to place who it was worried him, but as the man removed the sunglasses there was no mistaking Ogwang.

"Carver, I see you are visiting us, after all this time."

"Yes, I'm here for the celebrations," and feeling his vulnerability, added as an afterthought, "as a guest of President Ochieno."

"Ah, yes, you could always depend on rank."

Carver looked into the same rheumy eyes that had hidden the truth so often in the past. "I am sure you haven't just come over to enquire after my health. Are you still with the police?"

"I am not polisi." There was contempt in his voice for that word. "Here is my authority," and he produced a folded card from the breast pocket of the garish shirt. *Lieutenant Ogwang, Special Internal Security Force. Signed Musa Mulangi. Colonel, Officer Commanding.*

Mulangi. To see that name was a shock which brought back vivid memories – the brutality of the murders in the forest, the train crash and the death of Farnie de Hoek. That Mulangi had an official position was appalling, but what was more worrying was that Ogwang had approached him here; was it a coincidence or had he been watching for him? The crowd that had gathered parted hurriedly as though to be touched by either man might bring disaster. He made his way back to the hotel.

There were no further shocks. Tours had been arranged for the guests to see the public works started since Independence and these absorbed most of the available time. Carver knew he had to put Mohamed Ashraf and Ogwang from his mind now. That sort of thing was going to happen. There must always be a worry at the top about subversion and intrigue and now there wouldn't be the training and strict set of rules to deal with this.

With only three more days left before his return to England, he was luxuriating in his stay. The hotel was comfortable and his fellow guests were beginning to be interesting. There was only one more official function – the State Reception to be held in the Parliamentary Buildings – and then he would be on the flight home.

*

Bulandina stood in front of the shop window eyeing the shoes. They were dark red and shiny. Ever since she had seen Europeans wearing them when she first came to the Capital she had wanted shoes like these. If those women were able to balance and walk on heels so high why shouldn't she? And now she could afford them. Tomasi had given her the money to spend on herself. He would be so proud when she could master them.

She emerged from the Indian shop wearing the shoes, carrying her old flat ones in a paper bag. She walked carefully, slowly at first, taking sly looks at the reflections in windows to see that they were still on her feet. Now here she was outside the President Gideon Hotel, once the Imperial.

Slowly her eyes took in the whole grand building. It had always seemed a palace, inaccessible, with waiters in white suits as guards. Yet, with her new shoes why shouldn't she enter such a place and order tea. She climbed the flight of steps to the entrance and turned into the long enclosed verandah.

There was only one other person there, a man sitting at a table. She sat on a low settee at the opposite end and while she waited for the smiling waiter to bring her tea and sandwiches she looked at the man. He wore a heavy beard which was flecked with grey. Bottles and a glass were on the table in front of him.

There was something familiar about this man; did she know him? He looked directly at her as though jerked up by her gaze. Slowly he beckoned to her to come to him. She looked down and hoped that the waiter would hurry up with her tea and then she felt compelled to look again. This time he called her, "You there, come over here."

She rose from the settee and tottered the length of the verandah. As she reached where he was sitting, the waiter arrived. "Put it on the table," the man commanded.

Bulandina watched him. That he had drunk a lot was clear but despite the slurred speech she knew that voice.

"Are you the woman they sent me?"

She was held by the eyes. She knew those eyes too. The whites were coloured with red blotches and yellow streaks and the pupils were black. So black they hid all his thoughts.

"I've had you before, haven't I?"

"You… it's… aren't you… Japani?"

He scowled and leant forward to peer at her. "Bulandina. It's Bulandina. I didn't think I should meet you again." Was there a hint of tenderness? In those days in Jayanja he could show it. It quickly changed. "So now you are *malaya*." He used the Swahili word for prostitute. "You must be expensive with shoes like that and coming to the hotel."

"I'm not that… I only came to the Hotel for some tea."

He threw his head back and laughed. "You women are all the same. You have your dreams but you always end up on your back." He drained the glass. "Muzungu beer and whisky to drink and one of our own women. What is better?"

He stood up and gripped her by the arm. "Come on. You've got work to do. We go to the room they always keep for me."

As he pulled her up he looked into her face. "You must know I am Colonel Mulangi. Never call me Japani again."

Drunk as he was, she was no match for his strength and her screams brought no help.

"Stop yelling!" His free hand smashed into her face bringing blood from her nose and lips.

Still gripping her arm, he reached inside his coat pocket, found the key, opened the door and flung her onto the bed. Her new shiny shoes slipped from her feet. She lay there trembling with fright as he removed his flared trousers and pulled up the gaudy flower patterned shirt. Slowly he climbed on top of her. She felt suffocated by the bulk of the man for whom she had once kept house. Then, it had been so different. Now the smell of his body and the liquor sickened her. Saliva dripped onto her face. *So this is the famous Mulangi. He is the devil people say he is.*

He stopped moving on top of her and grunted. "You are no good any more. You do not help. You'll suffer for making me foolish."

He rolled to one side. She was now close to the edge of the bed. Distraught with fear and despairing that she would find anything, she felt around the floor with her right hand. The tips of her fingers touched something. She stretched a little further and grasped it. It was one of her shoes. He was trying to move onto her again and that was when she swung the shoe as hard as she could at his head. The pointed heel caught him fully on the temple. Japani – she could still only think of him as Japani – rolled off the bed and thudded onto the floor. She didn't wait to see any more. Clutching both her shoes she crept to the door, opened it and ran as fast as she could. Along the passageway, past the verandah and down the flight of steps to the street. All she could think of was getting back to Tomasi. She continued running, jinking her way through people on the pavements, stumbling as her feet caught pot holes.

In the house of a friend from his days as a policeman Tomasi Ngirenga played *muweso*, a game like chess using small stones and saucer like holes on a wooden board.

"You're not paying attention, Tomasi, that's the second game you've given me. You used to be unbeatable."

His host prepared the board again.

"Where is she? She should be back by now. I thought she would be safe in these crowds."

"Stop worrying. She'll be here soon. You know what women are like when they are free with money in their hands."

Tonight would be the last events. Fireworks and a band playing. The following day they would return to the village where he and Kipchai had now built up an impressive herd. And Bulandina. She had pleaded to go and look at the shops and against his better judgement he had agreed she could go out alone into the city. As he looked out all he could see were the crowds moving around waiting for the evening to come. As he stood watching he mouthed the words, "What would I do if something has happened to her?"

And then he saw her. Stumbling, careering into people, pushing her way through, blood on her face, dress torn. And what was she clutching to her breast? They looked like Muzungu type shoes. He shouldered his way through the crowd and helped her to the house. It was not difficult to wipe the blood away but in her mind Bulandina was so dirty, so soiled, she felt nothing would ever clean her body of the filth Japani had left on her.

Hesitantly she told the story of her afternoon. "I don't know if I killed him. I hit him so hard."

Tomasi listened, feeling his anger rise. It seemed they would never be able to shake that man out of their lives. And now he had violated his wife. He helped Bulandina to bed and then sat down in the shade of the compound with the former police sergeant who rented the house.

"How good are your contacts, Filipo, now you aren't a policeman?"

"People are careful about talking to strangers, but there's comfort in telling your troubles to someone you know."

"I want to know if Mulangi is still alive. I think his head is too hard for Bulandina to have killed him, but if he is still alive I want to know everything about where he goes. He must have his regular places."

Filipo let out a long breath. "Mulangi. I'll have to be careful with that one. People won't talk easily about him." He rose and as he went out of the door he looked back and said, "It'll cost you a cow. No, two."

Filipo returned two hours later. "Mulangi is still alive but he wears a patch of plaster on the side of his head. You'll have to watch out if you make Bulandina angry."

"Get on with it." Tomasi was impatient to know more.

"He will be at the Parliament Buildings all tonight. I have found out some of his places but I can only get to know where he is going on the day. At least he is a man of habit. Leave it until tomorrow and let's go and enjoy the fireworks and the band."

"You're right, Filipo, but that doesn't make me stop wanting to kill him this minute."

"Perhaps there is a way of finding out. You remember Ogwang? They used to call him a detective. He is one of Mulangi's lieutenants now. When it suits him he has a big mouth. I know where we can find him. Tomorrow."

Chapter 46

A long line of guests snaked slowly, haltingly up the flight of steps leading into the building. As Carver drew closer to the top he could see the reason for the bottleneck. There at the head of the stairs stood the President, his ample figure perfectly fitted into a dark grey suit, greeting guests with a handshake. As they moved on they were handed champagne and were ushered into the huge entertaining room. Carver arrived in front of the President.

"Paul. I am so glad you were able to come. I feel like the head master at my old school on prize giving day. I hope we shall find time for a longer chat before the evening is out," and while he was saying this his head was turning to the next guests. Carver took his champagne and carried on into the room. Ceiling fans were moving the air which was already clouding with cigarette smoke. The champagne was warm. The feeling he had always experienced at social gatherings returned.

"What brings you back to this place," said a Yorkshire voice behind him.

He turned. "Father Joe. I never expected to meet you again."

They talked, reminiscing of the times at Matamu. The football matches, the annual boxing tournament. "You never did do that exhibition bout with Kipchai," the impish humour still showing. Occasionally someone came to shake the priest's hand, but these interruptions didn't staunch the flow of conversation. The buffet was announced and they started inching their way with the flow of the crowd towards the doors to the next room. As they shuffled their way forward Father Joe whispered, "Take a look at that man standing in the alcove near the portrait of Ochieno. You're taller than me so you'll have a better view. Do you know who he is?"

He looked in the direction the priest had indicated and saw a tall, heavily built African. He wore a beard which covered the lower part of his face. The small round pink plaster on his temple looked out of place. Carver could imagine the eyes, hidden by sunglasses, taking in and mentally recording who were among the visitors.

"I've no idea. Looks a little too much like a Ton Ton Macoute to me."

The priest looked at Carver and shook his head. "You've lost me."

"Papa Doc Duvalier's bodyguard in Haiti. They're responsible for hundreds, probably thousands, of deaths there."

"In that case it's a fair description. He calls himself Colonel and commands the Special Internal Security Force. Everyone fears him and what he stands for. I'm sure the President is a bit afraid of him too. He's called Mulangi. Musa Mulangi... and I can tell you what you probably suspected.... Mulangi is in fact your old friend Luka Wamala. He hoards grudges like a bush dog harbours fleas. You'll have to watch how and where you tread for the rest of the time you are here."

Carver's heart raced. The scars on his neck burned. "How can Ochieno have that man in such a position?" He knew now that he had made the connection once before and had not trusted his judgement. "Ochieno can't know about him, surely."

The priest shrugged his shoulders. "Things have changed a lot since Independence. The President can appoint whom he likes to do what he likes. There is nothing anyone can do to stop him. He knows only too well what sort of man Mulangi is."

Carver glanced sideways to take another look. One thing was certain; Mulangi exuded power, raw physical power. He drank more champagne. He had now lost Father Joe in the crush. He took another glass. And then more. His mood of anger, threaded with despair, tormented him.

His mind must have drifted off. He had missed the President's short address. The crowd was thinning out, most of the guests taking advantage of the entertainment offered elsewhere. He must find and challenge Ochieno, whatever the consequences. He heard the President's voice coming from a small room off the entertaining hall. He pushed the door and as it swung open he saw Ochieno sitting at a desk, his jacket hanging over the back of his chair.

"Ah, old friend. I see you haven't gone to the fireworks and the band concert yet. Were you looking for something else?"

"I wanted to talk to you, Gideon."

"And why not? I was going to seek you out before you left. You've caught me at a good time. We can have a few minutes."

He moved from the desk towards a leather suite.

"Come and sit over here. It is more comfortable."

Everything was surreal. Carver was confused and realised the effects of the champagne when he found he had to fight hard to focus on what he had to say.

"As a friend, I want to raise a difficult subject."

Ochieno tilted his head expectantly.

"I have seen a man here today who I have known in the past. He is called Mulangi. You know all about him trying to kill me and one of my men when he called himself Luka Wamala."

The president sat expressionless. "So?"

"He murdered a defenceless woman at Mubindi prison farm, he derailed a train killing the driver, he murdered your political rivals in the Muvuli forest…"

"Yes, I knew all about him. He's good at his job – which is to make sure that any dissidents are under control. I would have thought that with your knowledge of our ways you would have understood this."

Carver's mouth hung open. "You're a lawyer. Where is your sense of justice?"

"My dear friend, What naiveté. As a policeman you should know that lawyers are not overly bothered about justice. Oh yes, they show great concern about it when it suits their purpose."

Carver was about to speak but the President held up his hand and continued.

"What lawyers like is power to overwhelm people. Subdue them with words and spin the law around until it comes out their own way. Chambers in England taught me this. But when you yourself are the government you can do what you want with the law. Change it; but why bother when you can ignore it if you wish."

He sat back, the voice lowered, a grotesque caricature of the man Carver had once known.

"So don't come to me talking of justice. Mulangi suits my purposes nicely."

If this had been a boxing match it would have been declared no contest. Carver's mind reeled. He was punch-drunk with the weight of the words, each one pounded into his head or driven into his guts.

With effort he pushed himself up from the settee. Shaking his head, he trembled as he walked out. He didn't recall negotiating the long flight of steps that led down from the Parliamentary Buildings into the night. Now he was on the street heading to his hotel. The air was fresh and scented with that natural fragrance that he always remembered from his first nights in the country so many years ago.

Colonel Mulangi stood at the top of the steps and watched until Carver was out of sight.

Chapter 47

Dawn. The skies were as heavy as if they had assimilated all the gloom and despair that he had felt during his meeting with Ochieno. His mouth tasted foul. Like the bottom of a parrot's cage, as they used to say in the army. His head throbbed, pounded. Thought came slowly, memory was blunted. He tried to slip back into sleep but his body resisted. He rolled over onto his stomach, kicking the thin sheet back. The nausea increased. Sitting up might help. He moved to the armchair and looked out of the window.

The encounter with Ochieno flooded his mind. No, not the mind. It was a visceral, not mental, sensation. *There is nothing you can do, nothing whatsoever, and this is what really hurts. You cannot raise a finger to change things. Failure yet again.*

He stood and looked around the room. Make some tea. That always helps. Three cups later and the answer was still the same. Get out of here while you can. Keep out of the way and get on the plane in one piece. Ochieno will do exactly what he wants and no-one outside the country will do more than cluck their tongues even if they know what is going on. None of Britain's Administration is going to risk the career-threatening stigma of being branded a latter-day colonialist. And most of all, there will be no images on TV of starving children to rouse popular indignation.

He took a late breakfast. Most of the other guests had finished and were in the foyer waiting for the bus for the final tour to a state distillery. Carver ordered paw paw and toast. He couldn't face more than this and hoped the curative juices of the fruit would settle his stomach. The coffee was good. He was beginning to feel a little more roadworthy when one of the fellow guests, a journalist, slipped into the spare chair at his table.

"I'm late for breakfast again. Good party last night. Fireworks set it off nicely. The band was a bit bizarre, though."

Carver grunted. Conversation was the last thing he wanted. He poured more coffee.

"Looks as though they are doing pretty well here. I've done a piece about their five years of post-colonial development. Perhaps you'd care to look it over?" and he started to reach into his brief case.

Carver flung his serviette onto the table and pushed his chair back. Last night's conversation with Ochieno still rattled round his head.

"What the hell do you know about it?"

He was gone.

"Miserable bugger," muttered the journalist and clicked his fingers for the waiter.

Chapter 48

Carver spent the rest of the morning and the afternoon in his bedroom. The notice board had said he was due to leave the hotel at 6.30pm and although this seemed early, the sooner he was in the airport the happier he would be. Now it was 6.25. He could just see a hall porter in his green uniform parading the foyer, holding up a small blackboard on a pole, ringing the bicycle bell screwed to the handle:

> T
> A
> X
> I
>
> F
> O
> R
>
> M
> R
> .
> C
> A
> R
> V
> E
> R

Carver's eyes swept the foyer. *No obvious SISF men.* In one of his darker moments he had wondered if Mulangi would make a last-minute appearance. Would the High Commissioner have enough clout to help him? He doubted it, even if he was able to communicate with him. He walked slowly from the lounge to the foyer.

"Here's Mr Carver now," called the receptionist to a man nearby. And then to Carver, "This is your driver for the airport."

A porter had already picked up his case and was carrying it through the door to the minibus waiting by the kerb. It was hoisted up onto the roof rack and secured while the driver opened a nearside door.

"You are the only one from here, sir. I have to pick up another from the Muvuli Forest Hotel."

"Muvuli Forest Hotel? I've never heard of it."

"It used to be a government rest house? It is on the way to the airport."

The taxi made slow progress through the suburbs of the city and Carver was glad it had been sent early. *You can relax. You're going home.* It was dark now and where a street light was to be found, half a dozen people gathered to catch the flying grasshoppers that swarmed in clouds around the lamp, only to fall as they hit the hot lamp. In his mind he re-tasted the delicacy as he remembered the first time one of his constables had offered him a plate of these. Grilled over charcoal they had the texture of prawns. Thank goodness not everything has changed.

It was now 7.30pm and they had just cleared the last of the small townships making up the outer ring of the city. They were on the Jayanja Road and passing the entrance to the quarry. Involuntarily Carver pulled his gaze away from the place. He couldn't bear to think about the death of Farnie de Hoek and the wanton destruction caused by the derailment.

Soon they reached the edge of the forest. The road became a tunnel, the canopy of the trees making a long dark hole with no end in sight. He recalled it wasn't far from here that the battered bodies of the 'forest murders' cases had been found. He pushed himself harder back in the car seat as if to hide from these memories. They couldn't possibly have any bearing upon today, could they? Yet they did. He hadn't resolved any of these cases and that still hurt him. *Snap out of it. Less than ten miles to the airport. Bright lights, dinner and a drink on the plane courtesy of BOAC and the sleep of the innocent.*

Further into the forest the taxi bumped over the railway level crossing. *Not much further to what was the old rest house. They call it the Muvuli Hotel now? They must have done it up since you knew it.* In the dim lights of the vehicle he could just see the entrance to the short approach road. The driver slowed, changed gear and the minibus bumped along the pitted track to the turning circle at the front of the bungalow styled building. There were no lights visible from the building and the trees hugging it intensified the darkness.

The driver switched off the engine and lights and made his way on foot towards the hotel. Carver peered intently. He heard, rather than saw, the door at the top of the steps open and he thought he recognised the form of the driver coming down followed by another figure. He heard the scrunch of the gravel as someone approached. The door behind Carver opened. There was no courtesy light.

The vehicle dipped on its springs as the additional passenger climbed in and settled into the third row of seats. It must be one of the Eastern Europeans he thought, since there was no greeting. They were not very communicative. He saw the form of the driver ease himself into the seat behind the wheel and the springs sank a little more. The engine started; there was a crunch of gears. Another quarter of an hour or so and we'll be in the airport, he thought, and settled back.

He could feel movement behind him as the minibus drove off, as though the additional passenger was leaning forward. Then the hot breath on his neck, the voice loaded with the weight of hatred stored for years. The trial in Jayanja flashed before him.

"So you have come back to me, Muzungu."

After all those years, there was no mistaking the voice, the voice he heard in the moonlight at Kaliso. The vehicle was barely moving. Could he hear another vehicle? He wasn't sure. If there was it was probably Mulangi's men.

"You and those two – the brown one and that barbarian with the ear loops – were the start of my trouble. You humiliated me. I went to prison and had to grovel to the Muzungu there. I made him regret that. Now you are going to suffer for all of those things."

He harbours grudges like a bush dog harbours fleas, Father Joe had said.

The blow at the back of his neck was sudden. His intuition had failed him when he needed it most. He was crumpling on the seat. His mind was between awareness and obliteration like that night at Kaliso. He clawed desperately at the rim of the black pit, momentarily staring down into limbo.

He mustn't yield. It would be so easy to do that, with only one outcome if he did. No surgeon, no Maggie, to see him through this time. The fingernails of his mind clung on. The vehicle bumped over the railway line it had crossed earlier. He heard the creak of the seat behind him as Luka leant over and he felt the hand brush along his chest.

"He's still out. Turn left into the clearing."

These were the old killing grounds of so long ago. Images of the decomposing bodies, skulls pounded to pulp flashed before his eyes. The acidity of his stomach made its way onto his tongue. He wanted to moisten his lips but dare not move.

You've survived so far. Your luck's going to hold. It has to. Lie still.

He lost track of the time he had been on his back. The vehicle's lights were out. He could see no sky, no stars and no moon. He was sucked in to the darkness and the disorientation that comes with the deprivation of the senses. A black void. *Keep stock still, it's the only chance you have.*

The vehicle stopped with a jolt. He heard Mulangi and the driver go around to the back of the vehicle and the rear door was opened. Mulangi spoke. Carver thought he heard, "go and dig," but he wasn't sure. He heard the ring of metal against metal. The blade of a spade? Now something hard and heavy was being dragged in the luggage area.

What defence had he got? Gurbachan's warning – *you haven't got a crown in your shoulder and the back up of a whole police force* – had lodged itself in his brain. The Sikh's insistence on having an 'ace in the hole' may have become an in-joke in Armadillo but at the first opportunity that day in the hotel kitchen he had picked up what he could.

Someone moved round from the back of the vehicle. The squeaking of the door as it was wrenched open hurt his brain. *Don't tense up. Slump, man slump.* He felt a wisp of the cool night air and the musty damp forest smell of dead vegetation.

He could sense the hands reaching forward, searching for him. It had to be Luka leaning over him. The hands touched him and were feeling along his body. The touch was repellent. The smell of the laboured breath was so close, thick, putrid, at one with the fetid odours of the forest. *Don't react, don't move yet.* He wanted to vomit just as he did on the roundabout in that fairground so long ago.

The hands had found what they wanted. He was gripped, fingernails biting into his back. He could feel the power, the strength. The beard brushed against his face. *The ace. Play the ace.* Carver eased the eighteen-inch-long meat skewer he had taken from the hotel kitchen from his sleeve into his hand, movements he had practised over and again in the privacy of his hotel room.

He drove the needle point of the stainless steel spike upwards and deep into the body stretched taut over him. Mulangi bellowed, through surprise as much as pain. Carver forced the skewer on with the heel of his hand. It slipped between ribs, in and on and into the lung. The body above him convulsed and writhed. A knee banged clumsily against his leg. No beast of the forest transfixed by a hunter's drop spear could have made as baleful a sound as the skewered man above him.

The sound echoed round and round the clearing, bottled in by the density of the trees. To Carver it seemed the inhuman noise would never end. The hands which had been trying to lift him thrashed but there was no power there; a fist caught him lightly on the lip. And suddenly there was no weight pressing him down on the vehicle seat. Luka (or Japani or Mulangi) had slid from the vehicle.

Carver dropped through the open door, feet first. He stood by the minibus and blinked as fast as he could to make his eyes work in the darkness. He couldn't see Luka. And he was still in danger while the driver was around.

There was a roar and an explosion of lights. The minibus driver was caught in the power of a vehicle's head lamp beams as he loped across the clearing, a spade in his hand. He dropped the tool and flung his hands up over his face but the vehicle crashed relentlessly into him and skidded to a halt. Carver was still reeling from the events. A vehicle. He could make out the shape of a long wheel-base Landrover. *It had to be more SISF men arriving.*

And then he heard a voice above the sound of the vehicle's engine. "Are you there Mr Carver?" *The situation must be playing tricks with my mind. It sounds like Tomasi Ngirenga, yet that isn't possible.* A torch beam dazzled him and he shaded his eyes.

"It is you, Mr Carver. It's good we were in time."

Whoever the man was, he now stood in the glow of the Landrover's headlights. It was the coppery skin, the sharp features. It was Tomasi Ngirenga who had stepped down from the vehicle. Five years had not changed him, but gone was the ever-present grin.

"Where is Mulangi?" There was no longer concern in his voice, just anger.

Another voice. "Where is Mulangi?"

The unmistakable figure of Wilson Kipchai moved through the light to where Carver was barely supporting himself against the taxi. The tall African swung the beam of his torch carefully around the clearing. There was a muffled groan, a watery wheezing and then slight movement of the long grass. Kipchai strode over and shone his torch. Lying on his back, blood ringing his mouth and gulping for air, was Mulangi.

In one movement Kipchai bent and swung the man they had sought so fruitlessly for so long up and over his shoulder as a hunter would carry his quarry. Ngirenga had opened the minibus's door and Kipchai dumped Luka into the seat. As he did so he spotted the ringed end of the skewer and tugged it from the body. He held it up so that it glistened in the headlights.

"You have chosen some bad meat for your barbecue, Mr Carver."

He flung the spike into the bushes and his laughter reverberated round the clearing as Luka's roars of pain and anguish had echoed earlier. With the crushed corpse of the driver loaded into the minibus he took a rope and coupled the vehicle to the Landrover.

"Let's get out of this place of death," he said, wrinkling his nose in disgust. He helped Carver into the Landrover beside Ngirenga and climbed into the driver's seat. They towed the minibus along the track on to the metalled road, where they stopped when the taxi was straddling the railway line at the level crossing. Kipchai removed the tow rope.

"Now let us go to the airport."

"No, Kipchai. There is still plenty of time. We must know this is finished. Drive over there where we can see the crossing."

Driver Ben Kagwa eased the regulator and wound the gears and locomotive 5901 lengthened her stride. The brass work of the cab and the pipes along her length still gleamed. Ben hated this section of the line. The forest hugged the permanent way, the trees fingered the wagons as they passed and colobus monkeys claimed the canopy as their world. If he kept the speed up in a few minutes the train would be out of it and running the last leg to the Capital.

Not long now until he would whistle the tribute to Farnie that he always gave as he came to the quarry siding points. *Faaaar-nie. Faaar-nie de Hoek-Hoek-Hoooooek.* Ben would pull the lanyard and the proud Beyer Garratt, would give voice, a powerful, loving voice. Wrapped in his memories, Ben nearly overlooked the level crossing, a few hundred yards round the left-hand curve, out of sight until nearly on it. A quick blast now, just in time.

There wasn't time, though. A vehicle was astride the track. Ben screamed for the fireman to keep blasting the whistle. He stared harder down the headlamp beam. The damn thing wasn't moving but with luck no-one was in it. Regulator right off, gear wheel spun down, brakes hard on.

The locomotive needed nearly a quarter of a mile to stop at this speed and there were now only eighty yards between 5901 and the stationary vehicle. Sparks spewed out as the locomotive's wheels fought with the burnished metal of the rails. The steely squeal split the night air and the low cow catcher ploughed into the minibus. Metal scrunched, glass shattered into tiny shards, the vehicle was lifted into the air, turned over onto its roof and catapulted along the track. The tyres burst one by one. It was now barely recognisable as a motor vehicle. The locomotive slid triumphantly to a halt on her shiny rails, unscathed, her headlamp staring contemptuously over the debris.

The Landrover crept quietly away along the road to Ndubi, no lights showing until it was far away from the level crossing. Ben Kagwa had only a few yards to walk from his cab to the wreckage. He tried to look inside the ball of metal but it was hopeless. If there had been anyone in the vehicle they could not have survived.

There were so many questions racing around Carver's brain. He didn't know where to start but Tomasi Ngirenga read his mind.

"When Luka was made SISF chief he said that he would kill Kipchai and me. I couldn't wait for that to happen so I ran away from the police and went home to keep cattle. Kipchai came as well. We have a big herd now and two trucks and are rich men."

Carver smiled. He could never picture them as rich.

Ngirenga continued, "Wamala sent people out to look for us but they didn't know our country. We put their bodies where we couldn't be blamed."

"But what brought you here tonight? You're a long way from your home."

"We came for the celebrations. Like you. But Luka tried to rape Bulandina. I wanted to kill him for that, but as long as he is dead it doesn't matter who killed him."

"I still don't understand how you knew to come to the forest."

"This afternoon we found Ogwang. One of Luka's hunting dogs."

Carver grimaced and nodded. "Yes, I met him the day I arrived."

"At first he didn't want to tell us where his boss was. Then Kipchai held him by his throat. He told us. Also he told us Wamala was going to kill you at the hotel in the Forest. Ogwang will not lie to anyone any more."

"And then…"

"We went to the Mvuli Forest Hotel looking for Luka. We were too late. He had just left. We heard him go to the taxi bus but when we got to our Landrover the minibus was gone. And then we saw the lights in the clearing."

"And I know the rest."

"Now we go to the airport."

"With all that's happened I'd almost forgotten that was where I was going. Oh, hell, I've lost my luggage in that wreck."

"Your case is in the back. Kipchai took it off the minibus. You will still look like a proper traveller."

The Landrover moved steadily along the road to the airport. In the distance he could see the orange glow of the street lighting of Ndubi. He looked at his watch. The time was now eight forty-three. How could so much have happened in so short a time?

The vehicle slowed and Ngirenga said, "There will be SISF men at the airport. We stop near the hotel and you can get a taxi from there. We will get Bulandina and go back home. And see our cattle."

Screened from view by the high hibiscus hedge, they stopped near the hotel. The three men climbed down.

"I don't know where to begin to say thank you. I am well aware you risked your own lives in helping me."

"Very many people would thank you if they knew you had killed Mulangi. We were only the night soil porters who cleared up the mess. I am sad I wasn't the one who killed him."

Ngirenga's imagery was perfect, thought Carver. Night soil porters. Those men who did the unsavoury but essential work of emptying the toilet buckets.

The rest of the farewells carried no words. The mighty form of Kipchai and the slight frame of Ngirenga were gone into the night. By the light of a street lamp he looked down at his suit. The jacket was dirty and torn and he brushed down those parts he could reach. Then he noticed the blood on the front of the lightweight material. He took the jacket off and turned it inside out and with it hanging over his arm, he picked up his suitcase and walked round to the hotel entrance.

Chapter 49

Nine-fifteen. The taxi from the hotel pulled up in front of the airport building. A gaggle of porters vied with each other to be the first to reach Carver's case. He looked at the clock mounted high on the wall. There were just another nine minutes until boarding. With the earlier arrivals already in the departure lounge there was no queue at the check-in desk. He searched inside his coat for the ticket and passport, praying that these had not been lost in the turmoil of the evening. His hand gripped the familiar documents. As he offered them to the official he noticed the two men in the shadows, unmistakably SISF.

A last minute rush. A few more people filled in the queue behind him. He took a deep breath and kept his gaze on the official in front of him.

"How much of our currency do you have, Mr. Carver?"

Keep your voice down, damn you. The man was eyeing him from under lowered lids. He realised he had not answered.

The man continued, "You know you may take no more than twenty shillings of our currency beyond this point."

"I've only got about that much." *Come on, come on, man. Let's get going.*

"If that is so you will not mind me seeing inside your wallet."

What now? Let's get away from where those damned goons keep watching. Carver felt his hip pocket for his wallet. Good, he still had that, too. He wanted to refuse, to say what was in his wallet was his business, but the last thing he now needed was a scene. He offered the wallet to the man who opened it, removed and pocketed all the English money and left the few notes of local currency. Carver stared. *Fifty quid, that's a fortune.*

"It is all in order, Mr Carver."

As he replaced his wallet he turned his head slowly and glanced at the SISF men. His heart beat faster. The nearest looked in his direction, turned to his companion, pointing towards the check-in. He wanted desperately to sprint across the tarmac to the steps leading to the plane. He wanted to put this country and all its contradictions behind him. He closed his eyes and felt the burning inside the lids. Now, after all he had been through he was going to be detained.

He heard the upheaval near him. They had pounced on an African in the queue behind him. He was struggling, yelling, pleading, until one of them hit him. Inert, he was dragged away.

A woman's voice implored, "Leave him, leave him, he is an important man, don't you know he is the Vice-Chancellor of the University?" She flung herself to the floor, sobbing.

Carver was stunned; people as eminent as that being brutally abducted and taken away to heaven knows where. *Why was it that journalists like the one at the hotel were never around to report the brutality of such scenes across the world instead of slavishly following the official press releases?*

"Mr Carver. Sir… Sir…"

The official leant over and tapped Carver, still in the thrall of what had happened so close to him.

"Your boarding pass. I trust you enjoyed our hospitality. I am sure you found our country delightful. You must visit us again."

Carver smiled at the irony of the situation. If only the man in front of him could know what he had been doing in his last hour in this beautiful country, a land where the life expectancy of people as decent as Mohamed Ashraf, Tomasi Ngirenga and Wilson Kipchai and the tens of thousands like them had dramatically shortened over the past five years.

"Thank you. I shall look forward to that."

He made his way to the aircraft with as much composure as he could muster. It was only after he had been shown to his seat by the stewardess, the aircraft doors had been secured and he had fastened the seat belt, that the uncontrollable ague started.

Chapter 50

The plane was on time at Heathrow. It seemed an age since he passed through here in 1956 on his first ever journey to Africa, when the airport was just a collection of unmatched buildings. How much water – and blood too – had flowed under the bridge since then.

It had been a wearisome flight. His bouts of fitful dozing were coloured by those near-dreams when you are neither asleep nor awake. He was being hunted by Africans in sunglasses in Peugeot taxis, brandishing pangas. He turned in his seat and the dream changed. Maggie Baird, as he had first seen her at Matamu, stood at the end of a tunnel, smiling, beckoning. The positions changed. He was at the end of the tunnel now trying to attract her attention. What brought on this dream… at this time? It was so long since he had seen her.

The plane's engine note changed. Now it was 'Fasten your seat belts, extinguish your cigarettes for landing'. He longed for just one more smoke and at this moment he wished he had never given it up. The patchwork of factories, housing estates, settlement ponds. and golf courses that marked this part of London was clear now.

A smooth landing, the cardboard cut-out smiles of the cabin staff as he left the plane. Nearly the last bag off the luggage belt. Then the trolley push along the customs corridor, the burst out into the babbling crowd of friends and relatives, meeters and greeters. And chauffeurs. Cards held up. ICI for Mr Grogan. Mr Findlater for the BBC. No-one from Armadillo Security, though. He sighed. A chauffeur would be nice. A relative with a car even better. But it would be the Airways coach to Knightsbridge,

Underground, and then a train from Euston to Watford. What an inaccessible place Heathrow was.

The passengers were moving slowly along the narrow exit channel, finding their land legs and scanning the crowd looking for familiar faces. Carver's overnight bag slipped from his shoulder. As he bent to pick it up he saw the African standing back in the crowd. Impassive. A gaudy shirt, printed all over with large flowers. Was he wearing flared trousers? He couldn't see. Sunglasses. *Oh God, not again. Nothing can happen here. Not in London. But it could. They've got a High Commission in London and every country has its spooks.*

He looked around the concourse for escape routes. There were no uniform policemen to be seen and the plain clothes Special Branch men would be inside by the immigration desks. Head down, he pushed on slowly, still scanning the crowd.

Carver wasn't looking for any one he knew. No-one would be there to meet him. But somehow this woman's face just insinuated itself from the collage of other faces lining the waiting area. Maggie? *No. Of course it can't be. It was just that I wanted to see her there. The dream about her on the plane.*

He was drawn to look at the African again, watching, mesmerised, as the man slowly removed the dark glasses. Mulangi, the vision of Mulangi again, here in London. The man was looking straight at him and was starting to move forwards. He was raising his hand. Carver stopped dead and felt the blow as the trolley behind him hit his calves. He was now so close that Carver could touch him. He wagged a finger at Carver in admonishment. "Watch it, man, you're holding the traffic up." And then he was leaning over the flimsy barrier and kissing the woman behind Carver. "Hi, honey, good to see y'back."

With all your years in Africa, you can't tell an American from an African. You're paranoid. The pulse raced; there was still sweat on his forehead but at least he was able to take in the crowd more easily. Yes, she was still there. Yes, she was so like Maggie. It was that damned dream come back.

"Paul. Paul. Over here."

The familiar voice rose above the babble and the public-address system. She waved, a tentative uncertain wave. The crowd had thinned and getting close was easy now.

"Maggie! You're the last person I expected to see!" And then as an after thought, "Are you meeting Jonathan?"

"No, I came to meet you."

Maggie was close now. She touched his arm, as though checking he was really standing there in front of her.

"Paul, let's go and have a cup of coffee or something. Somewhere we can talk."

They managed to find a table in Departures where it was quiet enough.

"I don't understand. You're not meeting Jonathan but you came to meet me?" He shook a sweetener into his coffee. "But how did you know I was coming to Heathrow today?"

"You used to take two spoonfuls of sugar, heaped." Then, "You're not the only detective. I'd read about Mr Carver, security chief, in the local paper. and Gurbachan was only too pleased to fill in the rest."

Her voice changed. "You wouldn't have heard that Jonathan died?"

"He's dead?"

"There's no reason why you should have heard. It was eighteen months ago. Lung cancer. Ironic, isn't it, for a man selling tobacco. So now I've nursed you both."

She looked up at him. Carver felt himself held by the brown eyes that were as deep and bright as they ever were.

"Saying I'm sorry about Jonathan isn't much help, but I am. Truly."

Abstractedly he searched his pockets for the cigarettes he knew he didn't have.

"It was going wrong before that. Everyone tells me I married on the rebound."

He gave up the search and looked at her. Her hair as dark as he remembered it, the complexion smooth, no makeup – she didn't need it. She was sitting upright, stiffly, on the uncomfortable metal chair. She was as lovely as in the days in Matamu, which now were like yesterday, or a century away.

And Jonathan. Jonathan who made us laugh, who could produce a Fats Waller record to fit any mood, Jonathan who took Maggie away from me. Jonathan's dead.

He was about to speak when Maggie whispered so quietly that he had to strain to catch what she said. She was touching his arm, as though not quite sure whether she should.

"I ought to have waited. I ought to have been more patient, ought to have known that after all you had been through it would take time for you to…."

Tears welled. They stopped her seeing Carver's eyes watering too. She opened her shoulder bag and rooted around for a handkerchief.

"Not very tidy for a nurse is it?"

She clicked her bag shut. Carver passed her his handkerchief.

So much had happened here in Heathrow in such a short time. His misreading of the menace of the man in sunglasses, news of the death of the old friend, a reunion he never in his most optimistic moments thought could happen. He stared into his coffee, took a sip.

Maggie broke into his silence. "Paul, please say something. How's the weather been... are you keeping well... will you come home with me... clear off. Say something, anything... Please."

"Sorry. It's been a lot to take in."

He stopped talking and for a moment he was back by the lake in Africa; he now had the chance he never took then.

"Look, what I really want to ask you..."

She leant forward and touched his hand.

"You'll never change, will you? The answer's 'yes', in case you never get to the question."

HISTORICAL NOTE

119up ('The Long Train') was a reality. In the 1950s and 60s it was one of the daily goods trains on East African Railways main line.

For over half a century, EAR&H (East African Railways & Harbours) operated one of the finest railway networks in Africa, outside South Africa. Regular goods and passenger services were provided throughout Kenya, Tanganyika, and Uganda, not only by means of the rail network but also by the lake and river steamer services.

The line from the Kenyan coast to landlocked Uganda was started at Mombasa in 1896 and eventually reached Kampala in 1931. Its construction was only accomplished through epic and ingenious civil engineering work. The terrain to be crossed – deserts, swamps, the Rift Valley and the fast-flowing River Nile where it emerges from Lake Victoria – presented formidable difficulties. Lack of clean water, hostile tribesmen, and man-eating animals were just a few of the other ever-present problems. It is not surprising that in its early days the railway was known as 'The Lunatic Line'. From the coast at Mombasa the line climbs to 9,136 feet above sea level at Timboroa Summit in Kenya, before gradually descending the five and a half thousand feet to Uganda.

Such was the British experience of railways in India, that it was natural to enlist key staff for the construction of this line from the sub-continent. Also, the relatively narrow metre gauge in use there was adopted for the new line in Africa. But India contributed much more. The labour necessary to construct the new line was hard to find. Local Africans had no experience of such work and to train the required numbers – even if they were willing – would have delayed progress at a time when budgets were under intense scrutiny. Some 30,000 Indians worked on the construction of the Kenya/Uganda railway. Some were rewarded by the allocation of parcels of land alongside the railway and from this grew the Asian population which contributed so much to the commercial success of the East African territories.

There were major engineering difficulties during the building of the line – for example, how to get trains down into the Great Rift Valley and then how to get them to climb out after crossing it. But once the track was laid, operating was also beset with enormous technical problems. To cope with the terrain there were numerous gradients and sharp curves which could not be negotiated easily by conventional locomotives. The Indian experience under similar conditions showed that the Beyer Garratt was ideal and in 1926 the first of these was acquired second hand from Indo-China. Built by Beyer Peacock of Manchester, the Beyer Garratts were of unusual design. The boiler was mounted between bogies front and rear with an engine located on each of these bogies. Each engine took its steam from this common boiler. This lay-out made the locomotive articulated.

The wheelbase of each of the bogies was short and adapted well to the severe curves. Since the wheels supporting the locomotive were spread more evenly than was the case with conventional locomotives, it enabled them to operate over tracks with light rails, thus substantially reducing building costs. The '59 Class', weighing 252 tons, had an axle load of 21 tons and could pull train loads of 1000 tons.

The 'Harbours' part of EAR&H operated an interesting range of services. Conventional steamers operated on Lakes Victoria and Tanganyika, but until the early 1960s there was a little-known route from the source of the Nile to the Mediterranean.

From Jinja a train took passengers to the river port of Namasagali. From there a stern-wheel paddle steamer towed steel lighters across Lake Kioga, through which the Nile flows, to Masindi Port. Since the river passes through the Murchison Falls near here, the next part of the journey was made by EAR&H bus and lorry to the port of Butiaba on Lake Albert. A steamer took passengers and cargo across the lake and these were then transferred to another stern-wheeler and the journey continued along the Nile to Nimule where it enters the Sudan; then onwards along the Nile. This was one of the earliest routes into Uganda from the outside world and was used by some during World War Two as a safer route than going through Mombasa.

OTHER BOOKS BY THE SAME AUTHOR

A QUIET NIGHT AT ENTEBBE

It is 1952 and the 'Winds of Change' are beginning to blow. African nationalism is gaining strength – unrest and rebellion are in the air. The unscheduled refuelling of the new young Queen Elizabeth's plane at Entebbe Airport presents the perfect opportunity for a lone assassin. Rosemary is facing her own 'winds of change'. Has she lived too long in the shadow of her District Commissioner husband? With the help of Flora, an outcast 'soul stealing' sculptress, Rosemary's life begins to take a new path – a route that leads straight to the would-be royal assassin.

ELEPHANTS DON'T SNEEZE

A variety of short stories. Ideal as a bedtime read!

Catch up with the deeds of unwittingly accident-prone Great Uncle Wilbur, linger a while with five different shades of the supernatural, and even find out what 'A Late Summer Evening' was like 70 or so years ago.